THE MYSTIC'S ACCOMPLICE

Mary Miley

SEVERN
HOUSE

First world edition published in Great Britain and the USA in 2021
by Severn House, an imprint of Canongate Books Ltd,
14 High Street, Edinburgh EH1 1TE.

Trade paperback edition first published in Great Britain and the USA in 2022
by Severn House, an imprint of Canongate Books Ltd.

severnhouse.com

British Library Cataloguing-in-Publication Data
A CIP catalogue record for this title is available from the British Library.

ISBN-13: 978-0-7278-5042-3 (cased)
ISBN-13: 978-1-78029-783-5 (trade paper)
ISBN-13: 978-1-4483-0521-6 (e-book)

33614082294785

All Severn House titles are printed on acid-free paper.

MIX
Paper from
responsible sources
FSC   FSC® C013056
www.fsc.org

Typeset by Palimpsest Book Production Ltd.,
Falkirk, Stirlingshire, Scotland.
Printed and bound in Great Britain by
TJ Books Limited, Padstow, Cornwall.

THE MYSTIC'S ACCOMPLICE

Also by Mary Miley

Roaring Twenties mysteries

THE IMPERSONATOR
SILENT MURDERS
RENTING SILENCE *
MURDER IN DISGUISE *

available from Severn House

ONE

I didn't learn *exactly* what my husband did for a living until the day of his funeral, when two dozen men wearing black suits shuffled into the nave of Santa Maria Incoronata, pulled off their fedoras, crossed themselves with holy water, and funneled into the pews. After the mass, they followed the hearse all the way to Chicago's Mount Carmel Cemetery, twenty-odd miles to the west, and stood motionless in the brisk May wind as the mortal remains of Tommaso Pastore were lowered into a cold, wet hole. I must've looked like I was going to faint, because soon as I'd thrown the widow's handful of earth on Tommy's casket, a burly man with slits for eyes took my elbow and steered me to a stone bench beside a fancy mausoleum. Sheltered from the wind, I greeted a line of mourners through the black netting of my veil. Several pressed money into my hands.

'Sorry for your loss, Mrs Pastore. This is for the baby.'

'Thank you.'

'Tommy was a good guy. Don't worry – he'll be avenged. And this'll help you when the little one comes.'

'Thank you.'

'It's a sad day, Mrs Pastore. We're all gonna miss Tommy. Here's a present for the baby.'

'Thank you.'

And then the boss of the Outfit limped over, trailed by his Number Two. He stood over me with an envelope fat with cash that he laid in my lap. I'd never met either of them before, but I knew who they were. Everyone in Chicago knew Johnny Torrio and his young sidekick, Al Capone. I hated them.

'This is for you and the baby, Mrs Pastore,' the boss began, his words flavored with southern Italy despite all the years he'd lived in America. 'Tommy was a good boy. Loyal. Honest. Hard-working. His loss, it's a tragedy for all of us, especially with him not living to see his own baby come into the world. We don't take these things lying down, Mrs Pastore.'

'Thank you, Mr Torrio,' I said, stealing a glance at the silent thug beside him. The ugly scar was there on his cheek like people said, but it was his snakelike eyes and thick lips twisted into a sneer that made me shiver.

'And the funeral,' continued Mr Torrio, 'it's paid for. Plus money for masses for his soul.'

'Thank you, Mr Torrio.'

'And you tell the man what to put on the gravestone, and it's done. Finito. We take care of our own. You let me know if you need something.'

I nodded my appreciation. I wished he'd leave. I wished they'd all leave and let me go home, out of the wind that wouldn't stop, someplace where it was warm and safe and none of this was real. A large tree beside the mausoleum had died and no one had cut it down yet. I felt like that tree: wooden, bare, maybe alive somewhere down deep, but dead to all appearances.

Of course, Tommy had told me he made deliveries for the Outfit. I'm not stupid; I knew he was involved in supplying bootleg hooch to Chicago's speakeasies, but there was nothing to that. Everyone had some sort of role in the long-running drama that played out day and night at the thousands of speak-easies scattered throughout the city, sometimes as many as six or seven on a single block. An army of men and women tended bar, served drinks, played jazz, kept the books, cooked, and cleaned, while another, much larger crowd drank, gambled, danced, smoked, and mingled. Cops and feds played their parts too, collecting bribes to look the other way or raiding the joints when the pay-off chain broke down. Dusk-to-dawn caravans of trucks and men were needed just to motor all that rotgut from warehouse to watering hole. What I hadn't known was that Tommy had been promoted from regular runs to bossing the fellas that did the runs. The night he was killed, one of Johnny Torrio's trucks strayed over the invisible line into the North Side territory of Dion O'Banion, and O'Banion's boys took offense. And the truck. Tommy and some others went to get it back. Three people ended up dead.

The fight was about more than geography. O'Banion bossed the North Side and Gold Coast Gang; Torrio had the Outfit on the South Side and in Cicero. The micks and Jews looked down on the wops, and the wops despised them back. Everyone was touchy, all the time. The bad luck of it was, a bullet caught my Tommy in the forehead. None of this story seemed true to me. I felt like an actress on the stage playing the part of an inconsolable widow for the entertainment of an audience. And a pretty poor actress at that, unable to squeeze out a single tear for her dearly departed husband. I found myself looking around for Tommy, who should have been there beside me at this funeral for someone else.

'You got someplace to go to?' asked Mr Torrio. 'Family?' He frowned as he surveyed the meager assembly of mourners, none of whom were behaving like grieving relatives. 'When the baby comes, I mean.'

'Yeah, sure. I'll be fine. We'll be fine.'

Except that I was missing a husband and my baby would be missing a father, we'd make do. I'd see to that. Two years ago, Tommy had bought us a house on the Near South Side; small, but paid for. Last year he bought a Ford coupe. We weren't big spenders – neither of us came from money so we respected it. There was ready cash in the bank. Three banks, in fact, in case one of them failed. 'Don't like putting all my eggs in one basket,' Tommy liked to say. I could hear him say it now, as clear as if he was standing behind me. I turned my head just to make sure.

Mr Torrio gave the nod that signaled the Outfit's departure. When the gang had melted away, I looked back toward Tommy and saw the gravediggers tamping down the dark, wet earth on top of him. A rough gust of wind tore some of the flower petals from the wreaths that guarded his plot and carried them toward the clouds.

The undertaker drove me home in the hearse.

Back in my own kitchen, I stared at the plates of food delivered by people I barely knew. I was real hungry, but ever since I got word about Tommy, everything I ate came back up. Nonetheless, I needed to put something inside me for my baby's sake, so I took a bottle of milk out of the icebox, lit the stove, and warmed some in a pan. That stayed down. Then, though it was only four o'clock, I got in our big bed alone and cried for

the first time since Tommy had died. I cried until my pillow
was soaked, until there was not a teardrop left in me, until I
fell hard asleep. I dreamed of Tommy, and in the dream, he
was alive and laughing and I was giddy with relief knowing
he wasn't really dead. When I woke up, it was late the next
morning, and he was really dead.

Coffee steadied my nerves. Remembering the money the men
had given me the day before, I rummaged around in my pocketbook and fished out the crumpled bills and envelopes. Then
I sat on the davenport in our living room and counted out more
than nine hundred dollars! Tommy's voice inside my head was
saying, 'You'll be fine. You'll be fine. You'll be fine,' like a
record skipping. The baby and me, we'd be fine. We had the
house. We had money. I could take care of both of us.

A sharp knock at the front door broke my trance. Panicked,
I stuffed the cash back into my pocketbook, careless of the
mess. Nine hundred dollars was a princely sum – more jack
than a lot of people made in a year. A woman eight months
gone would be an easy mark for even a puny thief.

But it was only my neighbor, Lucy, with more food. 'Good
morning, Maddie. I brought you this for supper tonight,' she
said. 'How are you doing? Would you like some company?'

Lucy Dillingham lived with her husband, Bob, and their two
lively boys in the house beside ours that was its twin. I didn't
know them well, but we were friendly. She was already inside.
There was nothing to do but invite her to sit a minute.

'Want some coffee?' I asked.

Lucy said the things people say when nothing they say can do
any good, and she let me persuade her to take one of the cakes
home to her sons. As soon as she left, I set out for the nearest
bank.

I'd walked the route many a time, along wide avenues where
streetcars bullied motorcars out of the way and pedestrians
scampered across street corners dodging the traffic, but I'd never
been as skittish as I was on that day. It felt like there was a
sign on my belly shouting to all the world, 'Clumsy, pregnant
woman carrying fortune in handbag!' My head bobbed right to
left, alert for suspicious-looking passers-by, and I took a deep
breath each time I rounded a corner in case someone should

jump me. I heaved a great sigh when I stepped through those massive doors into the bank. I was safe here. My baby was safe. My money was safe.

The bank had that leather-and-floor-polish scent that reeked of stability and permanence. The men all wore three-piece suits and slicked their hair with Vaseline. I felt out of place in the cavernous main hall – no surprise, seeing as how I was the only female in sight. Banking was a man's world. I felt the message keenly.

'I'd like to make a deposit,' I said to the teller, pulling out handfuls of wadded bills and pushing them under the bars of his station. Tightened lips telegraphed his disapproval at this disrespectful treatment of money, but he smoothed each crumpled banknote and counted them twice.

'Nine hundred thirty-five dollars. Is that correct?' he asked at last, eyeing me like I stole it or something. Jeez.

'Yes,' I replied, handing him our bankbook – *my* bankbook – and watching him enter the amount in the ledger and initial it. There was now over $3,000 in that one account, and there was more in two other banks. Enough to take care of me and the baby for years, if I was careful. And I would be very careful. How grateful I was that Tommy had put money aside! You'll be fine, his voice reassured me. You'll be fine. It was my life raft. Me and the baby, we were safe now. We'd be fine. I headed home.

As I walked up my street toward my house, I noticed with surprise that there were two men on my front porch. One was on his knees, fiddling with the lock. The other was wearing a blue uniform.

'What's the matter, officer?' I asked, lumbering up the steps, my voice squeaking with anxiety. 'What's wrong?'

'You live here?' the cop asked.

'Yes!' A jolt of panic streaked through my veins. 'Has someone robbed my house?'

He consulted some papers in his hand. 'This house belongs to Mrs Tommaso Pastore, who's evicting you. I'm sorry, lady—'

'But *I'm* Mrs Tommaso Pastore! My husband died Thursday. The house is mine now. And it's paid for! No mortgage.' There was clearly some mistake here. For a second, I wondered if

Tommy had a mother whose name was the same as mine, but no, he'd told me when we got married that his only living relatives were some cousins in New Jersey. 'There's been a mistake.'

'If that's so, lady, you'll need to clear it up with your lawyer. I'm just doing my duty here.'

The locksmith had finished. He gathered his tools, and, without the guts to look me in the eye, picked up his toolbox and walked off. The cop made to follow him. I laid my hand on his sleeve.

'Wait!' I said, panic stinging my throat. 'I don't know a lawyer! And I need to get inside my house! Everything I own is in there. Don't go!'

He thrust away my hand and left without a backward glance. Before I could focus my addled brain on what to do next, I heard a voice behind me. It was Lucy, on her porch just a few feet away.

'What's wrong, Maddie? I heard you shouting . . .'

Shocked speechless, I could only turn and stare at her like she was a ghost or something. She hurried down her steps and over to my porch.

'Lordy, girl, you look like death warmed over. Here, sit,' she ordered, gently pushing me into the wicker chair.

'I'm evicted. They changed the locks.'

'That's nonsense. It's your house, right?'

Dazed, all I could say was, 'Paid for.'

'There's been a mistake. You'll sort things out. Everything'll turn out jake.'

'That cop, he said I need a lawyer. I don't know any lawyers.'

'Banks have lawyers,' she said helpfully.

Relief flooded through my limbs, and I stood. 'Of course. You're right. I'm just not thinking straight. I was just at the bank. I'll go back there right now and talk to a lawyer.'

'Are you sure you're OK? You've had a shock. You're kinda pale. Let me get you some water.'

I shook my head. Tommy's calming voice was back inside my head. Mistakes happen. You can fix this. You'll be fine. You'll be fine. Everything was going to be fine.

The bank teller I'd seen just an hour earlier pointed me to a portly man with a waxed mustache seated at a glass-topped wooden desk, who asked me why I wanted to speak with a lawyer. Like he was suspicious I would be wasting the lawyer's time on something frivolous. In a few sentences, I told him my name and my problem and said I was a bank customer who needed legal advice.

Within minutes, I was escorted up to a fancy office on the second floor that smelled of cigars. In it were soft leather chairs, a window overlooking the busy street, and a thin, white-haired lawyer named Mr Anderson, who asked how he could help me. It didn't take long for me to explain what had happened.

'I can prove all this. I have a deed and a marriage certificate and a death certificate, but they're inside my house.'

'When did your husband pass away?'

'Thursday. Thursday night.'

'My condolences, madam. Did he make a will?'

'No. He didn't know he was going to die.' I could see him getting ready to give me the lecture on how everybody needs a will no matter what, so I said, 'The house was in both our names, and someone told me wives always inherit from their husbands, even without a will.'

'That's generally true, at least in part. Did he have any debts?'

'Not that I know of. But if he did, we've got the money to pay them.'

A knock at the lawyer's door interrupted us. The man with the mustache came in and handed some papers to Mr Anderson, who spent several long minutes looking them over. When he raised his eyes to meet mine, they held a grim glint that made my pulse skip a beat.

'I'm afraid the house belongs to Mr Pastore's wife—'

'*I'm* his wife! We've been married more than two years!' I held up my left hand with its plain gold wedding band that was engraved inside: *Maddie and Tommy, February 24, 1922.* 'I have a ring and a marriage certificate to prove it!' And a baby. Instinctively I put my hand on my belly where Tommy's child, curled up and sleeping, waited for his birth day.

The lawyer motioned with his hands to quiet me like I was some hysterical female throwing a temper tantrum. 'Unfortunately . . . *unfortunately*, it seems he had another wife, one before you whom he neglected to divorce. With a name like Tommaso

Pastore, I presume he was a Roman Catholic?' He pronounced the words like they left a bad taste in his mouth.

'So what? So'm I.'

'Then you should know that your religion forbids both divorce and bigamy. I'm sorry, Mrs uh . . . miss, uh . . . madam. This happens more often than you might think. Bigamy. In any case, Mrs Pastore's lawyer has notified us that Mrs Pastore – the real Mrs Pastore – is the legal owner of her late husband's property.'

As the clock on the wall loudly ticked off the seconds, I stared at him like I was some lunatic just committed to the asylum. This couldn't be happening. Another wife? Was this man crazy? There had to be some mistake. Tommy, with his laughing eyes and handsome face, Tommy would never have married someone else. He was mine.

But whether this lawyer fella was right or not, I had no place to sleep tonight. And suddenly, the other shoe dropped. The lawyer, he hadn't known about the house. The bank had no connection to my house. We didn't have a mortgage. The papers in his hand were not about my house; they were about my money. This lying woman's lawyer had seized our money from the bank as well as our house. My money. That's what the papers in his hands said.

I had to act quickly and calmly. I stood up and said, with as much dignity as I could muster, 'Thank you, Mr Anderson. There has been some mistake, which I will sort out shortly. Good day to you.'

And I walked out of his office, down the stairs, and over to the sullen teller I had used earlier in the day. 'I made a mistake in depositing that money this morning,' I told him coolly. Handing him my bankbook, I continued, 'I'd like to withdraw all my money, please.'

It was a good bluff. It should have worked, but it didn't. The teller said he'd need to clear such a large withdrawal with the higher ups and of course, that was the end of that. I explained, pleaded, threatened, screamed, and cursed, but the guard dragged me out of the bank and thrust me on to the sidewalk – none too gently, considering my delicate condition.

Furious and frightened beyond words, I made my way by

streetcar to the other two banks where Tommy kept our money, hoping the lying witch and her hell-bound lawyer weren't aware of those accounts. No such luck. The accounts at both establishments were frozen. My money belonged to another Mrs Tommaso Pastore, not to me. I was numb. I couldn't take it all in.

Clinging doggedly to the belief that this was all an unfortunate mistake, I worked my way home in a fog, only to remember after I climbed the front steps that I could no longer get inside. I had nowhere else to go. I didn't think it was possible to feel any worse than I did on the day they told me Tommy was dead, but today was worse. My neighbor, Lucy, found me sobbing on the porch.

Taking me inside her house, she gave me a stiff shot of whiskey and some warm broth while I told her what I could.

When her boys came home from school, she handed out hunks of cake and shooed them outside to play in the street. When her husband got home from work, she told him what had happened and announced that I would be staying with them for a few days until this mess was sorted out. Bob made no complaint. He was a good man. He worked in a bottle factory and brought home his paycheck every Friday without detouring to any of the local gin joints. When he understood my predicament, he nodded solemnly, then went to the closet and pulled an old towel out of the ragbag.

'Come on,' he said to me. 'No, Lucy, you stay here.'

We walked to the rear of my house where he chose a window that couldn't be seen from the sidewalk. With one sharp blow of his rag-wrapped fist, he smashed the glass and unlocked the sash from the inside. 'You stand here, Maddie,' he said, hoisting himself through the window. 'I'll pass everything you want out.'

It took the better part of an hour, but Bob and me working together cleared the house of my clothing, my jewelry, and my papers – I wanted my marriage certificate and the deed to the house – before he asked what else he should bring out.

'There's a few dollars in the sugar jar on the kitchen table,' I said, 'and you may as well hand me out the food. And I have some baby clothes in the extra bedroom. Oh, there's a picture of Tommy and me on our wedding day on the mantel.'

What else . . . what else? Inside my head, I toured the four rooms of the house I might never see again: the parlor with its matching set of oak furniture, the dining room where we put the new high chair we'd bought last week from Sears, the kitchen with our large icebox and gas stove and the café curtains I'd sewn out of yellow gingham, and our bedroom, where I'd held him in my arms just five nights ago.

'Oh, yeah, and Tommy's gun is in the drawer of the night-stand by our bed.'

TWO

Baby Tommy was born at Hull House on Sunday, June twenty-second, 1924. Everyone knows about Hull House, how it was started by a woman to help poor immigrants – well, I wasn't *exactly* an immigrant, but my parents had come from Quebec up in Canada, and I sure was poor. I sure as hell wasn't going hat-in-hand to the Outfit, no matter what Johnny Torrio had said, so I was grateful that Hull House took me in and looked after me during my labor.

Once upon a time, Hull House was a big brick mansion that belonged to a rich man, name of Hull, but then Jane Addams turned it into a settlement house. Over the years, she added a dozen other buildings to it and around it, until nowadays you can't even see the original mansion, except from the inside rooms. Everyone in Chicago knows Hull House is smack in the middle of Little Italy, but it's not just for Italians – they welcome Greeks, Jews, Germans, Poles, Russians, Lithuanians, anyone who's trying to scratch out an existence working twelve-hour days for pennies and living in a filthy tenement – and they teach useful things so people can survive the chaos of America's second biggest city.

I'd never been inside Hull House before that day in early June when I walked through its front door. I didn't know what to expect, but I was desperate enough to look for charity. Turns out Miss Addams really understood desperate people.

A tiny, bird-like woman with a hawk nose showed me into the parlor where they were serving tea to a dozen women. She guided me to a gray-haired lady in a plain brown dress and white lace collar who was perched on the edge of a fancy damask sofa. That lady rose to her feet and set her cup on the tea table as I came up.

'Miss Addams,' said the bird woman, 'I'd like to introduce Mrs Pastore, who's come to Hull House for the first time.'

With one delicate hand, Miss Addams gently pulled me to a

place on the sofa beside her. 'Won't you join us for tea, Mrs
Pastore? Mrs Mackenzie in the kitchen has just taken these
lovely current scones out of the oven. Perhaps you'd care for
one?' Suddenly ravenous, I buttered a scone while Miss Addams
poured tea in a blue willow teacup. 'Milk or sugar?' she asked.
I nodded, feeling like I was inside a fairy tale. 'And when is
your baby due, Mrs Pastore?'

My mouth was full. I chewed and swallowed hard. 'In about
two weeks.'

I saw her look at my left hand. 'And your husband?'

The hot tea in my throat kept me from crying. In a few
sentences, I explained about Tommy's death and told her I had
no other family. A lie, yes, but a necessary one.

'If you would care to stay with us until after the baby's birth,
my dear, we have an empty room on the third floor – you can
make it up two flights, I trust? It's very plain, I'm afraid, but
you will be quite safe there. And we have a midwife who can
assist when the baby comes.'

I could no longer hold back my tears. In seconds, my cheeks
were wet, and I couldn't speak for relief. Miss Addams just
patted my hand in a matter-of-fact manner and turned to speak
to someone else while I pulled myself together.

'Do you have belongings, my dear?' she asked when I had
dried my eyes.

'Yes, ma'am. Not furniture or anything big, just some clothes
for me and the baby and a few other things.'

'And where are these belongings?'

'In my neighbor's house on the South Side.'

'Lydia?' She motioned to a young woman across the room.
'Lydia, please find Elmer and ask him to come here.' To me
she said, 'There will be more than you should carry in your
condition. Elmer will accompany you to the South Side and
help you bring everything here.'

And so I moved into Hull House, where I had a narrow bed,
two decent meals every day, and educational lectures, recitals,
plays, art classes, and readings every night. I moved numbly
through the days like I was in a dream, not noticing much that
was going on around me, not talking unless someone asked me
a question. Miss Addams gave me a job in the kitchen where

I helped cook and wash up until my labor pains started, at which point they summoned Nurse Wilkie – no novice when it came to birthing babies – who stayed by my bed throughout the ordeal. As she cut the cord, she congratulated me on a healthy baby boy and an easy labor. The ten hours of agony didn't seem easy from where I was lying, but what people say is true: I soon forgot about the pain and exhaustion, so caught up was I in the joy of my lovely little boy.

You can't stay at Hull House forever, though, so when Baby Tommy was two weeks old, I moved to a nearby boarding house that Miss Addams recommended and began looking for work.

Mrs Jones charged ten dollars a week for a room that had nothing in it but a bed, a small wooden table, and a battered chair, painted green. The price included clean sheets once a month and dinner every evening. Chicago had cheaper places and nicer places, but Mrs Jones had one big plus in her column – she would take in a woman with a baby. And she let me use the backyard laundry hut where I could wash and boil Tommy's diapers every day or two. The room she showed me was crawling with ants and worse, and human stink seeped through the thin walls from the toilet room located beside mine. I had no choice but to clean up the filth as best I could and keep Tommy away from the other boarders, particularly the woman next door whose tubercular-sounding cough rattled the window glass. I took the room – what choice did I have? – and vowed to spend as little time as possible there. Soon I would find a decent job and make enough for someplace respectable.

The food Mrs Jones served her boarders was plain and heavy on the potatoes, but at least there was no shortage of it. One meal a day would have been enough for me by myself, but now that I had Tommy to nurse, I had to eat more often to make enough milk to keep him growing. The boarding house was just a few blocks from the Maxwell Street Market where I could buy a few pennies worth of fruit, hard-cooked eggs, and bread each morning before I went out looking for work.

A person could've gotten lost for days in this enormous market with its hundreds of stalls, stores, tables, and wagons that lined both sides of the street, block after city block. Carts carrying onions, potatoes, and squash from outlying farms jostled for position between canopied tables piled high with trout, salmon, whitefish and herring from the lake – fish so fresh, their gills still pulsed. Bakers offering pumpernickel warm from the oven were squeezed in among the egg women and the cheesemongers. It was Chicago's biggest market and you could buy anything there, not just food, like at regular markets. Some say it was the biggest market in America. I don't know about that, but I do know that it didn't matter whether you were black, brown, yellow, or white – not like some stores. If your money was green, you were welcome at Maxwell Street. Vendors hawked clothing, flowers, furniture, books – most goods were second-hand, which was good for me when I needed to sell off most of my nice clothes for ready cash. Gawking at the merchandise could be dangerous, I soon learned, as it required a delicate dance to avoid the carpet of rotten produce, dead rodents, and discarded bits of wrapping paper and filth that littered the ground. It was my third day out when I caught a glimpse of a face from my past – the mother of my best friend from school days.

'Mrs Burkholtzer?' I said, unsure at first, when I spotted her beside the fishmonger's stall. 'Mrs Burkholtzer! Remember me? It's Madeleine Duval. Alice's friend.'

Her dark eyes widened in surprise, then shifted to the right and left, like she was checking to see no one nearby had heard me call her name.

'Yes,' she said, drawing out the word a bit nervously as she took my arm and led me across the way where an empty stall afforded some privacy. As soon as she caught sight of Tommy, asleep in the sling around my neck that I'd made from a scarf, her mouth opened in an expression of delight.

'Lordy, yes, Madeleine, dearest Maddie. And you all grown up now! My oh my, who is this little tyke?'

'Tommy. He's seventeen days old.' I stroked the dark fuzz on his head with one finger and he opened his eyes wide and blinked his long, curly lashes. Mrs Burkholtzer gave a smile so big I could see the holes where her side teeth had been.

She hadn't changed much since the old neighborhood in Chicago's Near South Side. Older, of course – her gray hair pulled up under an out-of-style hat, her face creased with lines that had deepened, and her waist stouter than it had been. I'm sure I'd changed far more than she had in the dozen or so years since I'd last seen her.

'Lordy mercy, aren't you the lucky mother! He's a precious little mite, isn't he? Do you live in this neighborhood now?'

'I moved to Mrs Jones's boarding house just three days ago. And you?'

'I'm nearby. But never mind me, child. Just wait 'til I write my Alice and tell her I've seen her old friend, Maddie Duval! You'll never believe it – Alice is married now with *four* children, three boys and a girl, and they live in southern California where it's sunny and warm all year long.' She looked a bit wistful as she gazed at Baby Tommy, thinking, I supposed, of how far away her own grandchildren were, and how she wasn't likely ever to see them in the flesh. 'She sends pictures now and then . . . My, my, I remember when you two chicks went off to school together. Thick as thieves you were in those days. And how you used to read to that old blind woman after school. What was her name?'

'Mrs Nickerson.'

'That's right. You took turns reading to her.'

'We sure did. Sometimes we went on for hours. She used to give us a nickel every day we read to her.' I had fond memories of old Mrs Nickerson, whose 'job' gave me a safe place to go after school and some pocket money – at least, until my father discovered my tiny hoard and beat me for keeping it from him. 'She put us through the ringer with the books she chose: Dickens, Austen, Dumas . . . and poetry too, Longfellow and Whitman were her favorites. I think Alice and I ended up learning more from Mrs Nickerson than we ever learned at school, what with her explaining the big words and talking about what the books meant. She was one smart lady. I wonder what happened to her.'

Mrs Burkholtzer frowned as if in thought. 'I don't remember hearing that she'd died, but I don't get back to the old street too often.' The way she said it made me think she didn't get back to the old street at all. I knew why I didn't go back, but I wondered about her reasons. 'What about little Janey Mason?' she continued reminiscing. 'She was a pistol, that one.'

'She married after high school and moved to Pittsburgh with her husband. He had family there.'

'And those pretty little twins you and Alice used to play with? Clara and . . .?'

'Maria. I'm afraid the influenza took them. Five years ago.'

She gasped. 'Both of them?'

'And their mother too.'

She made pitying 'mm, mm, mm' noises in her throat and left Memory Lane where it belonged. The sad truth was, I had no girlfriends left from my school days. And no way of tracking down any who were still alive unless I knew the husband's name.

'What brought you to the West Side?' she asked. 'You leave home to get married?'

'I left home, yes, but that was ten years ago. And I'm a widow.' She gasped her dismay. I nodded in sad agreement. 'My husband died in May.'

'Oh, you poor dear. How sorry I am to hear that! No wonder you're out and about so soon after the birth. Is there no one to take care of you?' I could hear the unspoken question behind that: why hadn't I gone home to my parents? I didn't feel like telling her, and, honestly, she could guess the answer as well as anybody who knew us Duvals back in the day.

'I can take care of both of us. In fact, I'm looking for work now.'

'With a baby so new as this one?'

'I'll find something where I can take him with me,' I said, with more confidence than I felt, 'or I'll find someone who has a baby who could nurse him while I'm gone. Do you know of anything? I'm getting . . . I have to find something soon. I'm nearly out of . . .' I swallowed hard and then choked, as reality crushed any optimism I could muster.

She put her arm around my shoulder, and suddenly I was spilling the whole sordid tale to this sympathetic person from my past – how I'd lost my husband, my home, and my money in the same week and how I'd gone like a beggar to Hull House to have my baby. 'I was so sure it was all a mistake,' I hiccupped, blotting my eyes with my handkerchief, 'but it wasn't. I got a lawyer – a real lawyer, not a bank lawyer – and he found out that Tommy really did have another wife – he'd just never thought it was important to tell me – I was so mad at him then I woulda killed him myself if he hadn't already been dead – and this awful woman lived somewhere outside the city, and she read about his death in the paper and knew about us and moved fast to get everything he owned, and she got our house and all our money, and I wanted to kill her too but I couldn't find where she lived, but at least she didn't know about the motorcar Tommy bought last year, so I was able to sell it before she could find out, and that gave me enough to pay the lawyer and get this boarding house, but it won't last much longer, so please, if you hear of anything, I'm lodging at Mrs Jones's a few blocks from the corner. That way . . .' I pointed.

'Lordy, child. I can't think of a thing right this very moment, but I'll ask around and keep my ears open.' And as she gave my arm a pat, I saw something in her eyes as they raked over me and Tommy, a speculative look – the kind a housewife at the butcher shop gives a piece of beef when she's calculating how far it will stretch. A little bubble of hope rose inside my chest, but when she said her goodbyes and walked off, the bubble popped. I found a stool at a coffee stall where I could eat my hard-cooked eggs and watch shoppers haggle with vendors. Buck up, girl, I told myself. You're not the only woman in the world without a job or a man to support you. You'll be fine.

I'd had a job since my father made me quit school, but the sort of work I was used to – retail – wasn't something a woman could do with a baby on her hip. Little Tommy was my greatest joy and my biggest problem at the same time. Hull House had an infant nursery, but every crib had a hundred mothers wanting to leave their babies there. Heck, Little Tommy would be married before his name came to the top of that list! I had found no mothers who wanted to nurse an extra baby, nor had I come across any mothers who were weaning their own and could continue with mine, so I couldn't leave him. It would be months before he was weaned, and my money wouldn't last longer than a few more weeks. My dismal prospects brought a sick, panicky feeling into my stomach, so I tried not to think about the future.

After I'd stored up some strength, I took off for Hull House to ask if anyone there knew of work or a mother who could nurse two. No one did, but they gave me a bag of oats, some rice, and a sausage, and said to come back in a day or two. Maybe my luck would change.

THREE

The following day, I spent the dime for a streetcar to State Street to visit Marshall Field's, the largest, fanciest department store in the world and the place where I'd worked once upon a time, so I could ask about my old sales clerk job. I'd left Field's when I got married. Naturally Tommy didn't want his wife working – what man did? – and we didn't need the money back then with Tommy so flush with doing Outfit deliveries. But circumstances had changed. I needed work bad, and although most managers didn't hire married women, I thought there was a chance I could persuade somebody to give me my old job back.

Not much about the elegant department store had changed since I'd left – the cheerful, brightly lit atmosphere and the high-pitched drone of excitement that filled the air were as familiar as my own face in the glass. As I passed through the Rotunda, I looked up for the thousandth time at the enormous Tiffany dome and breathed in the sweet scent that came from the cut flowers someone had arranged in vases like living works of art. 'Look, Tommy,' I said, holding him so he could see the blue and gold ceiling high above. 'This is where Mommy used to work. Isn't it beautiful? This is where Mommy met Papa.'

I wove my way through the first-floor departments where counters were stocked with perfume, jewelry, handbags, gloves, accessories, and hats on my way to the elevator I would ride to the office floor. I saw several clerks I knew, but they were all waiting on customers, so I didn't dare distract them with a greeting. From force of habit, my eyes scanned the countertops and displays like it was still up to me to make sure everything looked tidy. The merchandise was different, of course – styles had changed. Now the hat department's blockheads were topped with sleek cloche hats instead of the large feathery ones that had been the rage when I worked there. In ready-to-wear, racks

displayed dresses with above-the-knee skirts for the young
flappers who followed the fashion. In the jewelry department,
long ropes of matched pearls and beads dangled from neck
mannequins. Shoppers, mostly women, clustered at every
counter as clerks displayed merchandise, wrapped packages,
and sent the customers' money shooting through pneumatic
tubes to the cashiers who made change and launched the receipt
back to the correct clerk with a satisfying *tha-wump*.

My same supervisor was still there. He remembered me with
a smile. I was a good worker back then.

'I'm sorry, Maddie. You know I don't hold with married
women working,' he said, glancing at the baby in my arms.

'But that's just it, Mr Wilson, I'm not married any longer.
I'm a widow, and I really need the job bad. And as for the baby,
I've hired a woman to take care of him while I work.' That last
was a lie, but if I could get my old job back, I'd make it true
somehow.

He looked thoughtful for a moment, then his eyes swept
across my face and along my body like he was evaluating some
new store merchandise just arrived from the docks. He cleared
his throat, leaned back in his chair, and tented his pudgy fingers.
'Let me give you some fatherly advice, Maddie-my-girl. Your
best bet is to find another husband.' He held up one soft hand
to stave off my protest. 'No, hear me out. You're a fine-looking
woman, if I do say so myself, with clear skin and womanly
shape. Let me be honest, any man would be attracted to you if
you just bat those big blue eyes at him. And praise god, you
haven't gone and bobbed your hair like so many of these foolish
young flappers! A good man would see your long, black hair
as a symbol of your virtue and respectability – your crowning
glory, as they say, and he would honor you for your traditional
ways. And you're still fairly young at – how old are you?'

'Twenty-seven,' I said, shifting Tommy's weight to the
other hip.

'And there's the proof, right there, that you can produce a
beautiful, healthy baby boy, something every man wants!
Remember what we always say in the store? "Success is in the
merchandising". Create an attractive display, and customers will
flock to buy the product. I know a hard-working, modest girl

like you could attract a decent man if only you set your mind on the merchandising. That would be the best solution for you and the baby, now wouldn't it?'

Anger burned so hot in my throat I could barely choke out a reply. The best solution for Tommy and me would be to avoid starving next week! I managed to take my leave of Mr Wilson without exploding – at least until I'd rounded the corner when I let loose with all the bad words I knew and some I didn't. Yes, we did say that success was in the merchandising, but we weren't selling people! If I was so virtuous and hard-working, how come I couldn't have my old job back? Find another man, my eye! I wouldn't take another man if he was first prize at the Illinois State Fair. Never mind, never mind, I heard Tommy's calming voice in my head. You'll be fine. There are other retail stores. You'll be fine.

I'd gotten over blaming Tommy for my troubles. It wasn't his fault he was so happy-go-lucky. His marriage to that witch was probably some arranged thing he couldn't get out of – I was sure he didn't love her – and he probably walked out figuring those chickens would never come home to roost. And they wouldn't have if he hadn't been shot so she read about it in the newspapers. Or maybe he thought he had gotten a divorce only he'd not signed a certain legal paper, or something like that. Tommy tried his best to take care of us. He did a good job of it. I could never stay angry at him for long. He was everything to me, my lover, my husband, my best friend.

Going inside Marshall Field's made Tommy seem almost alive. I gave in to an impulse that struck me as I stepped into the elevator. 'Basement level, please,' I told the boy. I wanted to see the receiving dock where Tommy used to work back when we first met. Maybe I'd feel his presence there. Right then, I needed to feel like he was still with me.

The elevator door opened and immediately I saw a man I recognized. One of the foremen, walking past with a sheaf of papers in his hand.

'Mr Spencer, hello! Remember me? I'm Maddie Duval who married Tommy Pastore.'

'Sure thing, Maddie, uh, Mrs Pastore. A pleasure to see you again.' He paused in what he was doing and wiped his damp forehead with his sleeve. 'I . . . uh . . . I heard about Tommy. I'm real sorry. We all are.'

'Thank you.'

'He was a good employee. Reliable, on time, honest. Nothing ever fell off his truck.' He came closer to have a look at the baby. 'Nice looking kid. Boy or girl?'

'Boy. I named him for Tommy.'

'That's something, then.'

'Yeah. Something.'

'Anything I can do for you?'

'No, I was just wanting to have a look at Tommy's old place of work. Seems like it would bring back some good memories.'

When I'd first met Tommy, he was driving a truck for Marshall Field's, one of dozens that picked up deliveries from the freight train station or the docks and transferred the merchandise to the basement storerooms where it could be unpacked, inspected, priced, and taken upstairs to the proper display or shelf. He had started when he first came to Chicago from New Jersey. He did a good job. Got a raise twice. Still, when someone at the Outfit offered him four times his salary to do what was basically the same job – picking up merchandise at the docks or warehouses and delivering it to retailers – he jumped at the chance. Who wouldn't have? 'We'll have enough to buy us a house, a flivver, and anything we want,' he told me. He saw no difference between delivering booze and delivering socks or lamps. Neither did I, back then. But it turns out, people don't kill people over socks or lamps.

'Well, look around all you want, just don't get in the way.'

'Thanks, Mr Spencer. I'll take my leave now.' With a final look around the huge basement, I rang for the elevator boy to hoist me back up to the first floor.

When I arrived back at Mrs Jones's boarding house, there was a scruffy young man with jug-handle ears hanging about the steps, looking like he was waiting for someone. Before I could walk past him, he closed in on me.

'You Mrs Pastore?' he asked as I approached.

I shifted Little Tommy to the other shoulder to give me a second to consider denying it – the hungry look in his eyes

made me wary – but curiosity got the better of me. I had told
several prospective employers where I lodged, maybe one of
them had had a change of heart.

'I am,' I said with as much dignity as I could, considering
Tommy was fussing over his empty stomach and smelling like
a cesspool.

'I come from Mr Alphonse Capone with a message. He said
tell Mrs Pastore that he avenged your husband, just like he
avenged his own brother last month.' His lips twisted in an ugly
smirk that bared buckteeth as big as a horse's. 'And it wasn't
pretty neither.'

In spite of the sun shining on my back, I shivered. Another
killing. On the one hand, I was glad; on the other, what did it
matter? Would the killings never stop? What could I say? Thank
you for shooting someone else's husband? Someone else's
father or son or brother? A story I'd heard back in school came
to me, something about ancient Greece when the women banded
together and refused to sleep with their men until they stopped
fighting. Had it worked?

'Thank you for bringing me the message.' Before I had
climbed two steps, he laid a hand on my arm. His fingernails
were long as claws and filthy. I shuddered but managed to
refrain from pulling away.

'Beggin' your pardon, Mrs Pastore, but there's more.'

'Yes?'

'Is the baby a boy?'

'Yes. I named him Tommy after his father.' A proud mother
would have uncovered her baby's face and shown him off. I
was plenty proud of my baby, but I didn't want this grubby
messenger to lay eyes on Little Tommy. It was almost like I
thought his gaze would hex him.

'That's nice. Real nice. Mr Capone, he said, if it's a boy, tell
her that when he's thirteen, send the boy to him, and he'll give
him a good job. We take care of our own. That's what he said.
We take care of our own.'

I shuddered and escaped into the boarding house. No way
in hell would Tommy and I have anything more to do with
Capone or Torrio or their stinking Outfit. I knew how the recruit-
ment game worked from my brother, years ago. They start with

little boys running errands. 'Here's a dime, kid. Run buy me a Clark bar. And get one for yourself while you're at it.' Next it's messages. 'Take this envelope to the man at the drug store, and tell him I said give you an ice cream soda.' Then it's money, small amounts at first to test their honesty. 'Run to the Three Aces and pick up a package from Sam.' In no time, the boy was in tight with the gang and carrying a weapon. My son was not going down that path. They would never get my boy. Never ever.

Two more weeks passed. Two more weeks of searching for jobs and wet nurses without any firm prospects. Office jobs and telephone operator jobs were beyond my reach. There were some that would've hired me in a minute but the pay was less than my weekly rent – those were jobs for married women who were looking for pin money and didn't need to support themselves – and none of 'em would let me bring a baby to work. I didn't have the schooling to be a teacher or a nurse. Retail was my trade, and I was good at selling, good at talking to customers, but Baby Tommy couldn't come with me to a store. I did finally get one job at a small dry goods shop, found a wet nurse, and left Tommy with her, but when I came to fetch him, he was wailing like a banshee, he was so hungry. She didn't have enough milk for two, and naturally she fed her own first. I had to let go the job and the woman after three days.

No matter how many times I told myself we'd be fine, we weren't fine. Sometimes I was so tired, I couldn't think straight, staying up night after night with the baby, feeding him every four hours. With no work and only a few dollars left in my pocketbook, I was forced to do what I once swore I'd never do as long as I had a breath in me.

I returned to the neighborhood where I'd grown up and paid a call on my parents. I wish I hadn't.

FOUR

They call Chicago 'the windy city', and the wind off Lake Michigan is pretty steady and sometimes fierce, but that isn't the reason for the nickname. It was the hot air coming from corrupt politicians that brought about the moniker. I'd sweltered through a lifetime of unspeakably hot summers without growing accustomed to the sticky heat, and this year was no different. I'd become resigned to the misery, that's all.

It was a week after the visit to my parents, on another sizzling day in the middle of July without so much as a whisper of wind off the big lake, when my thoughts were focused only on getting through the afternoon without so much as an electric fan in my room, that I caught sight of Mrs Burkholtzer at the Maxwell Street Market again. A basket on one arm and a fan in the other, she waved gaily from the far end of the cramped aisle. I had the distinct impression she was looking for me, waiting there at the same corner where we had accidentally met the time before.

'Why, if it isn't Maddie Duval!' she began, mopping her damp face with a hanky. 'Oh, that's right, not Duval anymore. What did you say your married name was?'

'Hello, Mrs Burkholtzer. It's Pastore.'

'Maddie Pastore. How nice to see you again! What lovely summer weather we're having!'

She was awfully cheerful about a miserable July day. 'Yes,' I agreed, 'although it's a bit warm.'

'And how is the little one?' She brushed Tommy's cheek with one finger.

'Growing fast, thank you. He's Mommy's sweetheart. Good as gold, he is.'

'Found work yet, my dear?'

I shook my head. I'd stopped in every retail store within a mile of the boarding house, scoured the 'Help Wanted – Female' section of the newspapers every day at the public library where

I could read it for free, and been back several times to Hull House, where they had no jobs but could usually give me some food to tide me over for a few days. What frightened me out of sleep was that I didn't have enough to cover next week's rent, and I wasn't sure how lenient Mrs Jones would be, even considering I was one of Jane Addams's girls. I refused to go back to the filthy Outfit and beg. The thought of finding another husband sickened me, but it was out of the question anyway – there wasn't enough time for a respectable introduction and courtship. I knew of one sure-fire way to make money – the way every woman, young or old, pretty or ugly, smart or stupid, could get money. I'd seen plenty of those women on the street with their dresses cut low where they should be high and high where they should be low, and I'd passed brothels on dark streets thinly disguised as boarding houses and speakeasies with rooms upstairs for men who had come in for more than a drink, but I swore I'd never get that desperate. But lately . . . lately, it was looking like the only way I could earn the jack to cover next week's rent. I would have starved before I sold my body for money, but I couldn't afford to starve now. I wasn't living for myself anymore. I had to think of Baby Tommy. Of course I would never tell Mrs Burkholtzer any of that.

'What about . . .?' she started to ask, then stopped mid-sentence. I know why – she didn't want to seem to pry into my personal life.

I helped her. 'What about my parents, you mean? It so happens I went home last week. I vowed I'd never go back there, but I had to break that vow for Tommy's sake.'

'And?'

I couldn't meet her eyes. 'Nothing's changed.'

It had been more than ten years since I'd walked out of my parents' home, but the kitchen table was still laid with the same faded flowery tablecloth, and the same cracked-lid sugar bowl sat in the center. I had glanced up at the same yellow stain on the ceiling that came from a leaky pipe from the tenement above. I'd looked down at the same brown linoleum, scraped gray beneath the chairs and lifting up at the edges where the glue had let go. It felt like going back in time. I felt sixteen again.

'I hadn't seen them since before I got married. I went home then – once – to tell them I was getting married, thinking they'd want to meet Tommy, but they said I'd lowered myself to go with a wop. I thought, now that he was dead, they might let me move back into the room upstairs for a few months, just until I could get back on my feet and get Little Tommy weaned so I could leave him for work. I told them how Tommy had been killed, how another woman claimed to be his wife and took all our money, and how I only needed a place to stay for a short while. I thought they'd want to see their grandson.' I stopped cold.

'And?' she prompted.

'They wouldn't even look at him.'

'Your parents were always hard people,' she said, shaking her head in dismay. 'Troubled people. They wouldn't take you in?'

'They said I'd shamed them, that they didn't want the neighbors to know their daughter was a whore, having a baby with a married man. They called Little Tommy a bastard.'

'Oh, no!'

'My baby is *not* a bastard! I was married by a genuine justice of the peace, and I have a marriage certificate to prove it! Tommy may have committed bigamy, I don't know about that, but I didn't! I was legally married, and now I am a widow, and Little Tommy is not a bastard!' Rage brought hot tears to my eyes and, ashamed, I wiped them on my sleeve.

'No one will say otherwise, dear,' she said, soothing me with her words, 'and if you never speak of it again, no one will know any different. Now, now, Maddie, you look as if you could use a nice cup of tea. That would do you good, wouldn't it? And there's a dear little tearoom across the street that has the best sweet cakes. My treat, of course.'

Drinking tea used to be an everyday event for me when I was married and lived in a nice house. Nowadays, it was a luxury I couldn't refuse. Besides, I was hungry. We crossed the crowded street to a pretty yellow tearoom, so nice and clean, and Mrs Burkholtzer ordered a pot of Earl Grey and cakes for two. As we drank it and talked of nothing, my spirits revived a little. Baby Tommy began to fuss, so I rubbed my little finger in the cake icing and let him suck it off.

Mrs Burkholtzer prattled on as I stirred sugar and milk into a second cup. 'Just like you and my Alice, I've changed my name,' she said with studied carelessness. 'I haven't married again, but I don't use Burkholtzer any longer. I've gone back in time to a previous life and a previous name. Do you believe in past lives, dear?'

I blinked in surprise at the question. 'I never really thought about it.'

'Well, death is not the end, you know. It is a proven fact that almost all of us have lived previous lives. I discovered my re-incarnations – I have four – through hypnosis, and it made all the difference in the world. I understand the whole universe now.'

Unsure of what to say, I nodded silently.

'I go by an earlier life's name now, Carlotta Romany. That was my name a hundred and twenty years ago when I was a gypsy queen in eastern Europe. Isn't that amazing? Knowing about that life explained so much! It freed me from the bonds that were holding me back from my true vocation. I've always had the gift of spiritual connection, you know – or maybe you didn't know, but ever since I was a child, I've had strong feelings about the Far Beyond. And when I met my spiritual guide, bless his soul, I was able to unlock the door to my true essence and began using my unique gift to help others do the same. Mrs Burkholtzer was a lonely, unhappy woman, not much use to anybody. Madame Carlotta welcomes clients who are despondent, confused, or grieving and helps them move on with their lives. It is so fulfilling.'

'You mean, you tell fortunes?'

'No, no, no, my dear. Nothing so commonplace as that. I am a Spiritualist. A telepathist. A medium who connects the living to the souls of the deceased. It is my supernatural gift, my vocation, and I share it with as many as I can. I have a studio nearby.' She indicated the direction with the tilt of her head.

Spiritualism had been so popular in recent years, it was hard to imagine there could be anyone in America who hadn't heard of all the ways mortals were communicating with souls in the Spirit World. There were fortune tellers with crystal balls, astrologers who plotted horoscopes, and people who swore by tarot cards, palm-readings, tea leaves, and Ouija boards, to name a few. I'd never put much stock in any of it. Certainly I'd never been to a séance, but I'd heard about mediums and their spirit guides and how they went into a trance to connect with the souls of the deceased and brought news from the other side. Maybe there was something to it. But dumpy Myrtle Burkholtzer, Gypsy Queen? That beggared belief.

'How fascinating!' I said gamely. Well, at least I knew now what she wanted from me. Madame Carlotta was going to patch me through to Tommy's ghost. Even if I had believed in her psychic powers, I didn't have the jack. It was out of the question.

'Would you like another cake, dear?'

Might as well eat while I waited for her pitch. 'Yes, please.'

'I have been practicing for two years, honing my skills, if you will, and establishing contacts with my own spirit guide. But there are times – too many times – when my intermediary doesn't answer my call, or when he does – for it is a "he" who comes to guide me into the Spirit World, the archangel Michael – he cannot locate the particular spirit my client seeks. Or the spirits are there, waiting to speak, but I can't quite break through the veil to reach them. These occasions make it appear as if my powers are meager, and I disappoint people. I lose clients. They don't return. I can't help them. Do you understand?'

'I-I think so.' Tommy was squirming, rooting around for my breast like a baby bird with its mouth open. He needed feeding. I'd have to excuse myself in a moment and find a quiet nook, whether she'd finished talking or not.

'I have an assistant – a young man who enhances my spectral visions, but lately I've been thinking that . . . well, if I had someone who came to my séances on occasion to help when my spirit guide was unavailable or when my powers falter, it would be a great blessing.' My puzzled expression urged her to greater precision. 'You see, my dear, I have thought for some time that a female associate, someone who could act as though I had linked her to her deceased loved one, even when I had not been able to do so, would be a boon to my credibility because other clients at the table would be persuaded of the genuineness of my abilities, and they would return to give me another try, when I could truly help them.'

She wanted a shill.

'I don't quite understand,' I said, although I understood one thing very well. Dear Mrs Burkholtzer – Madame Carlotta – was a fraud. A huckster. She ran a confidence game. She needed an accomplice.

'Let me be frank, my dear. I'm willing to pay you one dollar to come to my séance tomorrow night and play the part of a grieving widow who wants to connect with her husband's soul in the Great Beyond. It should be easy for you, since it is all true, is it not? You do want to connect with your late husband, do you not? And it's always possible that I *will* be able to connect with him – wouldn't that be *marvelous*? Should that happen, I would still pay you, of course. And if we don't reach him, well, you'll pretend we do, so as to encourage others forward along the Path of Right Thinking. And . . . you could bring Little Tommy along.'

I swallowed the last bit of cake.

'What time?'

FIVE

Getting ready for the séance was simple. I put on mourning. My plain black dress with its below-the-knee hem, gray collar, and gray buttons. That plus the gray hat, gloves, and shoes I'd bought to match and I was set for the scam. First, of course, I had to sew the dress back to its original condition, since I'd altered it with a panel addition to fit over my big belly so I could wear it to Tommy's funeral. My hands shook a little as I stitched. When Tommy helped me choose this outfit a year ago, it was to wear to other people's funerals. In a million years, I couldn't have predicted I'd be wearing it to his.

I considered what little I knew about Madame Carlotta's expectations. I'd have to fake some questions, sure, but there wouldn't be anything fake about my grief. No phony tears required – they would flow like Niagara Falls the moment I let down my guard. But it was worth the heartache. A dollar would feed me – and therefore Tommy – lunch for the better part of next week. And I fully intended it to be the first of many dollars, although I wasn't sure yet how I was going to persuade Madame Carlotta that I was indispensable. That she needed a permanent shill.

In the old days, it was snake-oil salesmen who made the most use of shills. They would plant an accomplice in the crowd and, when they made their pitch, he or she would step up and volunteer to swallow a dollop of elixir and experience a miraculous cure. There aren't so many of those types around today, but magicians routinely use shills as part of their acts. A shill in the audience helps the trick appear magical. And auctioneers rely on shills to bid up the price of their merchandise. It may not have been an honorable occupation, but it was an ancient one. And it beat selling my soul to the Outfit or my body on the street.

The night was warm; even so, I threw a fringed black shawl

over my shoulders and settled Baby Tommy into a straw basket given to me by a colored woman at the market last week. She'd seen me carrying the baby in my shawl tied around my neck, and she'd called to me to come have a look at her two-handled baskets. Strong but flexible, they were made from coarse grass she collected from along the riverbank somewhere, and she was right – one would make a perfect baby carrier. When I said I didn't have the jake, she made me a present of it. I tried to refuse, but she insisted, telling me she'd raised eleven children and knew how it sapped a mother's strength, holding them like I was holding Tommy. I promised to find her and pay when my fortunes were on the rise. And I meant it.

So we set out together, Tommy and me, to find Madame Carlotta's house of horrors on the Near West Side. It was closer to my boarding house than I'd expected, so we arrived a whole hour before the séance was to start. Carlotta – as I must remember to call her now, not Mrs Burkholtzer – lived in a two-story, brick row house built back when people in that neighborhood had more than they did today. I wondered whether she owned or rented. None of my business, but I was the curious sort, then as now. You never knew when information like that would come in handy.

Her assistant was already in the parlor, slouched in a blood-red velvet easy chair while an electric fan rotated back and forth, providing relief from the heat. I had expected an adult. Freddy was a boy and an ill-mannered lout at that. He returned my polite 'How do you do?' with a scowl and a sullen mouth. His baggy clothing and scrawny limbs made judging his age difficult – my best guess landed somewhere between fourteen and eighteen. At least his rumpled clothes were clean, his orange hair had seen a wet comb only moments earlier, and his face had been scrubbed so hard the freckles shone bright on his pale skin. Maybe I was absorbing the clairvoyance that saturated the house, because I could feel the heat from his hostility all the way across the room. What had I ever done to him? Why was he so threatened by my arrival? I would have to handle him the first chance I got if I were to turn this one-night stand into a regular gig.

The transformation of Myrtle Burkholtzer into Madame

Carlotta Romany was worthy of the stage. Good thing I was expecting it or I'd never have spotted my old schoolfriend's mother underneath her gypsy get-up. Even her personality changed. She swanned into the parlor sporting a gaudy, striped skirt and red-ruffled blouse, radiating self-confidence. Gold hoops dangled from her ears and clanged from her wrists. Her gray hair – or at least the hank that stuck out from her turban – had turned jet black, and a jewel-box of rings sparkled on her stubby fingers. She had rouged her cheeks, lined her eyes and darkened her lids with kohl, and applied liberal amounts of ruby lipstick. To be sure, I'd never seen a genuine gypsy . . . but even so, this looked like a pigeon dressed up like a peacock.

Her entrance demanded a compliment. 'My word!' I managed. 'You look very gypsy-like.'

She preened. 'Thank you, my dear. I feel I am my true self again whenever I wear these lively colors, released from the mundane restrictions of our humdrum daily attire. This' – she demonstrated with a clumsy swirl – 'this is my true destiny! Olé! Now, sit beside me and listen carefully while I explain how the séance works.' I joined her on the plush purple divan, set the baby basket by my feet, and glanced about the room.

The décor matched her gaudy costume. Four crimson velvet chairs sat atop a bold Turkish carpet, and plaster angels and a blue-robed Virgin Mary adorned marble-top tables. An étagère stood against the front window, laden with crystals, fortune-telling globes, charms, and whimsies and topped by ornate brass scales with dried flowers on each pan. The three windows were hung alike with royal purple damask that puddled on the floor.

'I open with a prayer,' began Carlotta. 'That's so clients don't think I'm in league with Satan or some such nonsense. My gift comes from God, and I want everyone to know it. I'll begin by calling on Archangel Michael to join us. He's my spirit guide. Do you know him?'

'Um, I don't think so.'

'Revelation and the Book of Daniel,' she said, as if that explained it all. Protestants read the Bible a lot, or so I'd heard. Roman Catholics, not so much. At least, I hadn't. 'Michael carries the souls of the deceased to heaven, so he's perfectly positioned to find the ones he wants to find. He came to me in

a dream two years ago. It was he who told me God had given
me this gift and persuaded me to use it to minister to others.
From there, I undertook many past-life explorations through
hypnosis and learned the truth about myself. I don't have time
to tell you about it all now, but it's an amazing journey through
the ages. Mind you, I can't command Archangel Michael – he
will come tonight or he won't, as it suits him. I'll ask whether
he can bring the spirit of your beloved husband to us tonight.
Was it Timmy?'

'Tommy. Tommaso Pastore.'

'Of course. You'll go first, you see. Do you have any specific
questions I should ask Tommy? I always ask whether they are
happy in the afterlife. They always are – the afterlife is a
wonderful place – but I like to ask. It so reassures my clients.'

I had given this some thought on the way over. 'I might ask
if Baby Tommy and I should move back home with my parents.'

She gave a soft gasp. 'Oh, no! After what you told me? Even
if they were to reconsider their rejection, that would be a terrible
mistake considering . . .'

Evidently my parents' reputation had spread beyond our
family's block. 'Don't worry, I'm not really intending to move.'

'Then why do you ask? There's no point in asking something
if the question isn't genuine, in case he is really there, listening
to you.'

I felt uneasy. How should I react? Surely she didn't think
she was actually going to contact Tommy's spirit? Or did she?
I looked at Freddy for help, but his eyes remained firmly fixed
on his feet. Tread carefully, a voice inside my head warned.
The last thing I needed to do was cause offense.

'Well . . . I would like to have Tommy's opinion on the
matter.' Still, she didn't seem happy, so I shifted gears. 'Perhaps
I could ask whether I should move to St. Louis with my brother.'

'One of your brothers is in St. Louis?'

When my older brother had escaped from home a dozen
years ago, he mentioned something about St. Louis. I had not
the slightest idea whether he had gone there or not, or where
he was today, or if he was even alive, but I sensed that honesty
was the wrong response here, so I answered, 'Yes, my oldest
brother Benjamin.'

Satisfied, she nodded and twisted her biggest ring for a few moments before continuing. 'The spirits speak through me. Sometimes their words aren't very intelligible, and in those cases, Freddy helps make the words clearer.'

I looked at Freddy. Not a flicker of expression crossed that pale face.

'How?' I asked, becoming more confused as the conversation went on. Did she honestly believe she had psychic powers? Was it possible she really did? Spiritualists thought authentic mediums could reach the souls of the dead in the Spirit World, but even believers realized that many of those who boasted about having such powers were frauds. The most famous Spiritualist in the world, Sir Arthur Conan Doyle, was a man of stern honesty and intelligence, and a medical doctor on top of that. His beliefs were unshakable. That was about all I knew when it came to Spiritualism. I had never met anyone who had actually contacted the dead. Spiritualism had always seemed to me like a religion for the rich.

Madame Carlotta ignored my question – she wasn't about to give away the store on my first day at work. 'After we've finished with Tommy's messages, you'll make the appropriate comments about how happy you are to communicate with his spirit, and we'll move on to the Adler sisters. Their note said they wanted to ask their father about investing their inheritance. We'll see what their father has to say on that topic. Then, when all the spirits have departed and Archangel Michael has left us, I'll collect any donations and retire upstairs to rest. You have no idea how exhausting it is to connect to the Great Beyond. The strain leaves me weak for hours. You will go out with the sisters and tell them how pleased you are with my success, and if need be, encourage them to come again, when I can do a better job for them. Without being too obvious, naturally.'

'Naturally.'

'Séances seldom last beyond an hour or two, but with the spirits, one never knows.'

'I see.'

Freddy still refused to meet my eye. There was no time to probe how much of Madame Carlotta's game was real and how much was fraud, because at that moment, the front doorbell chimed. Freddy leaped out of his chair and scooted up the stairs on stocking feet. I gathered his work was done behind the scenes.

'Gracious! Everyone's early tonight,' said Madame Carlotta, rising and smoothing the flounces of her gypsy skirt. 'I trust the spirits will be prompt as well!' She giggled like a nervous girl waiting for a beau, then, with a glance in the hall mirror to make sure her blackened hair peeked out just enough from her turban, she flung open the door with a queenly gesture.

'Come in! Come in, ladies, and join us. Tonight is the perfect night for a visit from the Spirit World. Come meet your fellow spiritual traveler, Mrs Tommy Pastore. Mrs Pastore, these are the Misses Adlers.'

I said my how-de-dos and the Adlers gave their Christian names.

'I'm Leticia Adler,' said one, 'and this is my sister Andrea.'

'Pleased to meet you, I'm sure.' I said in my best high-society manner, the one I learned when I used to wait on rich customers at Marshall Field's.

Madame Carlotta took charge. 'Now, if you would be so kind as to leave your wraps and bags on the rack and, when you're ready, follow me into the Spirit Chamber.' And with a rustle of her skirt and petticoats, she swept out of the parlor, leaving the sisters to remove their outer garments and plain brown hats. The women – one stout, one thin – bore little resemblance to each other, except that both seemed to be in their fifties. Baby Tommy earned his keep as an excellent conversation starter.

'What a precious little one!' the spinsters cooed. Tommy obliged with a squeak.

'It's a boy. His name is Tommy, and he's three weeks old. Is this your first time here?' I asked, knowing the answer.

The Adler sisters admitted it was. 'We learned about Madame Carlotta from an advertisement in the newspaper,' said Miss Leticia, the stout one. 'Our cousins in New York are ardent Spiritualists, and they encouraged us to come. We've never done anything like this before. It's rather daunting.'

'Not at all,' I reassured her. 'This is my second visit to Madame Carlotta, and I promise you there is nothing alarming involved,' I said, hoping I was right.

'You must have had success on your first visit to have returned,' said Miss Andrea, the thin one, as she pulled the hatpins from her hat and patted her hair.

I frowned in a show of candor. 'In truth, I learned very little last week, but I am not so naïve that I think the spirits can be commanded by us mortals. I believe in giving things like this two or three tries before making a decision about continuing, don't you?'

'Oh . . . well, yes, I suppose you're right,' said Miss Andrea.

I'd already begun earning my dollar.

We moved into the darkened séance room where Madame Carlotta was seated at the round table in a chair facing the only window, which she had covered from ceiling to floor with a thick purple curtain. I took the chair opposite her and set Tommy's basket on the floor beside me. As we took our chairs, Carlotta struck a match and held it to the wick of a single white candle in the middle of the table.

'Let us join hands and bow our heads in prayer,' she began. 'Dear Lord, who commands the day and night, the heavens and earth, the past and future, look with favor, we beseech you, on our work tonight as we pierce the dark veil of death and commune with those who have crossed over to your everlasting glory. Amen. Now, as our savior Jesus Christ has taught us to say, "Our Father, who art in heaven . . ."'

As our voices filled the room with the soft chant, I peered around in the dim candlelight. Opposite me, Madame Carlotta leaned forward on the table, resting on her elbows as each hand clasped one of the Adler sisters' hands. Her eyes were closed, her chin raised as if stretching toward the ceiling. She seemed to have fallen into a trance. After a long silence, she spoke in a voice that was lower and harsher than I had ever heard her use. More masculine and raspy, more mysterious. My spine tingled. Was this real? Was it the archangel himself? '*Ave verum corpus natum . . . vere passum immolatum in cruce pro homine . . .*'

All us Duval kids had been dragged to church every Sunday of our lives, but after I left home, my parents couldn't command me any longer. The mumbo-jumbo Carlotta was chanting made me think of the priests we used to hear in church. I guessed the words were Latin. I wondered if they had any meaning.

All at once a gust of wind blew into the room from nowhere, extinguishing the feeble candle. There was no open window or door anywhere, and the only electric fan sat in the parlor behind a closed door. The skin on my neck and shoulders prickled. Both Adler sisters squeezed my hands nervously. We were now in total darkness – if my hands had been free and I had put my fingers in front of my face, I could not have seen them. Madame Carlotta must have expected the blackout because her monotonous chant never faltered. Freddy was doing this, I told myself sternly, but I couldn't be sure. Maybe Madame Carlotta did have special powers. Was it possible? Sir Arthur Conan Doyle certainly believed, and he was no dupe. I swallowed hard.

The breeze continued unevenly, in my face, then nothing, then in my face again like an oscillating fan. But there was no fan and no sound of a motor. Carlotta's voice grew more insistent as she moaned, 'Michael! Archangel Michael! Come, I beseech you, come to us this night. Give us the comfort of your heavenly presence. We are all believers who wish to commune with the infinite spirits in your world. We are all believers here, are we not?'

This seemed to require a response, so I led with a firm 'We are.' The Adler sisters followed timidly.

'Bless us with a visit from the spirit of Tommaso Pastore, the husband of one who is with us tonight, one who respectfully entreats him to speak to her through me, your humble servant. He crossed over only two months ago, blessed Michael, prince of angels, can you find him for us? His grieving widow wishes to know if he is well and happy in the Spirit World. She wishes him to know that she has his son with her, a fine, healthy boy named for his father. Can Tommaso Pastore be found, O Great Archangel of God?' And she continued in this vein for another few minutes until she lowered her voice almost to a whisper. 'I am here,' she said softly. Or was it really Tommy's spirit speaking?

To tell the honest truth, the voice sounded a bit like Tommy's. I waited, motionless, forgetting to breathe, my heart pounding like a bass drum in a marching band. Was I supposed to speak? Unsure of the rules, I hesitantly whispered, 'Tommy? Is that really you?'

Madame Carlotta provided the reply in a hoarse, whispered voice. 'Yessss.'

It really was Tommy! My heart nearly flipped over in my chest. She was real! 'We-we have a son, Tommy. Did you know?'

'I knowwww. He is beautifullll.'

My voice shook. 'I named him after you.'

'I am proud of himmmm. And youuuu.'

'I miss you, Tommy. I love you very much.' I couldn't hold back the tears. It felt like knives were twisting in my chest.

'I love youuuu.'

Then, recollecting my purpose, I went on, 'I wanted to tell you, all our money was stolen. I had to move out of the house. I'm living in a boarding house. I haven't much money left. Do you think I should take Tommy and go home to my parents? Or to my brother? I don't know what to do.'

'Neverrrr to your parentsssss. Tommy would be in grave dangerrrr. And you as well. Remember our wedding? Remember your father, so drunk . . . so drunk . . . how he beat your little brotherrrr? Find worrrrk. Stay awayyyy from your familyyyy.'

And that was the moment I knew it was all faked. My tears dried up. My heart calmed. Tommy and I never had a wedding. We were married at the courthouse by a justice of the peace. None of my family came. My father had forbidden my sisters and brothers from attending a wop wedding. Tommy never met my parents or my siblings. But I did remember – and so, obviously, did Madame Carlotta – that a few years earlier, my *brother's* wedding was marred by my father's violence when he took offense at something my youngest brother, Louis, had done and beat him bloody right in front of the shocked priest, who did nothing to stop him until my father had broken the boy's nose. Myrtle Burkholtzer must have been there too. I certainly hadn't told her about it; shame prevented me from ever mentioning the incident to anyone, even to Tommy. But she remembered it wrong – she thought it was my own wedding. It wasn't Tommy's spirit speaking to me. It was Myrtle the Fraud's wretched memory. I was embarrassed that I'd been taken in, even for those brief moments. Straightening my shoulders, I ended the charade with a few more questions that needed no answers. What I *did* need was to earn that dollar. 'I'm so happy to be with you again, Tommy. Will you come again?'

'Yessss, when you need me. You're not alone. I'll always be here for you.'

Madame Carlotta paused for a few minutes, then lapsed back into the Latin chants before calling on Archangel Michael again, asking this time would he bring the spirit of Mr Adler to his daughters?

Archangel Michael obliged, rousting out the late Mr Adler with prompt efficiency, but if the first spirit visitation was a victory, the second was a rout.

'Mr Adler . . . Mr Adler . . . your daughters await . . . are you here with us tonight?' Her voice lowered and she answered herself, 'I am here.'

Miss Leticia made some tittery sound in her throat; Miss Andrea, the skeptic, remained warily silent.

'Tell us, sir, whether you are content in the afterlife.'

'I . . . am . . . content.'

During the lull that followed, Miss Andrea inserted herself into the conversation. 'Father? Father, this is Andrea,' she said in a firm, quiet voice free from intimidation. 'We think of you every day and miss you. There is a matter of money we wish to bring to your attention. We wish your advice on the matter of the money we've inherited.'

A long silence ensued. I imagined that Madame Carlotta was waiting to hear more about this inheritance, more information that would guide her to an appropriate response, but the Adlers were not forthcoming. She didn't know the sisters. She had no memories to fall back on. After an awkward length of time, she began to spout gobbledygook in her own subdued tone, like a woman in a trance.

'I'm losing him . . . he's just out of reach . . . Mr Adler, don't leave us, please . . . *cuius latus perforatum* . . . golden silver, silvery gold . . . *fluxit aqua et sanguine* . . . Florida . . . railroads to Florida . . . investments . . . the land of flowers . . . land of soaring values . . . stocks and bonds . . . investments . . . beware, beware the false gods, beware mammon . . . almost . . . he's trying to speak, but it's so faint, I cannot—'

Suddenly another voice came into the blackness of our room.

It was a disembodied voice, a man's deep voice, one that clearly did not come from Madame Carlotta, but from the air around us. It had to be Freddy.

'Make no decisions, my daughters. Make no foolish moves. Remember what I taught you. Haste makes waste. Investigate all possibilities thoroughly. Plan and reflect. Let caution be your watch word.'

At that point, Madame Carlotta dropped the hands she was holding, gave an exhausted sigh, and buried her head in her arms.

The séance – such as it was – ended.

SIX

As Madame Carlotta came slowly to life, I picked up Baby Tommy's basket as gently as possible so as not to wake him. Subdued, the sisters and I put on our hats and wraps and made our way out to the street.

The heat had broken, but Chicago's dark streets were almost empty and our footsteps echoed off the pavement. The gusty lake breeze did nothing to rid the air of the stink of rotting fish and bad eggs from nearby garbage. One of the Adler sisters gave a soft cry when something scuttered along a clogged gutter. The other murmured, 'Only a rat.'

'Do you have far to walk?' I asked, breaking the otherworldly stillness with mundane conversation.

Miss Leticia roused herself. 'If it were daylight, we might walk to the streetcar, but at night, Sister prefers to take a taxi. We'll hail one at the corner.'

'May I walk with you? I'm headed your way,' I lied.

'Of course, my dear,' said Miss Leticia. 'You must be pleased to have reached your late husband. How sad that he was lost so young! Was he able to see his little boy before he died?'

'I'm afraid not. Little Tommy was born a month after my husband was killed.'

'Killed? Oh my! You poor dear!'

'He was shot by the O'Banion gang in May while delivering liquor.' I hoped they weren't too scandalized at his working for the Outfit. They were, after all, citizens of Chicago, and if they read the newspapers, they should have been used to the gangster violence and corruption that had leeched into every level of daily life. 'And someone stole the money he left me, so that's why I'm thinking about moving in with relatives.'

The sisters exchanged a long look, and Miss Leticia nodded, as if giving permission. Miss Andrea spoke. 'Those vicious gangsters have taken over Chicago and spread their evil ways even to decent families, haven't they? It's terrible! We understand because our own dear brother – our youngest brother, Alfred – was shot too. Murdered. Shortly before your husband, during the Cicero elections in April. The police blame the rival O'Banion gang in his case as well. You may have read about it in the newspaper?'

'Yes, indeed, I believe I did.' I could not afford to buy newspapers now, but we used to have the evening newspaper every day when Tommy was alive. These days, I read the abandoned copies I found on streetcars or the ones on the racks at the public library. But I remembered the violence during the Cicero elections when several gangsters were gunned down, including a high-up one named Frank Capone, brother of Johnny Torrio's right-hand man. Tommy had told me about the violence. 'I am very sorry. A tragedy for your family.' I couldn't help but note the introduction of yet another murdered soul. My own tragedy was hardly unique in Chicago during those years. Did Madame Carlotta's Spiritualism business attract more than its fair share of people seeking to contact murder victims? And how would Carlotta know if the departed soul had expired naturally or violently? Did that even matter?

Miss Andrea spoke up. 'He was our brother and we loved him, but like your husband, he chose the wrong path.'

'The path of crime and sin,' added Miss Leticia. 'It's his money we are concerned about. He was a bachelor, you see, and he left what he had to us, Andrea and me and our other sister, all of us unmarried.'

'Oh, I thought the inheritance came from your father.' More to the point, so did Madame Carlotta, who had very nearly stumbled over that important detail. 'At least it was good of your brother to remember his sisters in his will.'

'But you see the moral dilemma, do you not, my dear?' said Miss Andrea. 'Brother's money comes from sin. From gambling, bootlegging, white slavery, robbery, and God-only-knows what else. Leticia thinks we should consider giving it to our church to wash it clean. There it will do God's work, and there can be no criticism. But the three of us are not wealthy and have been able to put away very little for our old age. We wanted to consult with Father – he was a vestryman at our Episcopal Church and highly respected in the community. We wanted to see what he recommended.'

'Perhaps you should return to Madame Carlotta and give it another try.'

'The second time certainly worked for you, didn't it?'

'It did.'

'I'm sure we will consider following your example.' A black taxi pulled up to the curb, and we said goodbye.

As soon as their cab had turned the corner, I retraced my steps to Madame Carlotta's house to report. My thoughts raced. I knew now how I could make myself valuable to Madame Carlotta, if only she would listen to my proposal.

Freddy let me in. 'Carlotta's changing,' he muttered.

'I'll wait for her in the parlor, then. And you might be interested in what I have to say, too. I can see you are an important part of her business. That was an effective interpretation of the late Mr Adler's voice. How did you do it?'

The mantel clock ticked loudly for a long half-minute as Freddy struggled to decide whether or not I was worthy of confidence. Finally he said, 'I made a hole in the ceiling that you can't see in the candlelight. Then I use bellows to put out the candle. I lower a metal speaking tube to a point just above the table, and when I talk into it, my words come out the other end. I can make my voice sound lower, older, and the tube gives it a spooky feel.'

'You tried to cover for her. A shame you didn't know what to say. I think I can help with that, if the Adlers return.'

'She's a good person,' he muttered sullenly.

'Freddy, look at me. I'm not out to hurt her. I knew her from way back when, before you were born. Her daughter was my school chum. Tell me – be honest – does she have any real powers?'

There was a long silence before he replied, 'Maybe . . . some.'

Meaning none. 'I see. But she honestly believes she does, is that right?'

He nodded miserably. 'She's a good person! She only wants to help people, to make them happy. Maybe she really was a gypsy in her past life, I don't know much about gypsies. But she doesn't charge any money for her séances; she only takes donations and only when the clients feel like they've been helped. She's not a fraud. Well, maybe a little, but she's not a bad fraud. No, I'm the fraud. And I don't care if I am. I do it to help her.'

Before I could pursue that comment, Madame Carlotta started down the stairs toward the parlor. Freddy lapsed back into his silent sulk.

This much I remembered about her from the old days when she used to be Mrs Burkholtzer: she was always kind, and not only to me. I never heard her say a mean word about anyone. She didn't have to put others down to build herself up. She tried to understand people, to see life from their point of view. Walk in their shoes, as the saying goes. Maybe that made her psychic.

'How did it go, Maddie?' she asked.

'Swell, I think. I told them that this was my second visit and that the first hadn't been particularly successful . . .' Here Carlotta scowled, so I explained how I had persuaded the sisters that a second or third visit was advisable. 'I believe they will return in a few days. Meanwhile, I learned a little about their circumstances that will help you and Freddy meet their needs, should they come back.'

'What do you mean?'

'I learned that the inheritance they are referring to comes from their younger brother, who worked for Johnny Torrio's Outfit. He didn't merely expire; he was murdered back in April during the Cicero elections. There are three sisters, and they need the money, but at least one of them – I'm not sure which – considers it tainted and wants to give it to the Church to make it clean.'

Freddy snorted. I felt the same way. The sisters needed it more than some church.

'It wasn't investment advice they wanted from their father,' I went on. 'It was advice on whether or not to keep the money. He was a vestryman in their church.' Whatever that was, it sounded important.

Madame Carlotta blinked thoughtfully. 'You have earned your pay tonight, Maddie-my-girl. Thank you for encouraging them to return. And for the details. That will certainly help me break through the veil next time. If there is a next time.' She pulled a dollar bill from a pocket and handed it to me with a flourish far grander than the amount warranted. It was time to pitch my services to this odd creature. I chose my words carefully.

'Madame Carlotta, did you notice how much stronger your powers felt when you were summoning Tommy than when you were trying to contact the late Mr Adler?' I said, and without waiting for her to respond, rushed on. 'I believe that is due in large part to your knowledge of the client's background. Your knowledge of me and my family from the old neighborhood put you in a position to channel the spirits smoothly and accurately. Your powers were weaker with the Adlers, whose family and circumstances you knew little about. I can help fill that void with information I collect about your clients and their deceased loved ones, like I did tonight. With the details I'll dig up, you will have less trouble communing with the Spirit World and translating the spirits' messages to the living.'

'How would you do that?' she asked in a small voice that wavered uncertainly.

'Give me a dollar a day and the names of your upcoming appointments, and I'll show you. If you don't find my services valuable after the next few séances, you have no obligation to continue.'

She fidgeted a bit, then agreed. I left with the names of the clients scheduled for her future séances – only two – and told her I would return before the first one took place.

Then I felt so high, you'd've thought I'd won the Irish Sweepstakes. I'd bought myself some time – sure, only a week or so – but I was determined to make good on my end, so good Madame Carlotta couldn't live without me. If I could just parlay this into regular work, I would have enough for our room and board. I could keep myself and Tommy safe from the Outfit's grubby grip.

SEVEN

Through that summer and into fall, Madame Carlotta's client list grew as fast as Baby Tommy, and I had everything to do with both improvements. People returned two, three, four times to hear from the Spirit World, and they told their friends that Madame Carlotta was the real deal. She could afford to pay me twelve dollars a week and she raised Freddy's pay to the same, earning me his eternal gratitude if not his total trust.

At first I'd played my cards close to the chest, protecting my research methods until I realized there was no need for secrets. Freddy could no more have taken over my research gathering than I could have managed his 'séance enhancement', as Madame Carlotta called it. Once he realized I was going to improve Carlotta's gig, not ruin it, he started to come around. His devotion to her was touching. I couldn't work out how they were related, or if they even were, but each was highly protective of the other. Nowadays we worked hand-in-glove, Freddy assisting with my research and me helping him prepare new techniques.

I had made peace with my conscience by promising I would do this only until Baby Tommy was weaned and I could find respectable work. I had to admit what I was doing was dishonest, not to mention sinful in the eyes of the Church, but sin comes in degrees. This was a whole lot less immoral than selling myself on the street or letting my baby starve, and it kept us both out of Johnny Torrio's clutches. We never hurt anyone and we helped most.

Our clients were three sorts: grieving relatives who left Carlotta's much happier than when they arrived; thrill seekers who came for the excitement; and crooks looking for a short-cut. The thrill seekers required little research. For them, we were pure entertainment, and Freddy and I could provide that as I pretended to communicate with one of my deceased relatives.

Sometimes we connected them to a spirit – occasionally one they didn't even know about – who told them how lovely it was in the Great Beyond. The crooks were easy to deal with too. They were the ones who wanted to know which horses were going to win at the racetrack tomorrow or what corn futures were going to sell for next month at the Board of Trade. Madame Carlotta made it clear that the spirits frowned on such questions. The grieving relatives were the ones I targeted for investigation. My natural curiosity and persistence stood me in good stead – by the end of the first week, I'd crafted a series of successful investigating procedures; by the end of the second, I was feeling like a regular Sherlock Holmes.

Carlotta doubled her income the first month I worked for her and doubled it again the next. She wasn't one of those crooked mediums who urged clients to turn over all their money; she never even mentioned money. She kept a basket on a table in the parlor where, after each session, I would make a show of depositing a ten-dollar banknote, thus giving others the idea of a donation. Most took the hint. All in all, we got along well enough.

'I've been thinking about music,' I said one wet October evening when Freddy and I were alone in the upstairs enhancement room. Madame Carlotta had concluded her regular Monday night séance, her clients and the spirits had departed, and I'd finished nursing Tommy, who had fallen into a deep sleep in the straw basket he was rapidly outgrowing. Freddy was putting away the evening's enhancements.

'Music?' he said.

'What about a bell or two with deep tones? You could ring them from up here to signal the arrival of Archangel Michael.'

He thought a minute. 'I could muffle the clappers so they sounded distant and spooky.'

'Good idea. You don't play the violin by any chance, do you?'

Freddy barked a short laugh that gave my question the scorn it deserved.

I grinned. 'Well, I didn't think so, but how hard could it be to saw away with a bow on the strings? I saw a violin for sale yesterday at Old Man Jeter's junk shop, kinda battered but only two dollars. I was thinking we might buy it and find a bow somewhere, and you could play some eerie notes that sounded otherworldly.'

Not one to rush to decisions, Freddy pondered the violin idea for some moments before agreeing to broach the topic with Madame Carlotta.

Just then, she came upstairs, a wad of donations in one hand. Freddy proposed the bell and violin idea. 'Music *would* enhance the experience, wouldn't it?' she agreed, and feeling flush, she peeled off two bills. 'Why don't you buy that violin before you come back tomorrow? And keep your eyes open for a suitable bell. Here's your ten back, Maddie, and one to grow on. Now, a new assignment. Tonight Mrs Beasley said she was sending a friend – a recent widow – to us. Tomorrow.' She pulled off her garish gypsy headdress and began wiping away the red lipstick with a handkerchief. Freddy and I swapped pained glances. A new client was always good news; a new client with only one day for background investigation was a serious problem. 'I told Mrs Beasley that any friend of hers was welcome at my séances, but I thought it would behoove the bereaved lady to spend her first visit observing so she could judge my clairvoyant powers before committing herself. All I know is her name: Mrs Charles Weidemann.'

Weidemann . . . Weidemann . . . the name tickled something deep inside my brain. Unusual name. German origin. I'd come across it somewhere before. Probably from the newspaper. Tommy used to bring home the afternoon paper every day, and we'd read it together each evening.

The delay was excellent news! It meant I still had a few days for research before Mrs Weidemann's own séance would be scheduled. I should have had more faith in Madame Carlotta's talent for turning dross to gold. Nonetheless, time was ticking, and as Freddy and I finished cleaning up and putting away the props, we laid our plans for the following day.

Madame Carlotta's capacity for self-delusion continued to astonish me. She rationalized my research as something that sharpened her psychic powers and saw Freddy's enhancements as gilt on her lily. Sometimes it felt as if Freddy and I were her parents, shielding her from the crass, day-to-day realities of life, and yet it was she who mothered us and paid our wages. I continued my attempts to find a respectable retail job, one that would pay more than the survival pay I was earning as her shill, one that would let me shake off the shame that was never far from the edge of my conscience, ready to rebuke me at every turn, but nothing had panned out so far. We weren't hurting anyone – that was my defense whenever my conscience flared – but even I had to admit we were taking advantage of people in their sorrow. That was something I could not reconcile or wish away. For his part, Freddy had no conscience. He had no emotions at all other than his love and loyalty for Carlotta. And Carlotta? There was a woman on a mission to save the world from grief. Delusional, to be sure, but sincere . . . as far as I could tell. One thing was certain: Carlotta's clients usually left her séances happier than when they came in.

And, to be honest, I was enjoying my work. As it turned out, I was pretty good at the investigating business. Chalk it up to a devious mind, if need be, but not much got by me when it came to digging out facts and thinking beyond the obvious. I'd quickly learned to probe a little deeper into human behavior and emotion and to push past superficial answers. The job didn't pay much – the money I made covered the boarding house with almost nothing to spare – but at least Tommy and I had a roof over our heads and food in our stomachs, and I'd discovered that setting the feet of the bed in pans of oxalic acid kept the ants and roaches out of my sheets.

I met Freddy the next morning on the steps of the Cook County Courthouse on the Near North Side shortly before they were due to unlock the doors. Baby Tommy was with me. I'd learned pretty quick that a baby can disarm the gruffest of people, something that usually worked in my favor, particularly in my current position. Freddy greeted me, then chucked the baby under his chin and squealed, 'Oooo, there's a new tooth!'

'There are two coming in on the bottom. It's making him drool a lot and fuss.' But I was proud of this further proof of Tommy's superiority to the average baby. I shifted his basket to the other arm as the doors opened. 'Here we go. You're on.'

Freddy took the lead. In the beginning, I'd come to the courthouse alone only to face blank looks and unyielding disapproval.

The courthouse clerks, all male and immune to Baby Tommy's charms, would wait on every man in the room, including those who came in after me, before they'd acknowledge my presence, and then, only with a sneer. Once it took four hours before the room was empty of men and even then, they ignored me until an alderman walked through the office and asked why no one was waiting on this woman. Then they were forced to call my number. I refused to let the system beat me. I couldn't afford to give up, so I went home that very afternoon and bought a cheap, second-hand suit for Freddy. From then on, he came to the courthouse with me. They waited on Freddy. They thought he was an office boy at a law firm.

Within twenty minutes, one of the clerks produced the last will and testament of Charles Francis Weidemann. A probated will is public record, so there were never any raised eyebrows when Freddy asked to see one. He took the document to a counter in an adjacent room where I waited with pencil and paper to take notes.

A will is a huge help to a medium. It usually lists the names of family members and often includes tidbits that can be incorporated into the patter, such as a significant ruby brooch for a daughter or a summer house on Lake Michigan for a grandson. Clients are dazzled by this sort of detail. And remarkably clueless as to its origins.

I wrote Weidemann at the top of the page and skimmed through the usual sound-mind-and-body blather until I came to things Carlotta could use: to wife Daniela Gettler Weidemann, the house and half of the estate; to nephews Noah Bristow and Richard Gettler, one quarter of the estate each; to nieces Rosalee Abbott and Fannie Abbott, three hundred dollars each; to Bessie Jackson, cook, two hundred dollars; to each servant employed at the time of death, fifty dollars; to Ralph Manderly, friend, his choice of ten books from his library; the remainder of all law books to the Northwestern University School of Law.

'He was a lawyer,' I remarked to Freddy in a low voice. 'They had no children of their own. At least, none that survived.' I would need to check that last assumption.

Freddy couldn't help me with this part. He couldn't read.

He'd been forced to confess the first time I brought him to the courthouse. When I'd handed him a pencil and paper, expecting him to speed along the note taking, he'd stood there like a statue until I asked if he was feeling poorly. He didn't answer. He didn't need to. I divined it instantly. We didn't discuss the matter until several days later.

'I quit going to school,' he told me. 'I just couldn't learn that stuff. I can write my name and I know my letters and numbers and I can read some.' That last was an exaggeration, as I was to find out. The boy wasn't stupid – far from it – but he was right: he just couldn't learn to read. I tried once to work with him, but he grew angry when he couldn't sound out the easiest words. We hadn't spoken of it since.

I continued my note taking, listing Mr Weidemann's legacies to the United Charities of Chicago, the Chicago Legal Aid Society, the Cook County Poorhouse, and St. James Episcopal Cathedral to help pay for its new organ. Clearly, Judge Weidemann had been a prominent Chicago citizen and what was even better, he'd been flush. Adding a wealthy widow to Carlotta's client list would do no harm to our balance sheet. I'd make sure we took extra special care of Mrs Weidemann.

'Done!' I pocketed my pencil and folded the paper into my handbag. Oozing servility, Freddy returned the document to the haughty clerks and we walked out of the office, through the halls, and into the autumn chill. Without another word, we turned our feet toward State Street and made our way to the public library a few blocks away.

Not knowing the exact date of death causes only a short delay in finding a newspaper obituary. I usually estimated it at a week before the will was probated and started there, working my way in both directions. Freddy requested a week's worth of back issues of the *Chicago Tribune*, and I began paging through the Ws in the obituary section.

Obituaries are usually full of family names and often include personality traits of the deceased. Women don't always have obituaries, but men do, even not-so-important men, and Carlotta's business was heavily skewed toward widows. Mr Charles Francis Weidemann's obituary took an hour to dig up, but once I'd found it, provided a gold mine of detail because he'd been such a prominent Chicago citizen. If it hadn't been for the steely-eyed woman behind the library desk who was more clairvoyant than Madame Carlotta would ever be, I'd've torn the page out of the newspaper and saved myself the trouble of taking notes. No such luck.

The man had been seventy-three and was in poor health when he was carried off by a sudden attack on October the second, 1924. He had been the second son of Mr and Mrs Henrich Weidemann, originally of Bonn, Germany, who had immigrated to New York in the 1840s. A good student, Charles Francis Weidemann had enjoyed a college education and gone on to study law at Columbia University, then moved to Chicago where he practiced law for twenty years, was elected to the circuit court for two six-year terms, and taught at Northwestern University's law school until his death. His relatives we already knew from the will, but I double-checked for accuracy. The obituary reported Judge Weidemann's many sterling qualities. He was widely acknowledged to be an honest man – this was always said of the deceased, even though an honest judge in Cook County was as unlikely as snow in July – and was praised as a dedicated teacher who nurtured and inspired hundreds of law students during his many years in the classroom. He adopted two nephews and raised them as his sons. If half what they wrote about Judge Weidemann was true, he would have been a paragon.

The obituary also gave us the name of the church where his funeral took place and the cemetery where he would lie. That was always helpful.

Freddy returned the stack of newspapers to the reference desk while I picked the latest *City Directory* off the shelf and looked up the judge's home address.

After the library, Freddy and I split up – I to the Weidemann house, he to the newspaper office to pay for another month of Madame Carlotta's advertisement. This ad was a revision of the one she had been using. I'd persuaded her to include a little picture of a gypsy in the corner as a come-on. 'Madame Carlotta,' it read in bold type, 'Spiritualist, Clairvoyant. Sees all, knows all.' Then in smaller letters: 'Will reunite you with the spirit of your departed loved one. Satisfaction guaranteed.'

It was a safe promise. Not since I'd been hired had anyone left disappointed.

Whenever possible, I liked to pay a visit to the client's home. Just seeing the outside would usually provide some useful morsels, like a picket fence, a tin roof, a flower garden out front, or a porch swing. That sort of detail woven into her delivery made Madame Carlotta sound like a genuine psychic. With the Weidemanns' address in hand, I set out on the streetcar toward Chicago's fashionable Near North Side, Baby Tommy snuggled against my chest in a warm shawl. I found the house without much effort and lingered around the corner out of the wind where I had a good view of the front door.

It was a pretty house, large, unattached, with lots of gables and a turret on the side, and it stood third on a moderately busy street among others like it. People who lived on this street were well off but not filthy rich, at least not by Chicago standards. A cluster of white wicker chairs sat on the wraparound porch and an empty birdcage hung from the ceiling. Several motorcars hugged the curb. No way of telling which of them, if any, belonged to the Weidemanns. Something about the house drew me, and I stood there until dusk turned on the gaslights, waiting for some sign of life on the porch or at the windows, but no one went in or came out.

I couldn't linger any longer – I had a séance to prepare.

EIGHT

At seven o'clock, Madame Carlotta retired to her upstairs room to dress and put on her face. She would spend part of the time reviewing the information I'd gathered on tonight's clients and the rest on her gypsy queen get-up, while Freddy and I assembled the evening's spiritual enhancements.

'Who's coming tonight?' Freddy asked. The kid who couldn't read had a better memory than any stage actor. He knew very well who was coming; this was just his way of asking for a final rundown. Already dressed and made up for his role, he looked like a chimney sweep at the end of a long day, with black trousers and shirt, black socks and gloves to cover his hands and feet, a black scarf tied around his orange hair, and burnt cork to darken every inch of his pallid face. A slender lad, he had found tight-fitting clothing so he could move through the dark without the slightest swish of fabric against fabric. Tonight I wore my mourning dress, something I had abandoned in my everyday life.

'We've got six tonight. Plus Mrs Charles Weidemann, who's observing. We'll sit her in the corner by the spirit cabinet. I'll keep a close eye on her. There's Mr and Mrs Lowthen whose son Daniel was killed in the war. It's their first visit.'

'In France, right?'

I nodded. 'If Carlotta doesn't use any French, you know what to say.' I'd taught him some phrases that I remembered from my French-Canadian grandparents. 'Then there's Mr and Mrs Vecchio back again – she's the one who can't carry a baby the whole nine months. Miss Felicity Hunt is back to talk with her mother about her romance with Mr Anthony Braithwaite. They've been courting for two years. I've checked him out and he has a job in a bank and seems quite respectable. And Miss Wilhelmina Devon is a first-timer: she's grieving for her fiancé whose fishing boat went down in a storm on Lake Michigan. Very sad. I'll handle the water for that one. I hope Carlotta starts with her so I can spill it early on before it leaks all over my sleeves.'

'Did you tell her to start with him?'

'Sure, but you know what she says: the spirits decide the order, not her.'

Freddy rolled his eyes. We viewed Carlotta's clairvoyant abilities through the same lens but seldom voiced our skepticism. She was a fraud, but a generous fraud who genuinely believed she was ministering to the bereaved. We were grateful for our jobs. If she wanted to believe she was psychic and her clients wanted to believe she was psychic, who were we to ruin the game? It's what fed us all.

If Freddy had asked, which he didn't, I'd have struggled to explain my own beliefs about the supernatural. My heart believed we could commune with the dead; my brain had its doubts. I talked to Tommy in my head at night and sometimes out loud when I visited his grave, and he answered in my head. I was sure he was in heaven – Mr Torrio had paid for enough masses to get a murderer's soul out of Purgatory if it had been stuck there, and I didn't honestly think God would punish Tommy for delivering booze when his own son had turned water into wine. Sometimes on a quiet morning when I was not quite awake and time was flowing upstream, I sensed I was back in our house in our big bed, feeling his warm presence beside me and hearing the soft rhythm of his breath inches from my cheek. I would try to hang on to that state as long as I could, for once I'd opened my eyes, I could do nothing but weep for what I'd lost. That was my psychic experience, and it was nothing like the hocus-pocus of Madame Carlotta's séances. She had no powers I could see, but I couldn't measure all mediums by her yardstick. My heart said some of her powers could be legit. My head scoffed.

'And who are you playing tonight?' Freddy said.

'The usual.' My regular role was that of the young widow with a baby who contacts her husband about moving out of the boarding house. None of these people had experienced my performance, so nothing original was required.

'But you didn't bring Tommy.'

'Too risky. I can't mind him when I'm rigged out for the

water trick. I might spring a leak. He'll be fine. I left him with Mrs Jones back at the boarding house. She has a grown daughter who is simple-minded, and the girl loves to play mother. Tommy is better than her dolls.' She loved the quarter I gave her too.

'Is the window open?' he asked.

I nodded. 'I think we're ready. I'd better go.' I needed to leave the house before the first clients arrived and wait at the corner until several had been admitted before I knocked, so it wouldn't look like I was part of a scam.

Madame Carlotta greeted me as she did all her clients, with sympathy and respect. To all outward appearances, she worked alone. Everyone was introduced and we removed our wraps and chatted nervously about the weather as we waited for the last person to show up.

I took special note of Mrs Weidemann, as I was in the midst of investigating her and her late husband. She seemed pleasant enough, with a short, plump body atop sturdy piano legs barely visible below her mid-calf hem. Her gray hair had been braided in two side plaits and wrapped over her head like a tiara. As befit a recent widow, she wore a black dress relieved only by a large cameo brooch at the center of her collar. A treasured gift from her late husband, perhaps? My investigation might let me answer that sort of question.

After the last guest had come through the door, Carlotta invited everyone into the room she called her Spirit Chamber so she could seat them in their predetermined locations. That's when I excused myself to the water closet upstairs, only that's not where I went. As soon as the last client was out of the parlor and the adjoining door was shut, I doubled back to search the ladies' handbags for anything – a photograph, a letter, a memento – that would reveal something useful. It wasn't as chancy as it sounds. No one ever came back into the parlor until after the séance was over, so I was confident that no one would catch me in the act. And I left no traces.

Often there was nothing to find, but tonight I hit pay dirt. Miss Wilhelmina Devon was carrying a photograph of a man standing in front of a boat – it could be no one but her lost-at-sea fisherman. I studied the picture for details and noticed the name of the boat painted on the side: *Illini*. The original Indian tribe that had lived along the lake before the white man came, a hundred years ago. French fur trappers had named the region Illinois after them.

I went into the hall and sat on the bottom step, as though I'd just come down the staircase, and I called out to Carlotta in the adjacent room, 'Madame Carlotta! Excuse me, please, but I am feeling quite unwell,' I said in a voice loud enough that everyone in the room could hear. 'I'm afraid I will have to leave and return on another night.'

The picture of concern, Carlotta rose from the table at once. She knew what my appeal meant. 'Please, remain seated. I'll only be a moment,' she said to the group. Then, when she had joined me in the hall, she fussed over my forehead and wrist and insisted on taking me to the kitchen for a glass of water. Out of earshot, I whispered my discovery.

'Miss Devon's fiancé – his boat's name was *Illini*, like the Indians. He had dark hair and broad shoulders.'

It was enough. Minutes later, she led me back to the séance room where I apologized profusely to one and all. 'A thousand apologies. I was feeling a little light-headed . . . all's well now. I only needed some water to chase away the dizziness. Please excuse the delay.'

Everyone murmured polite nothings as I took the chair next to Carlotta where I usually sat when I participated in a séance. That way, when we all held hands under the cover of darkness, I could let go of hers whenever I needed to perform some trick. Mrs Weidemann settled herself in the straight-backed chair we'd placed in the corner, next to the antique spirit cabinet we would not be using during this session. Tonight's performance would decide whether or not she returned – and whether the investigative work I'd done on her husband thus far was for naught.

A whiz at tinkering and building things, Freddy had fitted out the séance room with trap doors and sliding panels that were accessed from adjacent rooms, the basement, or the floor above – most of which even Madame Carlotta didn't know about. Her three-story house pressed tight against another similar house on one side, but there was a narrow alley on the opposite side that allowed for a window in the middle rooms.

Each floor had three rooms. The first floor consisted of a front parlor, a middle dining room that now served as our Spirit Chamber, or séance room, and a rear kitchen. The second floor contained three bedrooms and a modern bathroom at the end of the hall with a toilet, sink, and porcelain tub. Madame Carlotta rented the front bedroom to Mr Pearson, a traveling salesman who seldom spent more than two nights a week here. On séance nights, Mr Pearson kept to himself. If clients saw him, a boarder was easily explained. Carlotta had the quiet bedroom at the rear of the house. Our workroom was between the two, above the séance room – that was where we stored our 'enhancements', our equipment, tools, and disguises – and it had several trap doors that Freddy had cut through the floor to access the séance room from above. In one corner was the pallet where Freddy slept. He had moved in not long after soft-hearted Carlotta found him huddled in the alley. The basement was generally out of bounds, as she sub-let it to the shopkeeper next door for his excess stock, but Freddy had installed a trap door directly under the table to allow him to agitate the table legs from below.

Once we had all settled into our seats, Madame Carlotta lit the single candle in the center of the table and asked us to join hands. We were eight. She began, as always, with her own invocation followed by a recitation of the Lord's Prayer.

'Now, hold on to the flame with your eyes, with your heart,' she chanted in a soothing monotone. 'Concentrate on the flame, on your faith, on your journey, on your love for all people and all creatures of the earth, on the duality of the world . . . the invisible forces that connect you to the spirits . . . I call on the archangel Michael to come and lead us into the Spirit World, to connect us to the spirits we seek, to guide us in our spiritual dialogue. Let us receive your knowledge and wisdom . . . Come, Michael. Come to us. Speak. Bring us peace. Speak through my humble body, unworthy as it is.'

Her head dropped, her breathing seemed almost to cease. The self-induced trance was beginning to take hold. A distant bell, muffled, tolled three times. Wind stirred the air and the candle flickered wildly, then went out. Several clients gasped in surprise. We were in utter darkness. I bit my lower lip – one never knew what Carlotta would do or say when she was in her trance.

'I come forth.' The deep voice, raspy and delivered in something resembling a Middle Eastern accent, came from Madame Carlotta's lips. 'Understand that I come into this female vessel to deliver a simple message. I bring the transmutable flame of invisible forces.' Several long minutes passed before Michael's voice came again. 'Can you feel his presence? He is here. He is with you.'

'Mother? Father?' From the speaking tube came Freddy's natural voice.

'Daniel? Is that you, Daniel, darling?' said Mrs Lowthen. 'It sounds like Daniel! We miss you so much, dearest one!'

'Prove that you are Daniel,' demanded Mr Lowthen, more skeptical than his wife.

'My . . . school . . . Lake View . . .'

A gasp from both parents confirmed the accuracy of what I'd found in his obituary, published a month after his death in 1918 on a French battlefield. Freddy went on.

'I . . . am . . . with . . . you . . . oftennnnn,' he said, laboring over each word as if it cost him tremendous effort to push it out. 'Whenever the wind blows on your face, I am there. Whenever the sun shines on your back, I am there. I am the moon in the eastern sky, the stars at night. See them and know I am with you and love you.'

During the long silence that followed, the only sound was that of Mrs Lowthen sobbing softly and her husband clearing his throat several times. My own eyes were wet with tears. Losing a son . . . I could only imagine how it would feel to lose Little Tommy. I hoped Freddy's words would bring them some comfort.

My turn. Carlotta usually positioned me at the beginning of her séances so as to create a positive opening mood and build trust in her spiritual powers. None of the six clients tonight had heard my widow's routine, so we repeated that, with Freddy providing Tommy's voice, me exclaiming that it sounded just like Tommy, and me being told I shouldn't move back in with my parents. It took about ten minutes.

Carlotta resumed with her own voice, speaking in a hesitant

manner. 'I-I cannot see clearly . . . Michael, are you there? Help me, Michael. I sense . . . I sense . . . a presence . . . an Indian. Does anyone here seek an Indian?' A negative murmur around the table suggested Indians were in no one's thoughts. 'The red Indians who roamed this land before the white man came . . . noble savages . . . the sensation is very strong . . . the natives who hunted and fished these woodlands . . . the Illini . . .'

A gasp from Miss Devon cut through the dark. 'Oh, dear Lord, it's Carl! That's my Carl's boat, the *Illini*, not an Indian. Carl? Carl?'

That was my signal. I let go of Madame Carlotta's hand and stretched my arm toward into the middle of the table, while squeezing my elbow against the bladder in my armpit. Water streamed out through the tube that ran inside my sleeve, pooling on the tabletop, reaching each clients' hands at a different moment as I aimed in every direction. Their exclamations told me where the water flowed. To define the illusion, I said, 'Golly, it's water! Water on the table! What can that mean?'

Miss Devon supplied the answer. 'It's Carl. It's a message from Carl. It's how he died. Drowned. A storm . . .' Her voice broke.

'Carl is with us,' said Madame Carlotta, 'but he does not speak. I sense dark hair, strong, broad shoulders. A quiet man. I sense sorrow . . . grief . . . loss . . . great, great distance . . .'

'Carl, are you there? Speak to me, Carl, I implore you.'

'He does not speak,' continued Madame Carlotta, 'but I sense peace and contentment and love. I feel his thoughts . . . they come not in words but in emotion . . . you must not mourn me, he wants to say. You will carry on with God's work and find happiness.'

'I don't want happiness! I want you, Carl!'

'Happiness comes in many guises. The coming year will bring peace and contentment.' I wasn't sure if that last was Madame Carlotta speaking as Carl or as herself. Whatever, it was our final contact with Carl. I held my breath in anticipation of what was coming next. My eyes, now somewhat accustomed to the dark, had seen nothing, but my ears had picked up a faint noise from behind the heavy curtain as Freddy came through the open window. I coughed to cover any slight noise and, as intended, the clients were too caught up with the water to pay attention to the window behind them.

'What's that?' cried Mrs Weidemann from the corner. I heard nothing. Then I felt it. A flutter that stirred the air and moved quickly around me, around us all. Once it came so close to my face, I thought I felt a softness brush my cheek, and I made a startled noise and jerked.

'I felt something!' I cried out in alarm. No pretense necessary.

'Silence!' commanded Madame Carlotta. 'Listen.'

The ruse worked brilliantly. No one was focusing attention on the area by the curtain, where Freddy stood, half behind it, half outside it, his blackened form wholly invisible against the darkness of the room as he held the end of a black thread tied to the leg of a blackbird. The creature fluttered about the room, frustrated in its search for a suitable perch. Whenever he alighted on the chandelier, Freddy would give the thread a gentle tug and get him flying again.

My role was to guide the clients' thoughts, so I remarked in an awestruck voice, 'It sounds like the wings of angels. I could feel them against my cheek!'

Archangel Michael was back to provide the explanation through his medium. 'Infants . . . unborn souls await your arrival . . .'

'Our babies!' cried Mrs Vecchio.

The blackbird grew more agitated, fluttering wildly – I presumed Freddy was reeling it in. It wasn't smart to trust such things overlong. The impression had been made. When the fluttering had ceased and Freddy slipped out the window, the séance entered a period of low moans and Latin gibberish from Madame Carlotta, after which Archangel Michael conducted a spiritual monologue about unborn souls and hope for the future, all of which was designed to give Freddy time to return to his position above the chandelier for the final visitation.

Miss Felicity Hunt and her mother had been close, and Miss Hunt, now in her late twenties, felt unable to give her heart to a man without her late mother's approval. I had tracked the young man down to the bank where he worked, and then followed him home to the modest house where he lived with his parents and younger sister. When I saw a house for sale across the street, I pretended to be interested in buying it. As a potential buyer, I knocked on several doors, spoke with a few neighbors, and learned the family was regarded as upstanding citizens and their son as a sober, decent man. There are no guarantees in life, but this young man seemed like a pretty good bet. With the archangel Michael's help, we conveyed the late Mrs Hunt's support for the engagement, and Miss Felicity seemed satisfied. Perhaps relieved was the more accurate word.

'Go forth,' rasped the archangel Michael. 'Go forth tonight and reflect the love of God and the souls inhabiting the Spirit World in your daily lives, now and forever.'

We let go our hands and wordlessly made our way back into the parlor, where we put on our coats and wraps. There was very little conversation. I put my ten-dollar bill in the basket and everyone followed my example, some with bills larger than mine. As I left through the front door with the others, I noticed that Mrs Weidemann had held back to speak with Carlotta privately. A good sign. I'd get back to work on her case first thing tomorrow.

On the sidewalk, I paused beside Mrs Vecchio who was waiting for her husband to start their motorcar. 'I am sorry for your troubles,' I began, mindful of the fact that I, as a client, would not know anything about their childbearing problems other than what was revealed in the séance. 'I believe I share them, for at first, I thought the angels' wings were my own babies that I could not bear.'

'You, too?' she exclaimed.

'These difficulties are not so unusual. It only seems so because we seldom speak of our private sorrows to others. I now have a little boy who is the joy of my life.'

'How fortunate you are! How blessed! You finally carried one to term!'

I shook my head. 'I found another way. A friend told me about the orphans at Hull House, where there are babies hoping for mothers, and I found my son there.' It was true, in a way. I did get my son at Hull House. And I did remember seeing several orphaned babies when I was there, babies whose mothers had died or abandoned them and who had no known family. They were delivered to an orphanage if no one claimed them after a certain interval.

Mr Vecchio came around and held the door for his wife. She said nothing, but I hoped I had planted a seed.

NINE

'Wanna come with me to the juice joint around the corner?' Freddy asked when I'd returned to Madame Carlotta's after the séance.

It is said by people who know such things that someone counting Chicago's speakeasies would find ten thousand of them inside the city limits. I believed it. I'd walked down many a city block where four or five speaks operated bold as brass, with signs out front and unguarded doors, sometimes flaunting themselves on the same block as the local precinct station, and that didn't reckon the blind pigs that hid behind false fronts and locked doors. They all stayed open for one reason: people wanted to drink. And other people – like the Outfit – wanted to oblige them. Tommy once told me that distilled spirits cost next to nothing to make, but a bottle could sell for just about any price, even more when you broke it down by the glass. There was so much money in illegal liquor that men thought nothing of killing to get it.

Tommy and I used to go to speakeasies now and then, back when we were courting, just to get a drink and a bite and listen to the colored musicians play their jazz music. Tommy loved jazz. I liked it when it was peppy and we could dance to it, but I didn't tell him I was bored by the gloomy, everlasting sort that seemed to have no beginning or end. I hadn't been to a speakeasy since Tommy died. Didn't want to and couldn't afford it if I did. And what would I have done with Little Tommy? Just about anything could happen in a speak – colored could dance with white, women could smoke, kids could drink – but take a baby to a speak? I'd never seen that.

Freddy and I were evaluating the séance while we put away the enhancements. The last client had departed. The blackbird was back in his cage, feasting on seeds and bits of fruit. Carlotta had retired to her room to rest. She seldom remembered much about what went on during her séances. Freddy had changed out of his black clothing and wiped the burnt cork off his cheeks. Now he sported a clean white shirt and a pair of wide trousers too big for his skinny waist – suspenders kept them from falling and two large safety pins took up the slack in the back. 'A stiff drink would go down good. It's early still. And you said you got the crazy girl to mind Tommy.'

'Elsa is not crazy!' I snapped. As if I'd leave my baby with a lunatic! 'She is simple-minded, that's all, and very sweet, and her mother keeps a close eye on her and Tommy both.'

He held up both hands to ward off my anger. 'No offense intended. I could use a drink, that's all, and there's never any spirits around here,' he joked. That was for sure times two. Carlotta was as dry as dead bones. 'Come with me. I hate going to those places alone. Everyone stares at me. Gives me the creeps. We'll get a cocktail. I've got money.'

I'd opened my mouth to refuse, but when he said he'd pay, I had a giddy, buoyant moment, like a cork bobbing on water. Or a cork on wine. Or a cork on champagne! All of a sudden, a cocktail sounded exotic and exciting. Freddy always had more in his pockets than I did. Carlotta paid us the same, but after I'd shelled out for the boarding house, there was almost nothing left in my purse. Freddy slept for free at Carlotta's and so had dollars to spare.

'As long as you're buying, I'm in.'

We walked two blocks, passing several raucous establishments, until we reached the speakeasy Freddy had in mind, a lit-up corner bar with glass jars of penny candy in the windows and a sign above the door that read 'Ben's Confectionary'. It was only a Tuesday night, but in Chicago, every day was payday and every night was Saturday.

'Have you been here before? Is it safe?' I asked.

I didn't mean the bar; I meant the liquor. There had been plenty in the newspapers lately about people getting sick and even dying from drinking rotgut or smoke or poisoned hooch supplied by crooked bootleggers. You couldn't tell the real McCoy smuggled in from Canada or Scotland from the bathtub gin made from denatured alcohol, juniper flavoring, and embalming fluid. The bottle labels were no help – it was nothing for men to reuse genuine bottles or forge labels for their own rotgut. I couldn't afford to die of poisoned alcohol – I had Little Tommy to think of.

Freddy shrugged. What could he say? These days, no one had any idea what they were drinking unless they made it themselves, which wasn't a bad idea. If only I were still living in my own house with its kitchen and back yard, I could have bought beer starter and brewed my own beer. Lots of folks were doing it. Magazines advertised dried grape bricks for making wine at home – I could have tried that too. I could have walked down Ninth to Paddy's Market, a seven-block Mecca for wine-makers, and picked up all the supplies I needed. Tommy had told me once that running a distilling operation needed no special know-how, just some cheap equipment. Those who made their booze at home could at least rely on its safety, if not its quality.

There was no secret knock at Ben's Confectionary, no pass-words through a peephole like at some places. Ben must have been generous when it came to greasing the skids. We opened the door and walked right in, bold as brass. A harsh haze of smoke hung over the place like fog on a fall morning. It shrouded the piano man and the colored woman standing beside him who was singing a familiar favorite, 'I Wish I Could Shimmy Like my Sister Kate'. Her warm, throaty voice caressed the notes like a lover and made me want to sing along. Freddy and I sidled up to the crowded bar and ordered martinis. We surveyed the joint as we waited for the bartender to deliver.

'It must've been a real confectionary once-upon-a-time,' I remarked idly. Two long wooden counters cut the large room in half. Two bartenders worked between them, serving customers from both sides. On our side, a dozen café tables, each with two chairs, formed an arc around the musicians. The opposite side was busier, with half a dozen card tables, each ringed with gamblers. No one on the gambling side was paying much atten-tion to the music, which was their loss. That singer was good. I closed my eyes and concentrated on her song, and for a few moments, Tommy was beside me, enjoying his favorite music.

The martinis arrived and my own private séance broke down. Freddy put three quarters on the counter. 'Keep the change,' he said grandly.

At Ben's, men outnumbered women ten to one – not a comforting ratio for a woman in a speakeasy who didn't want to be accosted, but I had a man, sort of, next to me, so I wasn't much concerned. Raised voices from the table farthest from us told me the game there was heating up.

'D'you gamble?' I asked Freddy between sips. We'd worked together for several months, but I'd never broken through his stone wall of reserve.

'Can't afford to.'

'Me neither.' The gamblers' argument continued to heat up. 'Let's drink up and try another place. This looks like it could get ugly.'

Working with Carlotta must have burnished my prophetic powers – no sooner had the words left my mouth than a shouting match erupted at the corner table. A young man with a superior smirk flung taunts at an older fella. Cheating accusations flew . . . profanity . . . it was hard to catch the words. All too soon, words went out of style. One man hurled himself at the other, overturning a chair and scattering poker chips, playing cards, and shot glasses on to the floor. A couple of the other players tried half-heartedly to pull the two brawlers apart. Most stepped back to watch. The musicians played louder. More chairs toppled. Cheap bar glasses shattered into a thousand shards.

One of the fighters, a fair-haired youth with a handsome face and a bloody lip, was getting the worse of it. The older, heavier fella had faster fists and the bob-and-weave of a man not new to fisticuffs. The youth swung a couple of weak punches that never struck flesh, then, throwing up his arms in an attempt to shield his face, backed away until he was, quite literally, cornered. At that point, the bartenders came out from behind their stations to put an end to the fracas. A few of the gamblers helped them hold the combatants apart.

Most people would feel sympathy for the weaker man in a fight. Somehow, all I could feel was revulsion.

'That guy gives me the creeps,' I said to Freddy.

'The big guy?'

'The skinny one with the slicked-back hair. He looks like a smart aleck getting what he deserves.'

Pushing the stocky fella back into a chair, the bartenders dragged the younger man to the door and gave him the bum's rush. 'You're not welcome here anymore, pal,' the older one said. 'Scram! And don't come back!' added the other, unnecessarily, as they gave him a shove into the street. 'OK, gents and ladies, show's over,' said the first man as they ambled back to their positions between the bars. 'Who's ready for a refill?'

'And let that be a lesson to him what doesn't pay his lawful debts,' shouted one of the gamblers. A chorus of ayes filled the room. The piano man launched a chipper ragtime.

The man beside me leaned across the bar and spoke to the older bartender. 'So, Ben, if he don't come back, he ain't gonna pay his tab. Bad news for you.'

'Nah,' replied Ben, who, since his name was on the joint, must have been the boss. 'He paid up. That's the only reason I didn't throw him out before. I was waiting for the little weasel to make good. But now, I don't want to see his face again. That sap gives the place a bad name.' He looked at me and noticed my empty glass. 'Lady, you want another?'

'No, thank you. We need to be getting home.' I lowered my voice and said to Freddy, 'This place is too rough for me. Let's find another.'

When we left, I peered up and down the street to see if the ejected gambler was lurking somewhere nearby, plotting revenge, but there was no sign of him. We strolled for several dark blocks without seeing another likely speakeasy – everything was too large, too small, too coarse, too dirty – until at last we reached a bunch of flappers clustered under the corner streetlight. Judging from the way they were looking up and down the streets and pointing, they were wrestling with a similar dilemma.

'Evening, girls,' I said. 'I've been away for a while, so I don't know what's what with the latest watering holes. Do you know a respectable place nearby?'

One of them sized us up, then gestured with her thumb toward a short alley across the street. 'See that light bulb at the end of the alley? There's a place there. It's too quiet for us, but you've already got a man, so maybe it's what you're looking for.'

I smiled. In the darkness, it was easy to miss the ten-year difference in our ages, and I knew Freddy would puff up at having been referred to as a man. I thanked the girls, and we crossed the street.

Nothing announced the name of this speakeasy. In fact, there was no indication at all that the door led to a public place. But it was unlocked, so we turned the handle, only to encounter a dingy concrete staircase leading unsteadily down into darkness. We exchanged questioning glances.

'Well, the girls called it respectable,' I said. 'Let's give it a go.'

Respectable was the right word. Classy was even better. The windowless room was small but the floor was clean and the air was warm and cozy without the usual stench of cigars and cigarettes that I found so off-putting. The clientele looked upscale too, the sort of people you'd see in a swank club, with the men wearing dinner jackets and the women sporting as much jewelry as a Tiffany's display window, with long loops of matched pearls and dozens of bracelets decking out their beaded flapper dresses. Freddy and I were clearly under-dressed for this crowd, but no one gets too snobby at a speakeasy, so we made our way to an empty table. A three-piece band played the mood from the back corner. Candles burned on each table. A friendly waiter approached.

'Welcome, folks. What's your poison?'

I ordered a Maiden's Prayer, Freddy got a Tom Collins, and we both dove into the basket of fat, salty pretzels that came with the booze. The drinks were loosening shy Freddy's tongue, and soon he was spilling more about his past than Madame Carlotta could have discovered from her archangel. His mother had died when he was born; his father passed on when he was ten. The uncle and his wife who were obliged to take him in made it clear they didn't want him. When repeated beatings from his teachers didn't cure his stubborn refusal to learn, the uncle hired him out at a glass-bottle factory where he worked the assembly line for twelve hours a day, turning all his wages over to the uncle until he ran away. For two years, he lived on the streets, stealing, begging, and working odd jobs, sleeping in train stations in the winter and in abandoned buildings in the summer, until one day he ran into Madame Carlotta, a warm-hearted eccentric who was that very day moving into the house where she intended to embark on her new profession as a spiritual medium. She hired Freddy to carry boxes into her house, spoke to him kindly, and gave him a few coins, a hot meal, and a glimpse of what it was like to have a mother. Over the next few weeks, he found himself coming back again and again to do odd jobs, run errands, and eat. The reason for his hostility when I had first arrived was now much clearer – he'd been jealous. He saw in me a rival for the affections of the only person who'd ever been kind to him.

Feeling all of his sixteen years, Freddy signaled the waiter for another round.

'Do you think we should?' I asked, concerned more for his pocketbook than our growing state of inebriation. I didn't need a clock to tell me what time it was – my breasts were becoming tender. I was closing in on Baby Tommy's feeding time. 'Mrs Jones and her daughter will be expecting me home soon. I think we should head out.' Freddy nodded at the wisdom of my words and canceled the drink order.

Just as we rose from the table, a party of seven or eight men, some in suits, some in police uniforms, burst through the door and fanned out around the edges of the room. Talk about lousy luck! Two minutes earlier and we'd have been home free.

Their leader raised his night stick and shouted, 'All right, everybody, stay where you are. You're all under arrest.'

TEN

There was a moment of wild panic and a good deal of shrieking as the people at the tables nearest the back door ignored the order and tried to sneak out that way. No dice – the cops weren't born yesterday, and a pair of them was blocking the exit. Shocked into silence, Freddy and I froze in our seats until a federal agent with a weak chin and bad teeth lorded over us. 'OK, sister, you and him, get up and get outside. We've got a comfy little paddy wagon waitin' for you on the street.'

I stood. Freddy's thin frame seemed glued to his chair. Gently I took his arm and spoke in a calm tone, 'Come on, Freddy. People get arrested every day. It's our turn.'

He blinked back to life. 'Yeah, sure.' He stood up and stumbled toward the door. I held on to his hand as the agents herded us up the staircase and into the night.

A moment's thought let me know we were dealing with a mixture of federal agents – the men in suits – and blue-uniformed Chicago policemen with large brass stars on their chests. The mix made sense, because the Chicago police would not have raided a speakeasy by themselves unless it had failed to pay its fair share of bribes, a risk few establishments dared run. Word on the street had it Johnny Torrio had started paying Mayor Thompson to keep the police out of his territory all together, a deal that continued to be honored even after Big Bill Dever replaced Thompson as mayor. Chicago's politicians had never been keen on prohibition. There weren't enough tax dollars in the entire state of Illinois to enforce the federal prohibition laws, and Chicago's citizens, like those in New York, Detroit, Cleveland, and other large cities, refused even to pretend to vote for funds. It's a federal law, said the authorities, let the feds enforce it! But since the federal budget was as stingy as the states', there were hardly any prohibition agents in all of America, so you could pretty much count on never seeing one.

Unless you happened to have the bad luck to be drinking in the one gin joint in Chicago where they decided to flex their muscles.

Freddy's hand shook as we climbed into the paddy wagon. Squashed in with dozens of other suddenly sober people, we rode the short distance to the local precinct station. 'We'll be fine,' I reassured him, sounding just like Tommy when he used to reassure me. 'They'll slap a fine on us, and we'll be home before you can say Jack Robinson.' Not that getting arrested for drinking was good news, but Freddy was far more alarmed than he needed to be at our unfortunate turn of events. I wondered if it had something to do with his earlier life on the streets, something he hadn't shared with Madame Carlotta or me.

I didn't wonder for long. We reached the police station in ten minutes and were funneled, like cattle to the slaughterhouse, through the arched entranceway into the main room for processing. I had to pull Freddy along; he was stiff with fright. And then my reassuring words turned hollow as I thought ahead to the expected fine. 'By the way, how much money do you have on you?' I asked him.

'Five dollars.'

I'd never been arrested before. I didn't know the procedure. I'd heard you got booked, paid a fine, and left. But what was 'booked'? How much would the fine be? More than five dollars, I was sure of that. What happened to people who couldn't pay? Would they let us telephone someone? Carlotta had recently installed a telephone in her parlor – would she, with her teetotal opinions against drinking, help us out with an advance on our salaries? I didn't know anyone else with money who could pay a large fine. Except . . . except Johnny Torrio. But I'd go to jail before I'd ask the boss of the Chicago Outfit for help with something like this. And seriously, how would I get in touch with him, if I should even want to? I had no idea. On the other hand, I *really* needed to be home soon to nurse Baby Tommy.

Thirty drunks make a lot of noise complaining and squabbling, stuffed as we were in the small precinct station entry room while a single hapless cop behind a counter blinked nervously at us. It was late, so the desks behind the counter were empty and the glassed-in offices behind them were dark, but the commotion grew louder as the second paddy wagon emptied its carousers through the main door. The counter cop watched the commotion with mounting horror, no doubt trying to figure out how in god's name he was going to deal with this mob by himself. He fumbled for the telephone, and putting a finger in one ear and the receiver against the other, bent over to shout into the mouthpiece, probably calling for reinforcements. When he spied some more uniforms working their way through the crowd, he hung up the telephone and motioned them to come behind the desk to help him with the processing.

Women in furs with jeweled bandeaus around their heads clung to men in navy blue dinner jackets – this was no collection of low-life bums. In fact, if anyone looked as if they didn't belong, it was Freddy and me. Freddy had worn his one cheap suit; I had only the modest, drop-waist, woolen dress I'd put on for Carlotta's séance before I knew I was going out on the town. We didn't fit in with this snazzy crowd.

The crush became increasingly oppressive. The temperature climbed. There were no benches or chairs, so I elbowed my way toward the back corner where I could lean against the wall and breathe a little easier. Freddy followed. I needed to think. I had to get out of here, and fast.

The corner was no cooler. A woman began to scream that someone was manhandling her. A man spewed curses. Someone else hurled insults at the feds. Two men shoved each other and one swung a fist. I couldn't have said which ached more, my head or my full breasts.

'I'm feeling horrible,' I said, putting my mouth near Freddy's ear. Why I said it, I don't know. There was nothing he could do but sympathize, and he looked too scared to do even that.

Just then, the back door near my corner opened, and four cops stepped into the room. Reinforcements. Without giving me a glance, they pushed their way through the throng, shouting at people to form a line and shoving them against the walls. All but one, a tall man, who remained near us where he could oversee the whole room. He seemed to be looking for something. Or someone.

'Sir,' I said.

No response. He couldn't hear me over the din.

'Sir,' I said as loud as I could. He noticed me then. I thought the helpless female routine would work best, although in truth, it wasn't at all far-fetched. 'Please, sir, can you tell me how long we'll be here? I need to go home.'

'You shoulda thought of that before you went into an illegal gin joint, lady.'

'Yeah, yeah, I know. But what's happening now? I've never been in a police station before.'

He gave me the once-over. My dress was respectable and ended just below the knee, so he shouldn't have frowned so rudely. But at least he replied. 'You're gonna get booked, then you'll plead guilty, and the judge'll determine your fine.'

I craned my neck, trying to see into the far end of an empty room beyond ours, full of vacant desks and chairs and silent typewriters. 'I don't see a judge anywhere.'

'He's home in his comfy bed, lady. You'll see him tomorrow.'

'You mean—'

'You'll be spending the night in the pokey.'

'I can't do that.'

He snorted and looked away. I put my hand on his arm.

'No, wait, you don't understand. I have a baby. A little boy. And I need to be home to nurse him.' How could I tell this tall, stone-faced, steely-eyed man that my breasts were about to spout milk like a fountain? And Little Tommy was probably crying by now. Mrs Jones would have nothing to give him.

The cop gave me a disgusted look. 'You're a pretty poor excuse for a mother, leaving your baby to go out drinking all night.' He glanced at Freddy, who was holding on to my arm, and then did a double take. I could read his mind: what was I doing out drinking with this boy? I was clearly too young to be his mother and too old to be his wife.

I had to come up with something fast. 'My cousin and I were having a birthday celebration drink. That's all. It's my first time out since the baby came.' I fumbled in my bag for a handkerchief. The tears didn't need much encouragement to start flowing.

'Well, you can just hope your husband will come get you tomorrow morning.'

I should have held my tongue, but the liquor and my tears

and my anger combined to make red-hot fury. The police station
felt like a furnace and it seemed like the raucous crowd had
sucked every atom of air out of the room. I grabbed the cop's
arm when he turned to push into the fray.

'My husband is dead. Shot by the O'Banion gang in May.
And how dare you suggest I'm not a good mother! I'm tired
and I'm scared and I'm suffocating in this room and I can't
wait until tomorrow to feed my baby!'

The perspiration on my brow was proof I wasn't exagger-
ating. The noise, the strain, and the lack of air nearly
overpowered me. I don't recall ever fainting in my life, and
I didn't completely faint there in the police station, but my
head flopped backwards and my knees crumpled. Freddy
caught me before I hit the floor.

'Jesus,' said the cop.

I was vaguely aware that someone put his arm under my
knees and picked me up like I was a little girl. A moment later,
I was carried through the door and into a hallway that was
twenty degrees cooler and full of air. The cop set me on a bench
where I could lean back against the wall. I gulped in air like a
starving person inhaling food.

When I opened my eyes, I saw bars. For a moment, my heart
lurched and I panicked, unable to figure out which side of the
bars I was on. Freddy was kneeling beside me, mopping my
forehead with my handkerchief and the cop was holding a teacup
of water in his very large hands, urging me to take a sip. I was
sitting on a crude bench across from half a dozen smelly cells.
Thankfully, I wasn't inside one of them. Not yet anyway. But
I knew without a doubt, this was where I was going to spend
the night.

'You all right now, lady?' The cop had the decency to look
concerned. Maybe he wasn't so bad after all. Then I noticed
he was staring at my chest and my rising estimation of him
plunged.

'I . . . yes . . . no. Th-thank you for the water,' I said in a
raspy voice. 'I need to go home to Baby Tommy. I'll come
back tomorrow morning and pay the fine, honest I will! But I
have to go home now!'

Eager, I supposed, to ward off another swooning spell, he

glanced up and down the hall. The cells directly in front of us were empty – a circumstance that wouldn't hold true for long – and there was no one but Freddy within earshot. He took my arm, not gently.

'Come on,' he said, his disgust made manifest by his tightened lips.

With Freddy at our heels, he hurried me along the hallway past half a dozen cells until we reached another door. Taking a key out of the bunch dangling from his belt, he unlocked it. We made our way through to another hallway, dimly lit by a single, naked bulb but blessedly cooler with fresher air, and climbed a short flight of stairs, crossed a large, empty room, and descended another flight, until we reached a heavy metal door. With another key, he unlocked that and thrust it open. A dark alley stretched before me.

'There. Go.'

Confusion paralyzed me. 'Go where?'

'Go *home*, lady! For God's sake, go home and take care of your baby.'

'Oh. Th-thank you, sir. Thank you very much. I'll . . . we'll come back tomorrow—'

'Forget it. Don't come back, not ever. Just scram.'

Freddy and I scrammed.

We'd traveled an entire block before the cold night air seeped into my skin. 'Oh,' I said with dismay. 'I've lost my wrap.'

'It must still be at the speakeasy. I'll go back tomorrow and—'

'No! Don't go back there. Leave it.' We walked beneath a streetlamp. A glance down at my chest gave me to understand why the tall cop had been staring at my breasts and why he had taken the risk to sneak us out of the police station. The front of my dress was wet with two circles of leaked milk. I felt ashamed that a strange man saw me in such an immodest state – something no one, not even a husband, should ever see – but at the same time, I was relieved.

In ten minutes, Freddy left me on the front steps of Mrs Jones's rundown boarding house, where I could hear Baby Tommy wailing.

ELEVEN

Wednesday morning brought a pounding headache and a guilty conscience. What a sap I'd been, leaving Baby Tommy to go out on the town like some frivolous flapper throwing all cares to the wind! And I was painfully aware of the debt I owed the anonymous cop. I should have gotten his name; I should have shown more gratitude last night. The humiliation of being arrested would have been nothing beside the horror of spending the night – or longer – in one of those nasty cells, and I had missed both outcomes by a whisper. In the calm of daylight, the raid played through my head like a nightmare on film. How could I have been so thoughtless? What if I had been jailed for several days? What would have happened to Baby Tommy? What if Carlotta learned of our little misadventure? Would she, a teetotaler even before Prohibition, have cut ties with Freddy and me? Without my investigator's job, would I be forced to go to the Outfit?

I vowed I would never take such a foolish risk again. I would redouble my efforts on Mrs Weidemann tomorrow. That very night, I began feeding Tommy solid food, mashing up a bit of boiled potato in milk and patiently introducing it into his mouth, trying again and again after he spit it out. Mrs Jones, who counted herself an expert on such things since she'd had seven of her own, assured me that he'd learn to swallow food in a few days.

When Freddy and I met up at the Cook County Courthouse the next morning, I was glad to see he looked no worse for the experience.

'How did you sleep?' I asked him.

'Pretty darn good,' he grinned, 'seeing as how much booze I drank. I threw up last night after I got home.'

'Wish I'd done that,' I said glumly. 'We were very lucky, you know. You didn't tell Carlotta, did you?'

'Hell, no. Was Tommy all right when you got inside?'

'Screaming mad, but I fixed that pretty quick. Nothing like this will ever happen again. I'm starting him on solid food, so if I'm ever late for nursing, he'll have something to tide him over.'

We were making another call on our friendly courthouse clerks to investigate two wills, one for a Mr Roland P. Beasley and another for a Mr Francis Lintner. Mission accomplished, I sent Freddy home and continued on to the library to search the relevant obituaries. I found only the one for Mr Beasley – turns out not everyone who dies gets an obituary, maybe because they aren't important enough or didn't pay for one or no one cared enough to write it – and when I'd finished jotting notes, I caught the streetcar north to Graceland Cemetery, where, according to his obituary, Judge Weidemann had been laid to rest a few weeks earlier.

Cemeteries are full of helpful information tailor-made for a mystic, as long as you know what you're looking for, and by now, I did. The judge's family plot would probably shed light on other relatives, specifically any children he and his wife might have had who did not live to adulthood. That they had taken in two nephews probably meant they had no children of their own. Still, I didn't want to leave Madame Carlotta unprotected if Mrs Weidemann was to ask to contact the spirits of her deceased children as well as her husband.

The judge had been a member of St. James Episcopal Cathedral on Huron Street, but churches in Chicago had no graveyards. Some used to, but graveyards were no longer permitted inside the city limits. A waste of valuable space, I guess. Graceland Cemetery sat outside the city boundary line, and lots of important people were buried there. A toothless caretaker at the gate looked up in a register to tell me where to find the Weidemann family plot.

'He don't have no stone yet,' the caretaker said. 'It hain't come. But you can tell it by the bare dirt.'

Wrapping my shawl tightly around Baby Tommy, I buttoned the top button of my coat against the blustery October wind and took off at a brisk pace. Dried leaves rained on us with every gust and they crunched under my feet as I made my way along paths past beautiful Greek temples, pyramids, statues, mausoleums, fancy marble monuments, and simple gravestones, past family plots fenced by wrought iron or shallow marble walls, along a small lake, in search of the Weidemann name. And there it was, right where the caretaker said it would be. Located on a gentle slope with markers clustered around a central obelisk emblazoned with an enormous W, the family plot was surrounded by an elaborate bronze fence turned blue-green with age. The gate was locked, but by walking around the perimeter, I could read all the markers. I set Tommy's basket down on the leafy carpet and fished a pencil out of my bag.

Recently turned earth gave away the location of the judge's grave. Flowers not yet wilted lay atop the dirt, evidence that someone – his wife? – had visited recently. But it was not *his* grave that interested me. I examined the ones nearby, recognizing the headstones of his parents by their names in the obituary, and those of his siblings or cousins by their dates. And yes, there was one small flat slab with a delicate marble angel on it, her sharp features worn smooth by decades of harsh weather.

Anna Elise Weidemann
Beloved Daughter of Charles and Daniela
February 7, 1881 – April 18, 1881

Long ago, they had had a child they had loved and she had died. I picked Tommy up and hugged him so tight, he began to protest.

I looked around. Not a soul in sight and the wind had died. The park was as peaceful as sleep. The only sounds came from the birds above and the squirrels scampering through the dry leaves, so I found a white marble slab warm from the sun and sat down to nurse Tommy. I had plenty of information on Judge Weidemann. Carlotta would be primed for her séance tomorrow, and I'd also made good progress on Mr Beasley and Mr Lintner, whose widows weren't scheduled until early next week. There was no séance scheduled for tonight, so I'd have a few hours after dinner to take Tommy's dirty diapers from the bleach-water bucket out to the laundry shed for washing and then hang them on the line outside my window.

Tomorrow was free. We could spend the afternoon at the zoo if the weather held. I hadn't been to Lincoln Park in years and the prospect of an outing lifted my spirits. Back when I was a girl, I'd trailed along behind my older brothers when they went to the park and my memories of the place were good. But one thought kept intruding on this pleasant picture, the idea that I should make another effort to hook up with the servants at the Weidemann house. If it was possible, I liked to have a few details about the inside of the deceased's house. Some convincing tidbit like the color of the wallpaper in the bedroom or their dessert last night would clinch the deal with Mrs Weidemann. Clients were always impressed with intimate details that no fake medium could possibly know, and chatting with a servant usually gave me exactly that. I surrendered to my inner voice and decided to take time tomorrow morning for a stop at the Weidemann house before heading for the zoo.

I had one more errand this afternoon – one I had been dreading all day because of my shame. Reluctantly, I caught the next streetcar and headed to the precinct police station.

A great yawn shuddered through my body. I was dog-tired. Tommy and I had been kept up by noises from the little girl in the room behind ours who had come down with a bad case of measles. Despite her mother's efforts, she cried and fussed all night, and the wall between us was so thin as to be invisible. This morning, I overheard Mrs Jones recommended bathing the girl in barley water, but her mother couldn't afford it. Worried that Tommy would catch the disease, I planned to spend as much time away from the boarding house as possible and to take him with me every day, no matter how heavy he was getting. As soon as I had enough money, I was going to move out for sure. Not that Mrs Jones wasn't a decent woman and not that I wasn't grateful for her taking in a boarder with a baby, but the place wasn't good enough for Tommy. I was determined to give him a better life than growing up in one room of a stinking boarding house like the poor little measles girl.

The police station looked far less threatening in the afternoon sunlight than it did last night. And at three o'clock, the large room behind the counter was a hive of worker bees, with cops, clerks, secretaries, and telephone operators flitting back and forth, buzzing in and out with busy purpose. Telephones jangled, cops argued, and fingers clattered away on typewriters while six great overhead fans swirled the smoke and muffled the noise. I waited my turn at the counter.

'Next!' called the cop on duty. I stepped forward. 'Yes, ma'am, what can I help you with?'

'A name, please. One of your policemen was helpful to me recently, and I didn't have the chance to thank him. I don't know his name. He's tall and . . .' Too late, I realized I hadn't paid enough attention to his appearance to describe him. It had been dark in the crowded precinct, and I'd been too shaken to absorb much detail. I couldn't exactly say that I was looking for a policeman who wore a blue uniform with brass buttons and a cap on his head. 'He was working last night.'

The cop turned and called, 'Hey, Murphy!' A man sitting at a desk by a window looked up from his reports. 'Would that be him, lady?'

I shook my head. Coming here had been a mistake. All I could remember about the man was his height and: 'He had very large hands.'

He gave me a funny look that I countered with a steady, innocent stare. 'Murph! Lady wants to know, who was working last night who's tall and has big hands?'

Officer Murphy gave the question some thought before shouting, 'Sounds like O'Rourke, maybe?'

'That's the best I can do, ma'am. Could be it was O'Rourke. That'd be Kevin O'Rourke. He ain't here now.' He fished through a pile of papers, found the one he wanted, and said, 'He's on night shift the rest of this week.'

Of course he was. I should have figured that. 'Could I leave him a message?'

'Yeah, sure. Write something up and I'll stick it in his box. Next!'

I moved to the backless wooden bench against the wall, set Tommy's basket beside my feet, and rummaged through my bag for a notebook and pencil.

Dear Officer O'Rourke, If you are the man who helped me last night, I wanted to thank you for your kindness. I went directly home to feed my baby and all was well. Sincerely, Mrs Tommy Pastore.

TWELVE

The next morning was cold but sunny – a good day for investigation. I tucked Baby Tommy inside my coat where he was cozy and warm, and I set out early for the Weidemann house, where I took up my position at the street corner in a spot out of the wind and waited. Mornings were better for running into servants, since they usually came and went during those hours on kitchen chores, shopping trips, or taking messages. I was wearing my warmest coat, the blue one that came almost to my ankles that Tommy had bought me at Marshall Field's last winter because it matched my eyes. The temperature had dropped during the night and the sun was just starting to do its job. When I breathed through my mouth, it looked like a person smoking.

It didn't take long before my patience was rewarded: a servant girl carrying an empty wicker basket appeared from behind the house and headed up the sidewalk in the direction of the local market. A young kitchen maid. Perfect. I followed her carelessly, sometimes getting ahead of her on the opposite side of the street, since I was pretty certain of her destination.

Inside the market building, she unbuttoned her coat and removed her scarf, revealing a round face topped by a tangle of red-gold hair that had escaped the bun she'd tried to fashion on top of her head. She was younger than I'd thought. She strolled along the aisle between vendors who'd stacked their root vegetables, apples, and fall produce in piles on tables and in crates on the ground. When she stopped to examine some potatoes at a farmer's stall, I carefully bumped into her.

'Oh, excuse me,' I said with my most cheerful voice, meeting her eyes. And I moved on. No point in being too obvious. I'd made contact.

She picked out some potatoes and carrots, then cut across to the meat aisle where she talked to an elderly butcher about pork. He cut what she described and wrapped it in brown paper.

She continued toward a cheesemonger at the end of the aisle. Sensing where she was heading, I got there first and appeared to be deep in thought over the Wisconsin cheddar when she came alongside me. I looked up and smiled again, as if I had just recognized her.

'Oh, hello again. I don't suppose you've tried this cheddar, have you?'

Before she could reply, the vendor asked me, 'Would you like a taste, miss?'

'Yes, please,' I said.

'And you too, miss?' he asked the kitchen maid, no doubt thinking we were together.

'Yes, sir, I would that,' she said, and with that one phrase, I knew she was Irish. The fair, freckled cheeks and the hair should have given her away by themselves, but the lilt in her voice confirmed it. This girl had not been born in Chicago. I'd lay money she was not long off the boat. Young Irish girls had flooded the city in recent years; most of them found jobs in service.

Together we sampled the sharp cheese. I ordered a slice.

'How cold it is this morning!' I exclaimed. The weather was always a good place to break in. 'I hope you didn't have too long a walk.'

'Not too long,' she said, and she mentioned the street where she lived. 'What a sweet baby you have there! Is it a boy, then?' she said with a wistful note in her voice.

Having Little Tommy along made conversation with strangers easy. 'His name is Tommy and he's four months old. Just getting teeth.' I paid the cheesemonger and while he was wrapping my purchase, I glanced around and spied a corner stall selling coffee and pastries. There were three round tables and some spindly chairs out front. 'He's growing so fast, he's getting pretty heavy now and my back is killing me. I'm going to rest a bit over there and have some coffee.' Figuring the money in her pocket wasn't hers to spend, I added, 'I'd be honored if you'd let me buy you a cup. It'll warm us up. And I have enough that we could share a sticky bun.'

In no time, we were chatting like old friends. Her name was Ellen. She had come to America two summers ago to join her brother and had found work as a maid at the Weidemann's. She lived in. She was sixteen. Freddy's age.

I matched my own story to hers as closely as I could. I knocked five years off my own age and told her I had recently come from Canada to keep house for my father. To give me an excuse to walk home with her, I said we lived on a modest street a few blocks beyond the Weidemann's.

'And your husband, he didn't come with you from Canada?' she asked, her forehead creased with concern.

'He died.'

'Oh,' she sighed, crossing herself quickly. 'I'm very sorry.'

'Thank you. We're fine now, with my father.'

Ellen was my entrée into the Weidemann home. It was easy to steer the guileless girl where I wanted to go, and soon I had learned that the household was in mourning for old Mr Weidemann, that poor Widow Weidemann was bedridden with grief, and that Ellen was none too sure about her own future.

'Cook's a holy terror,' she said, 'but when you come to know her, she isn't so bad. I miss old Mr Weidemann. He were a kindly gentleman, always giving me a smile and a pat on the cheek when he saw me. And the missus is kindly too. But it's a sad house now, it is.'

'A death is always sad. But an old man . . . well, he lived a good life, didn't he?'

'It were sad before he passed. This past summer, little Dickie Gettler drowned in the river.'

'How horrible! Who was he?'

She nodded in agreement. 'He were only twelve years old, and a sweet boy. A nephew to the family. He and his cousin, the other young gentleman who lives with us, they went fishing in the river and Dickie fell in. The cousin, Mr Noah Bristow, jumped in after him, but he couldn't save him. It were a terrible time. And now old Mr Weidemann is gone too.' She gave a great sigh. 'Poor Mrs Weidemann can't bear losing the both of them so close together like that.'

This was important news – we assumed that Mrs Weidemann was looking to contact her deceased husband, but she might be wanting to commune with the spirit of her nephew as well. Madame Carlotta would be pleased to learn this.

Ellen and I finished our coffee and bun and left the market side by side, heading down Wabash toward her home, as I continued to feed her gentle questions to keep her talking. I learned that the pork roast was tonight's dinner and the cook's name was Bessie. Once she got going, Ellen was a chatterbox. Sad, in a way, because it probably meant she had few chances to socialize with girls near her own age. Then again, that could describe me too. From the first day I met Tommy, he was my entire life, and I'm afraid I'd lost touch with the girls at Marshall Field's who had once been my friends.

As we cut over to State Street by Holy Name Cathedral, Ellen clapped her hand over her mouth. 'Oh! I nearly forgot.' She pointed to the flower shop across the street from the cathedral, near the corner of West Chicago Avenue. 'I need to buy this week's flowers.'

'I'll come too.'

Inside, the shop smelled good enough to eat. Small buckets filled with bright blooms, common and exotic, lined the shelves; larger buckets sat on the floor around the edge of the room. A colored man with a wide smile greeted us as we entered. 'Hello, young ladies. What can I help you with today?'

Before Ellen could reply, a friendly-looking man about my own age limped out of the back room, wiping his wet hands on an apron. 'Well, well, if it isn't Miss Ellen! Top o' the mornin' to you . . . and to your friend. Such lovely young ladies will outshine my prettiest blossoms,' he said, giving Ellen a wink. 'Will you be needin' the usual?'

Ellen blushed 'til her freckles faded. 'Yes, sir, Mr O'Banion. Six roses, if you please.'

I blinked in surprise at the name O'Banion. Well, not too much surprise. This young employee at a florist shop was obviously not Dion O'Banion, the head of the fearsome North Side Gang, however, he could well be kin. Irish, like Italians, grew their families large. If anything, this one was to be commended for striking out on his own in a legitimate business instead of following the murderous route his relative had chosen.

'And what color will it be this week? The yellow ones are freshest.'

'Pink, if you have them. Pink is the missus' favorite.'

'You choose.' He lifted a large bucket off the floor and set it on the counter. Another customer entered and he greeted her with similar patter while Ellen selected four pink and two yellow roses.

'These are for Mrs Weidemann,' she said in a low voice. 'Bessie puts one on her breakfast tray each morning, and again at lunch and supper if she eats in her room. She keeps them in the ice box until she needs them, so they last all week.' I made a mental note of this little tidbit – something Carlotta might find useful. Pink roses, the mistress's favorite. Mr O'Banion took the stems from Ellen and wrapped them in a thin sheet of newspaper, folding the end so no water would drip on her coat. She handed him a dollar and waited for change.

Flowers . . . I hadn't thought about flowers in months. Now the memories stabbed my chest without warning. Tommy used to bring me a huge bouquet on our anniversary and another on my birthday and sometimes for no reason at all except that he loved me. I turned away so Ellen wouldn't see my eyes fill with tears, burning like I was standing beside a smoky fire. The colored assistant held the door for us, and we continued our walk home.

It looked like I'd have a full day of work after all. The Weidemann séance was tonight. There was no time to waste at the zoo if I was to visit Graceland Cemetery and the public library again to investigate the nephew's death. Two deaths in one family, and so close together? What a tragedy! I said goodbye to Ellen in front of the Weidemann house and watched her disappear around the back to the servants' entrance.

Just as I turned to go, the Weidemann's front door opened and a young man walked down the steps. Sparing no glance in my direction, he took in the busy street with a sweep of his head: the motorcars chugging past, the iceman delivering next door, the bread truck driver carrying a load into the house across the street, and the band of older boys riding past on bicycles. One shouted to him, 'Hallo, Noah!' and he raised his arm in reply. I stopped in surprise. I knew that face. I was certain I'd seen him before, and recently.

A moment was all it took. This was the young man Freddy and I had seen ejected from the speakeasy the other night. I could give him a name now. This was Noah Bristow, the cousin of the drowned boy. The other nephew of the late judge. The one who inherited a good deal of his money.

THIRTEEN

This time, I didn't need to hunt up the caretaker at Graceland Cemetery. I marched straight to the Weidemann plot and spotted the gravestone I was looking for right away, planted a few feet from the center obelisk. I'd seen it on my earlier visit; I just hadn't understood its significance.

Richard Simpson Gettler
Always Loving, Always Loved
April 12, 1912 – August 24, 1924

This was the boy Ellen had told me about, the nephew. Judging from the last name, he was the nephew of Mrs Weidemann, whose maiden name, Daniela Gettler, I already knew. It must have been her brother's child. What circumstances had brought him to the Weidemann house? Mrs Weidemann's brother and his wife must have died or become incompetent, so the childless Weidemanns took him in. Drowned last August. What a sad end to the boy's short life!

After nursing and changing Tommy, I rinsed his soiled diaper in the cold lake water and left the cemetery for the library. Now that I knew the date of Dickie Gettler's death, I could see if the newspapers carried any more details.

Boys don't drown in rivers every day – especially not boys from prominent Chicago families. I located the article about his death within less than an hour. A photograph of Master Gettler appeared on page two above a short article describing the tragedy.

Youth Drowns in Forest Preserve
Last Sunday the 24th saw the tragic death by drowning of Master Richard S. Gettler, known to all as Dickie, age 12. Master Gettler was the beloved nephew of Mr and Mrs Charles F. Weidemann, who adopted the boy when

his natural parents, Mr and Mrs Stephen S. Gettler of Cleveland, passed away.

Death struck cruelly and unexpectedly, while the boy was fishing from a dock on the North Chicago River in the Forest Preserve with his cousin, Mr Noah Bristow, at his side. Master Gettler fell into the murky water and quickly disappeared from view. As other fishermen watched in horror from the riverbank, Mr Bristow, 19, knowing his cousin could not swim, courageously leapt into the water to save him, repeatedly diving in a vain search for the lad.

Two brave Negroes, Samuel Brown and Earl Smith, who were fishing from the riverbank nearby, heard Bristow's cries for help and ran to the site. They jumped into the river to assist in the search; sadly their best efforts met with failure. When the boy's body was finally recovered only a few feet from the dock, it was too late to revive him.

The loss of a child brings with it exquisite sorrow that weighs especially heavily on the family and friends who grieve his passing and mourn the man he was meant to become. In the case of Richard Gettler, the whole city grieves with them for a life of unfulfilled promise cut tragically short.

Two days later, the *Tribune* carried an obituary.

Master Richard Simpson Gettler was the beloved nephew of Mr and Mrs Charles F. Weidemann, who adopted the boy when his natural parents passed away during the Spanish flu epidemic in 1919. A bright lad, he excelled at Latin and mathematics at the Latin School of Chicago, achieving the highest marks of his grade in both subjects, and placed first in the 100-yard dash. He enjoyed baseball, both as a third baseman on his school team and as a spectator. He was often seen with his cousin, Mr Noah Bristow, and his uncle, a former circuit court judge and currently a professor at Northwestern University Law School, cheering for his beloved team from the stands at Cubs

Park. Friends and neighbors described the lad as cheerful, well mannered, and full of potential.

Master Gettler is preceded in death by his natural parents, Mr and Mrs Stephen S. Gettler of Cleveland, and a sister, Marguerite Gettler. Funeral services will be held on Thursday, August 28, at St. James Episcopal Cathedral, followed by interment at Graceland Cemetery in the Weidemann family plot.

The young man I'd seen leaving the Weidemann house had been the one who had tried to save his cousin from drowning. The newspaper called him a hero. He hadn't seemed very heroic when he was getting the bum's rush at Ben's Confectionary for fighting and cheating at cards, but I was willing to allow that everyone has some measure of heroism in them. I regretted that I'd judged Noah Bristow unfairly, without knowing much about his character. Perhaps the trauma of his cousin's drowning had driven him to reckless drink and gambling. It wouldn't be the first time.

I made it back to Madame Carlotta's house where Freddy and I got ready for Mrs Weidemann's séance. She had asked for privacy, so there would be no one else there. Just Madame Carlotta and the spirits. And the two enhancements upstairs.

'What a sad turn Mrs Weidemann's life has taken,' commented Carlotta as she dabbed black shoe polish on a lock of her gray hair. 'Two terrible losses within a few weeks! I feel almost as much grief – in here – as she does, the poor lady,' she said, pressing her hand to her breast, 'to lose both her sweet nephew and dear husband. I know what it's like to lose a husband . . . as do you, my dear. Tsk, tsk. Tonight I am absolutely determined to contact at least one of those spirits. I will do whatever it takes! Communicating with her dearest departed souls will surely give her the courage to turn her face to the future. She has so much to live for – another nephew and perhaps other relatives who love her and need her love in turn.' She paused to dab her eyes with a handkerchief. I had never known anyone to feel the pain of others as intensely as Carlotta. I reached over and clasped her free hand in mine. 'I try so hard, Maddie,' she said, her voice quaking. 'I know I have the power. I feel it come over me. It's always been there, but more so since Archangel Michael called me to be his medium. I reach out to him and stretch, but I just can't seem to break through the veil. Sometimes his messages are confusing. Sometimes I hear them but I can't speak.'

'Don't be so hard on yourself, Carlotta. You have a good deal of success.'

'You and Freddy are my success, and don't think I don't know it.'

'We help, of course, but you are the reason people leave here encouraged, with a happier outlook on the future. Just give Mrs Weidemann your best, as you always do, and we'll handle whatever comes.'

Seven o'clock came; seven o'clock went. Mrs Weidemann never showed up.

FOURTEEN

If Thursday night's séance was a bust, Friday night's beat the band with five new clients, all of whom were ably investigated, if I do say so myself. Madame Carlotta slipped easily into her trance that night and was able to perform with exceptional fluidity. At the end of the evening, grateful clients made large donations and Carlotta gave Freddy and me a bonus. I went down to the Maxwell Street Market the very next day to spend mine on a larger carrier for Tommy.

The Basket Woman wasn't at her usual location. 'Excuse me,' I said, approaching a black-bearded man in a skullcap who was selling hats from a cart near the spot where I'd seen her before. 'I'm looking for the old colored woman who makes baskets. Would you happen to know where I could find her?'

He barked out a name and a lad of about ten appeared from behind the cart. 'Sorry, missus,' said the boy, 'he no speak English. I help. Are you wanting hat for your husband?'

The question struck like a stiletto, bringing the pain of Tommy's loss when it was least expected. I blinked, and drew a deep breath. 'No, not today, thank you. I'm looking for an old woman who weaves baskets like this one. She usually sells them in this area.' Considering her advanced age, it was not unlikely that she had taken ill or even died since I'd last seen her. The boy translated my question into a guttural language I didn't recognize.

The man – his father? – shook his head and answered. 'He say not today, lady,' said the boy. 'Some days she stay home and make basket or go to river for cut long grass. Most time she here on Sundays. Tomorrow.'

I thanked them and said I'd return then.

Saturday's mail brought a note from Mrs Weidemann, apologizing for her absence. She was taken with a sudden illness, she wrote. Privately, I chalked it up to nerves, but we were relieved to learn she planned to come again the following week.

I didn't want to think of all that excellent investigative work as so much wastewater flushed down the drain.

With the Weidemann widow safely inserted into next week's schedule, I returned to the market nearest her house to see if I might meet up with Ellen again and learn what had really happened to her mistress. I spied the young maid at the butcher's, and we arranged to finish our marketing and meet at the coffee stall in half an hour for some refreshments.

I bought coffee and a sticky bun for each of us. Ellen cooed over Little Tommy.

'Can I hold him?' she asked. 'Don't worry, I know how – I've seven little brothers and sisters myself, and where I come from, the oldest girl does as much mothering as the ma.' Tommy blinked big eyes at this new face, but adjusted happily to her funny expressions and bouncing antics. 'He's an easy one, he is. I can tell. And look at that smile! You're a charmer, you are, Master Tommy. There, now, he's smiling at me! You'll charm all the ladies soon enough, won't you?'

'You must miss your family,' I said.

'Whoosh, yeah, I wanted to go home so bad at first, I was nearly sick every night. It was just me and my brother over here, with an ocean between us and the rest. But I couldn't go home. There wasn't enough to feed us all, and here, there's so much food, even for poor folk . . . I just wish I could send some home.'

'Do you see much of your brother?'

'Tomorrow I will. Every Sunday I have half a day off. And my next sister is here in Chicago now, so I see her too, though not as much as I used to. She used to help out at the Weidemanns once a week when they needed an extra for cleaning, but now she has her own job at a school.'

'She's a teacher then?'

'Gracious, no! Brenda's only fifteen. She cleans the school. Our alderman got her the job because the judge asked him.'

I couldn't resist the opportunity to get inside for a peek at the Weidemann house. 'If the Weidemanns ever need an extra, I'm a good cleaner and a fair cook. I could leave Tommy with someone for a time.'

'Your da would look after him?'

'Oh, right.' I'd nearly forgotten my story about living with my father. A poor liar I made, unable to keep my stories in the front of my head.

She handed Tommy back to me and took a big bite of her bun before answering. 'They don't need anyone else now that there's just Mrs Weidemann and Mr Noah. There isn't as much work in the kitchen or the house as used to be – with them in mourning, you see, there's no dinner parties or teas or such like – and they send the laundry out to the Chinese. We used to have another girl working, Ursula her name was, but she disappeared sudden like.'

'Disappeared?'

Ellen glanced around as if to see whether anyone was close enough to overhear our conversation. 'One morning last spring, Ursula was gone. At first, Mrs Weidemann wanted to call the police because she was that worried about her. Then she looked in her room in the basement, and it was empty. All her clothes, gone. So we knew she'd not been snatched off the street. She'd packed up and left us, sudden like. But we didn't know why she'd taken off 'cause she didn't seem unhappy. Then a week later, Mr Noah noticed six silver candlesticks and a heavy silver tray had gone missing, which proved she was a thief. We saw no more of Ursula. The missus was going to hire another girl but before she could, Dickie drowned and, well, then the judge died and they just didn't need anyone else.'

'You must miss having someone your own age to talk to.'

'Whoosh, yeah, but Ursula wasn't such a good friend. She was older than me and always talking about boys. But I'll remember what you said, and if I hear them wanting to hire a temporary girl for spring cleaning or such like, I'll give your name. What's your address, in case I need to find you?'

I wasn't prepared for that. I couldn't let her know I lived in an entirely different part of town. I fussed with Tommy for a moment to give me a chance to think of a response that wouldn't backfire.

'I'll give you the telephone number of our neighbor. That would be easiest. We don't have a telephone, but Mrs Romany does. CAL-6949.'

Ellen repeated it and stored it in her head.

I turned the conversation in the direction I wanted it to go. 'Poor Mrs Weidemann. I'm very sorry for her. I know how hard it is to lose a husband.'

'Bless you, Maddie, I'm sure you do. That poor lady! She's taking it hard, she is. And then she fell ill on Thursday and couldn't go to the séance like she wanted.'

'A séance?' Too late, I realized my mistake. I'd been foolish to share Carlotta's name and telephone number with Ellen, who might connect it with the medium her mistress was planning to visit. Well, there was no correcting that now.

'You know, a séance. That's when the spirits of the dead come talk to the living. I couldn't do something like that – I'd be too frightened! And I don't think the priest would approve. But Mrs Weidemann, she wanted to talk with the judge so bad, she was going to risk it, even though Mr Noah didn't like her going to such things.'

'Well, I suppose he has his aunt's best interests at heart.'

Ellen shook her head. 'He thinks of nobody but himself. When Bessie – she's our cook – fell ill that same day and left me all alone to make dinner for Mr Noah, and you think he might appreciate that I tried my best, wouldn't you? But no. All he could do was make fun. And I never claimed to be a fancy cook.'

'How ungrateful! But isn't he the one who tried to rescue the boy Dickie? I read about it in the newspaper.'

She acknowledged the truth of what I'd said with a bob of her head. 'Because he did one grand thing doesn't make him a grand person. Now that the judge is gone, he's started making a pest of himself.'

'You mean . . . to you?'

She nodded. 'And Mrs Weidemann dotes on him and can't never hear a thing bad about him, so I don't have anybody to go to. Except Bessie. She says to stick close to her when he's on the prowl. I don't know what I'd do without her.'

'You'd find another job, that's what. Don't you dare let him bully you into anything shameful! There are other respectable jobs a girl like you can get.' It might have seemed odd for me to be saying something like that, with all the trouble I had finding work, but I believed my words in spite of that. Chicago was full of jobs for anyone willing to work. Anyone without a babe-in-arms, that is.

'Me and Bessie have a little space fixed up in the basement to sleep and Mr Noah doesn't come down there. And would you believe it, he's a thief himself! Why, once, not long after I'd come to work for the family, he stole some books belonging to the judge, books that were old and valuable, out of a trunk in the attic, and he sold them. Not very clever, that one, because he sold them to the same book dealer that the judge used, and when the dealer recognized them, Mr Noah told him the judge had sent him on this errand. Well, a week later, as luck would have it, the dealer saw the judge at his club and said something about how he was surprised the judge would have sold his special books. And you can see, the theft was exposed.'

I was shocked, and my wide-eyed expression showed it plainly enough. 'How despicable! To steal from his uncle!'

'His uncle who, mind you, took him in when he was a lad and paid for his schooling and treated him like a much-loved son! And you'll never believe the end of the story, but here it is: he wasn't punished neither. Bessie heard them in the library after he got caught, and he got nothing but a scolding and a lecture about the evils of gambling and drinking instead of a belting like he deserved. Bessie heard the judge tell Mrs Weidemann that Mr Noah was a good boy at heart, and that he – meaning the judge – had gotten into mischief too when he was younger, so he understood how a boy could fall in with the wrong sort, and he forgave the lad. I say that's no way to raise a boy!'

I didn't like to think what my own father would have done if one of his sons had stolen from him. I looked at sweet Baby Tommy and prayed for the wisdom to bring him up right.

By the time we parted, Noah Bristow's heroic sheen had tarnished. Ellen's denunciation aroused my curiosity, and I decided to stop at the speakeasy where Freddy and I had seen him fighting and ask a couple of quick questions, just to see what the bartender had to say about him. After all, Ellen's opinion could be just one side of the story. Ben's Confectionary was not out of my way. I'd pass by the place on my way home.

Ben's was pretty quiet when I walked in – things wouldn't heat up until later in the evening. The man I remembered as

Ben stood between the double bars with another man, just like he was last Tuesday, but the pianist and the singer had been replaced by a Victrola in the corner playing a jazz recording.

'Hello. It's Ben, isn't it? I'm Mrs Duval. I was in on Tuesday night when you tossed out a young gambler by the name of Noah Bristow.'

He squinted back and forth from Little Tommy to me, clearly puzzled as to a young mother's connection with a ne'er-do-well like that. 'What about it?' he said, not exactly rude but not friendly either.

'I couldn't help hearing that he owed you money. He owes my father money too, and Dad asked me to find out if you got paid or not. Anything you might know about the fella that would help us get our money back too, I'd appreciate.' I gave him my most innocent smile. Tommy always said I had an angelic smile.

Ben stroked his mustache with one hand as he turned my request over in his head. Evidently he found nothing in it that threatened him or his business because he agreed. 'Sure,' he said, pulling off his dirty apron and coming out from behind the bar. He was a bulky man with shoulders as wide as his belly, but he moved with surprising agility. 'I don't know as I can help, but there's no harm in talking when things are slow. Have a seat. Want a drink?'

I declined.

We settled at one of the small tables near the Victrola. Ben lit up a cigar. Tommy always told me a gentleman asks a lady for permission before he lights up a smoke, but we were in Ben's bar and Ben wasn't one to sweat the niceties. Leaning back in the chair and crossing legs thick as tree trunks, he surveyed me and the baby without making a single flattering remark about Little Tommy, who was behaving admirably.

'What do you want to know, sister?'

'Whatever you know about Noah Bristow is what I want to know.'

He blew smoke in my direction. I didn't flinch. 'He's a kiss-ass little twit who ran up big tabs and had to be threatened with a broken leg before he'd go crying to papa for the jack he owed. But that's not why I threw him out. He's a card cheat too. And he bothered my girls, always pushing them for free favors. He made my skin crawl.'

'So he owed others money? I mean, other than you and my father?'

'That was the talk. He paid up here because I don't stand for disrespect in my joint, see? After he paid, I told him he wasn't welcome here anymore, and we didn't see him for a while. But he come back a coupla weeks later – Tuesday, like you said – and he come in with a group of fellas and sat down over there, and I didn't want to chase out all of 'em so I let him stay. You said you were here that night, so you musta seen what happened. They got in a fight, like isn't unusual here, but by now I'm sick of the little prick. I got plenty of business without him.'

'Do you remember when he paid you?' Judge Weidemann had died on October the second. Had Noah Bristow paid his debts with his unexpected inheritance?

Ben gave himself several puffs to consider the question. 'Middle of September. But I know what you're thinking. His rich uncle or somebody died a few weeks back and he's rolling in dough now. Or so he says to everyone who'll listen. That don't mean he's gonna pay up.'

'Did he cheat at cards?'

'There's some that say so, yeah, but I don't know. He lost most of the time, so if he cheated, he was a lousy cheater. Tell your pa to lean on him with some serious consequences until he gets his jack. If he's too soft to do that himself, I got some connections that don't cost much.'

'Did you know he risked his own life trying to save his cousin from drowning last summer? It was in the papers.'

'You sure it's the same fella?'

I nodded. 'He dove in again and again. Nearly drowned himself.'

'The cousin musta had gold in his pockets is all I can say.'

'Do you know who else he owed money to?'

It was one question too far. Ben narrowed his eyes and took a few puffs on the cigar. Standing, he snapped, 'Why would I know something like that? I don't go poking my nose in other people's business. Maybe you oughta follow my example.'

FIFTEEN

I walked the short distance to Madame Carlotta's house so deep in thought I passed right by it and had to turn around at the corner. Noah Bristow was a young man with little conscience and big debts. He needed money. His creditors were threatening bodily harm. His uncle had bailed him out in the past, but not sufficiently, because he had to steal some valuable books for ready cash. Was it not possible, even likely, that he had stolen other things from the house as well? What about those silver objects – some candlesticks and a tray – that the maid Ursula ran off with. Odd to have two thieves in one house. Could she have been in cahoots with Noah Bristow? Could they have been lovers? Had Noah known that his uncle's will left him one-quarter of the estate when the judge passed away? The judge was old and ill, so that wouldn't be a long time. I tried to remember the will's exact wording.

No one was home at Carlotta's, so I took the spare key from behind the flower box and let myself in. I needed to look at my Weidemann notes.

We kept all our research in a file cabinet in the enhancement room. Nothing was ever thrown away, just in case. These days, most clients visited three or four times, found a measure of peace with their loss, and didn't return, but some became regulars and others reappeared months later for new reasons. Keeping hold of my notes meant I didn't have to redo anything. I pulled out the Weidemann file and sank into the upholstered chair to read it, with hungry Tommy at my breast. It didn't take long to find what I'd written about the judge's will.

Suddenly, the door to the enhancement room flung open and Freddy barged in.

'Oh, geez Louise! I-I'm sorry, Maddie!' His face flushed tomato red as he spun on his heels and wrung his hands in despair. 'I didn't know—'

'No, no, that's all right, Freddy, come on in. I didn't hear you on the stairs.' I adjusted my shawl to cover my breast. 'All babies nurse, there's nothing shameful about it. Sit down, I have something I want to talk to you about.'

'You sure?'

'Sure I'm sure. I'm covered. Come. Sit. This is important.'

Keeping his head carefully turned away, he pulled up one of the flag-bottom chairs and sat with his back to us. I couldn't help smiling, in spite of my concerns. The poor boy was far more embarrassed than I was.

'It's the Weidemann case,' I said. 'I've been thinking . . . We've got the Weidemanns with two nephews, one from her side of the family – that's Dickie Gettler – and the other from his side. That's Noah Bristow, the fella we saw thrown out of Ben's speakeasy. The judge is old. He's been sick. He's a lawyer so he knows how to write a will, and he leaves half to his wife and a quarter to each nephew.'

'I remember.'

'Noah Bristow has run up a lot of gambling debt in recent years, which the judge pays for him sometimes. He's forgiving, but he doesn't give Noah enough to live the kind of life he wants. So Noah continues that life on credit, letting people know he's going to be rich as soon as his uncle dies. That works for a while, but eventually, some of his creditors – like Ben at the Confectionary – don't want to wait anymore and threaten him. When that happens, he steals. He nicks his uncle's valuable books and sells them. Probably some other things too. And when the judge finds out, he doesn't do anything but scold.'

Freddy shook his head in disbelief. Clearly, such benevolence had not been present in his own youth.

I continued. 'Scolding doesn't slow Noah down. He runs up a lot of debt, maybe even more than his inheritance would cover. But he's seen the will and he knows what it says: the money goes to each nephew, "or the survivor of them". Those five words mean that if one of the boys dies, the other one gets his portion. The surviving boy would get half, in other words.'

Freddy spun around in his chair, his eyes wide with comprehension, his embarrassment forgotten. 'So you think Noah Bristow killed Dickie for his share?'

'The only good thing I've heard about Noah Bristow is that

he tried to save his cousin from drowning. So I've been thinking
. . . what if he wasn't trying to save him? What if he saw his
opportunity when Dickie fell in? What if he jumped in after
him and held him under? What if he pushed Dickie into the
river in the first place? He's nineteen and bigger and stronger
than Dickie, who's only twelve. And their uncle was failing, so
he had to do something fast, before the uncle died.' Freddy
gave a low whistle. 'You think I'm crazy?'

'No . . .'

'But?'

'But what do we do about it?'

'That's my problem. I can't go to the police with a bunch
of "maybes" and "probablys". And the Weidemanns are one of
Chicago's leading families. I, as you may have noticed, am not.'

He flashed a grin, then wiped it off his face as the serious-
ness of the situation reasserted itself. 'And you can't exactly
tell the police you discovered all this while investigating people
for a Spiritualist medium to help make her séances spookier,
can you?'

'Bingo.'

'What are we gonna do?'

I smiled at his use of the word 'we'. 'We can find some
evidence. I have an idea. Remember the newspaper article? It
mentioned two colored men who saw Dickie drowning and ran
to help.'

'Yeah, they jumped into the river but couldn't find him in
time.'

'If we could get to those men – we might learn something
from them. We know their names.' I checked my notes from
the obituary and added, 'Samuel Brown and Earl Smith.'

'How we gonna find two men with names like that in a city
this size? Chicago's got more than a million people, and I'll
bet half of them are named Brown or Smith. Samuel and Earl
are pretty common too.' To prove his point, he reached for
Carlotta's *Chicago Directory* and handed it to me.

I flipped a few pages and started counting. 'There are eleven
pages of Smiths but only twenty-four Earl Smiths. And . . .
and . . . geez, you're right. Fifty-one Samuel Browns!' I sighed.
Although most of the names had occupations listed beside

them, we didn't know what sort of work the two men did. Few had telephone numbers – these were people, not businesses, and telephones were expensive. I racked my brain for a way past this roadblock. Knocking on that many doors would keep me busy until Easter. Supposing Brown and Smith were relatives – cousins, say, or in-laws – might they live at the same address? I crosschecked the two lists without success. Freddy was right: this was hopeless. Stumped, I could only say, 'Well, here's an idea: the police know who they are because they questioned them after the drowning.'

'You're gonna walk into the police station and ask them for their files?' Freddy snorted.

'Maybe I can come up with an angle they'll believe.'

Carlotta's telephone bell interrupted my thoughts. Freddy jumped up. 'I'll answer it. You . . . um . . . finish what it is you're doing. I'll wait downstairs.'

SIXTEEN

Chicago was enjoying extraordinarily fine weather for October, and on Sunday, the sunshine encouraged Carlotta and Freddy to join me for an outing to Municipal Pier. We'd never done anything like that together, and it felt so comfortable – almost like having a family. The wind nearly blew off our hats as we walked along the pier, listening to a military band play marching music by John Phillip Sousa and joining in a sing-along with a church choir. I loved watching the children ride the teeter-totters and go down the sliding boards, and for the first time since Tommy had died, I could see into the future to a time when my little boy would run and play with the other children. He would be a healthy, happy boy. I would see to that, if it was the last thing I did, so help me God. Somehow I would make more money and get us out of that flea-infested boarding house into respectable lodging; I would buy him nice clothes and feed him good food and send him to a fine school. He would grow up to be a gentleman with an education and an important job and his own motorcar. No shilling for phony mediums for my Little Tommy! No delivering hooch for gangsters either. If I had anything to say about it, he would never know his father had worked for the Outfit.

On the way home, we took a slightly longer route through the market so I could look for the Basket Woman.

We found her in her usual position. But she had no ready-made baskets large enough. 'You come back in a day or two, missus, and I'll have just the thing for your little one,' she said. 'I just cut a mess of river grass yesterday. I'll start on it this very night.'

The next day would find me working a job at the Weidemann's. The telephone call that Freddy answered on Saturday had come from Bessie, their cook, who had heard about me from Ellen, who had mentioned that I would be interested in day work, if any was to be had. Lo and behold, Bessie wanted to hire me to polish silver.

'With just Ellen and me, there's no way we have time to shine a thousand pieces of silver and still keep the house up,' Bessie had told me on the telephone. 'I think it will take you two or three days. And Ellen says you have a baby – you can bring him along.'

I thanked her profusely. The extra money would be welcome, but getting inside the house was the jackpot. Surely I would learn something more about Noah Bristow and whether or not Mrs Weidemann had really been ill when she stood us up last week. The disreputable Mr Bristow had gotten under my skin.

Come Monday, I dressed in my oldest clothes and took special care with my appearance. It was likely I would meet Mrs Weidemann at some point during the day, and I didn't want her to recognize me from the séance she had attended as an observer. I would not have made much impression on her at that time: I hadn't spoken to her but to say hello during introductions when lots of others were present. The parlor had been dimly lit and the séance room was black as pitch, so she hadn't had a good look at me. But I had made that little disturbance about needing water and my contact to the Spirit World had been successful – those things she might remember. So I braided my dark hair in two long plaits, which made me look younger than my years, and put on spectacles that I'd borrowed from Madame Carlotta. They were real spectacles but not strong, and I could set them aside if Mrs Weidemann was not present. I brought Tommy along – he had not been with me during that particular séance, so his presence would not stir any of her memories. Other than that, I would just have to minimize my exposure to the mistress of the house and make sure she didn't connect the grieving widow at the séance with the shabby young mother polishing silver in her kitchen.

Bessie met me at the back entrance of the Weidemann house, wearing the same gray uniform that Ellen wore, with a plain white collar and matching apron. She was just as Ellen had described her, gruff and scowling while she showed me to the mountain of silver on the kitchen table and explained the job, but tender-hearted enough to ask if I'd had breakfast and give me some muffins and bacon when I said no. Mr Noah was away for the day and Mrs Weidemann was resting in her room, she told me, so the house was quiet. I could work undisturbed at the large kitchen table. Outfitted with an apron and rags and a jar of polish, I started into the first of twenty-four place settings of sterling tableware, singing quietly to Tommy as I rubbed each piece 'til it gleamed like a mirror.

I'd never seen so much silver in my life. Turns out rich folks have different sets for lunch and dinner, and they need four sizes of spoons, three of knives, and five of forks, plus dozens of serving pieces and odd-shaped utensils I couldn't even guess at. Ellen passed through the kitchen a few times to check on me, and Bessie was a constant presence. She wasn't chatty, but after a while, we fell into a comfortable rapport.

'You're a good worker, Maddie,' said Bessie as she surveyed the large pile I'd finished in a few hours. 'I'll run sudsy water and you can wash and dry those. It'll give your hands a rest from rubbing. The hot water will feel good. After I take Mrs Weidemann up her noonday tray, we'll have ours.' Being fed was a bonus, especially as Bessie was a fine cook.

'Is Mrs Weidemann feeling any better?' I asked when she returned. She and Ellen and I sat down at the end of the kitchen table for a bowl of thick split pea soup, pickles, and cheese toast.

'Better today. Poor lady has bad stomach pains and bowel troubles, like you'd get from eating spoilt food. But that isn't it. We all eat the same food here, and none of us is sick, so the doctor says it's probably grief causing most of her upset.'

'It must be dreadfully hard on her,' I said, 'losing her nephew like that and then her husband.'

'And them married so many years,' added Ellen.

'Nigh on to forty,' said Bessie.

'Have you been with the family that long?' I asked with surprise.

'Not me, but my mother did for Mrs Weidemann when she and the judge first married.'

'Sad that they didn't have children of their own,' I said, in an effort to steer the conversation back to Dickie's death.

'A little girl, years ago, but my mother said she didn't live long. They just weren't blessed in that way.'

'And then to lose her nephew like that. By drowning.' I shuddered.

'Dickie was a sweet boy,' Ellen said.

I picked a few soft carrots out of the soup, mashed them on my plate, and fed them to Tommy with the tip of my spoon. Practice had not yet made perfect, but he was getting better at tonguing the food to the back of his mouth where he could swallow it. 'Had he lived here long?'

'About five years,' Bessie said. 'They loved him like he was their own. We all of us loved him. If only he had learned to swim!'

'If only his cousin had been able to pull him out!' I added.

'Mr Noah, he has his faults, mind you, but when it mattered, he did his all for his kin.'

'And two other men who didn't even know Dickie jumped in to help too. I read about it in the newspaper. They didn't know him, did they?'

'No, they were fishing on the banks a ways away and heard the commotion.'

'Did you know them?' I asked.

'I misremember their names. Brown was one.'

'Smith,' prompted Ellen.

'That's right. Smith was the other. None of us knew them, but they came by the house when the judge asked. He wanted to give 'em some money in appreciation of their bravery.'

'How kind!'

'I showed 'em in and took 'em upstairs to the hall where he shook their hands and gave 'em some money. How much, I don't know, but they looked mighty happy.'

'What kind of men were they?'

'What do you mean?'

'I mean, young or old? Were they related? Did they have jobs?'

Her eyes narrowed and she looked at me as if for the first time. 'Why you want to know?'

'Just curious, I suppose. Wondering what kind of man would risk his own life to try to save a stranger.'

That passed muster for she said, 'They were in middle years, I guess. One was a shoemaker. Or at least he worked at a shoe company. I heard him say to the judge he worked at Elgin Shoes, and the other man said something else, I couldn't hear whether he worked at the shoe place or someplace different. They were good Christian men, that's all I know.'

'I'm sure they were,' I said as I helped clear the table and thanked Bessie for the food. 'I better nurse Tommy now and get back to work.'

The next time Ellen came into the kitchen, I took advantage of Bessie's brief absence to ask if there was a copy of a city directory in the house. I had a reason ready in case Ellen asked why I wanted such a thing, but she didn't; she merely brought the book from the judge's library. It was a couple of years old, but businesses didn't move that often. I looked for the address of the Elgin Shoe Manufactory, found it on South Michigan Avenue, and gave her back the book.

I finished the flatware at about four o'clock. After Bessie had examined some of the pieces closely, she indicated her satisfaction and told me to come back the following Monday to tackle the hollowware. I sped out of the house to the nearest white-striped pole and caught the next southbound streetcar – they were running every minute or two, so I figured there'd be plenty of time for me to reach the factory on South Michigan before it let out. With luck, I could ask at the office for Earl Smith and Samuel Brown and talk with one of them this evening at quitting time. As the only witnesses to the incident, they should be able to shed some light on the boy's death. My heart raced with anticipation.

The sun was fast setting behind the tall buildings as Tommy and I made our way through two streetcar changes until we came near the address I was looking for on South Michigan. The first conductor gave me a transfer; the last one showed me where to get off. The factory was not visible from the corner, but as I walked closer, I saw a large brick building set back from the street with E-L-G-I-N S-H-O-E-S painted above the third story windows in big white letters.

When I got closer, I stopped in my tracks. My jaw dropped. Thoroughly confused, I scanned my surroundings. The Elgin

Shoe Manufactory was an abandoned building. Rusty barbed wire fenced the scraggly yard. Years' worth of grass and weeds strangled its sidewalk and clogged the cracks in the cement around the front steps. The grimy, broken windows looked as if street urchins had lobbed stones through them for target practice. Clearly, Bessie had misunderstood what the one man had said to the judge or I had misunderstood Bessie, because Elgin Shoes had not been in business for years.

SEVENTEEN

Feeling like a balloon with the air let out, I turned to retrace my steps when engine noise caught my attention. On the far side of the deserted building, an old Ford truck was rattling out of a narrow alley. A second one followed closely behind. Curious, I walked toward the alley.

No barbed wire here. The alley did, indeed, lead behind the building. When the trucks drove off, an eerie silence descended over the block. I made a complete circle where I stood and saw no sign of life in any direction. The only sound came from the wind in the leafless trees lining the sidewalk and the scratching of a squirrel that scampered to the top branch.

I hadn't gone to this much trouble to be scared off now. Resolutely, I turned into the narrow alley and followed it the length of the factory building, down a bit of a slope. Rounding the corner, I peered down to a packed-dirt lot with a few automobiles and trucks parked at one edge. A vacant railroad siding led into the factory's lower level. Then came the screeching sound of rolling doors, and two more trucks pulled out and headed toward the alley where I was standing.

This was Chicago with Prohibition in full swing – I was clearly looking at some sort of illegal bootleg operation, one that used this abandoned factory to make or store booze and ship it out. When the colored man had told Judge Weidemann he worked at Elgin Shoes, I'll bet my life the other man spoke up to smooth out that mistake. No one wanted it known that there was anything going on at the old shoe factory, especially if the person they were talking to was an honest judge. This being the Near South Side, I could be pretty sure I was looking at an Outfit operation. Perhaps one like where Tommy had worked. Or maybe Tommy had worked right here, on this very spot. I felt a chill creep over me.

But it was no time to get sentimental. If caught, I could probably talk them out of anything they were of a mind to do, seeing as who my husband was and that I knew Johnny Torrio, but there was no guarantee this was an Outfit operation. I couldn't take any chances, especially not with Little Tommy along. Quick as a cat, I darted behind some overgrown bushes and pressed up against the building where the twilight shadows hid us both. The two trucks passed by within three yards of our hiding place. If the drivers had turned their heads, they would have seen me.

After the trucks had passed, I stepped out of my niche and stared down at the empty staging area again while considering my next move. There was no one around and darkness would soon fall. It would be quitting time for the workmen, wouldn't it? If I waited for the shift to end, wouldn't they walk this way? Wouldn't I have a chance to approach one of them and ask if Samuel Brown or Earl Smith was among them? I could wait across the street in a clear spot away from any danger where I would see them pass by. No, I told myself, too risky. Not with Baby Tommy along.

As if to reinforce my decision, Tommy started whimpering. He wasn't hungry, so it couldn't be that, and he wasn't wet, but he went from fussy to wailing without paying a lick of attention to any of my shushing. Before someone could venture out to investigate a baby's cries, I picked up his basket and turned to go.

And barreled straight into the chest of a man standing two feet behind me.

The wall beside us muffled my shocked cry. Shadows masked most of the man's features, but not the brutal stare that pierced through my eyes to the back of my brain. He wore dark, workman's clothing, and a cap covered his hair. He smelled like he'd been bathing in whiskey. His right hand held a small gun that pointed down.

My heart leaped into my throat. My first thought was to run, but even a cripple could overtake me while I was carrying Tommy, and this man was no cripple. He did not speak. It was for me to launch the attack.

'Geez Louise, you scared the life out of me! What do you mean, sneaking up on a woman like that? And a woman with a baby!' I snatched up Tommy from his basket to hold him closer.

A mother with a baby – that should bring out the gentleman in any man, even a gangster.

Except there was no part of a gentleman in this one. He made no reply, just grabbed hold of my arm with his free hand and marched me down the slope and around the wall to where a single light bulb cast its faint glow over the deserted staging area. As we came closer, the overhead doors rolled up again, revealing an enormous warehouse stacked to the ceiling with what must have been thousands of crates of what had to be liquor. The railroad siding had brought a boxcar all the way inside the factory. As I looked on in amazement, a dozen men were transferring booze from the boxcar into two trucks while others stacked boxes on shelves like toy blocks.

The only man there who was wearing a suit and tie turned and, removing the cigar from his mouth, looked from me to Tommy and back again with a bewildered expression.

'What the hell—?'

'Found her sneaking along the alley,' growled my captor, without releasing my arm.

As if joined together on a single chain, every man in the warehouse stopped what he was doing and turned to face me, a woman in old clothes clutching a baby.

'What was she doing?'

'Watching.'

My options had played out. I had to go with the odds and assume – pray – that this was one of Johnny Torrio's operations. If it was, the name Pastore would probably protect me. If it wasn't, the unwritten rule between gangs that forbade them to harm each other's wives and children would be so much dust. If this was an O'Banion operation, they would recognize the Pastore name too and conclude that I was a spy. I took a deep breath and prepared to roll the dice when a voice from the back of the warehouse said, 'Hey, that's Tommy Pastore's wife. I remember her from the funeral.'

Their boss squinted at me. 'That true, sister?'

'Yes.'

'So, enlighten me.'

'I'm not spying. I'm looking for two men who tried to save a boy from drowning last August. Their names are Earl Smith and Samuel Brown. I understood they worked here.'

All heads turned toward one man in the middle of the room, a thin colored man whose eyes bulged in alarm. He said nothing, but it was obvious that he was one of the men I'd just named.

'What do you want with them?'

'Just to ask some questions about the boy's drowning.'

'And how did you come to think they was here?'

I had no choice but to answer honestly, even though what I was about to say would go hard on someone. 'I work at the Weidemann house where the drowned boy lived. Last August, Smith and Brown came to the house so Judge Weidemann could give them some money to thank them for trying to save his nephew. When he asked where they worked, one of them said Elgin Shoes. I thought it was a normal factory, I mean, a going concern. When I got here and saw it was shut down, I was about to leave, but I heard the trucks coming from around back, so I went to have a look, to see if it was open. That's all. I didn't mean to interrupt anything.'

He looked pained. 'Earl, get over here. And the rest of you, show's over. Get back to work.'

The terrified colored man joined us and started pouring out a confession before either of us could speak. 'What she say is true, boss, but it wasn't me who said Elgin Shoes; it was Samuel. Honest, boss. I swear it. I tried to make it better by saying we used to work there but didn't no more.'

'Where's Samuel?' asked the boss in a voice that scared me.

'Gone back home to Mississippi. When he got the fifty dollars from the judge, he right away bought hisself a train ticket south. His daddy was dying and he was going to take care of his momma and little sisters. He's not in Chicago anymore so you don't need to worry 'bout him telling nobody 'bout nothing.'

The boss rubbed his chin a while, then he turned to me. 'What did you want to ask Earl?'

'I wanted him to tell me what happened that afternoon when the boy drowned.'

The boss gave Earl a nod that told him to proceed.

'Well, like we told the police, we was minding our own business, fishing in the Forest Preserve near a dock where two white boys were fishing. We heard one of 'em cry for help. The older boy was thrashing about and the younger one had disappeared, so we knew what was happening. I can swim. So can Samuel, so we ran to the dock and jumped in, but the water was too dark to see where the boy was at. We felt around at the bottom – it wasn't so very deep – but we couldn't find him. We figured the current might have pulled him south, so we moved thataway but when the older boy found him, he was right under the dock all along.'

'What do you mean, it wasn't very deep?'

'Me and Samuel, we could touch bottom.'

'Was it shallow enough that the boy could have touched bottom?'

'I guess not, or he would of stood up, wouldn't he? The water came up maybe chest high on a man. In some places, it was waist high; other places was deeper.'

'Did you actually see the boy fall in?'

He shook his head. 'We weren't so close as all that, and there were trees in the way. It wasn't until we heard the shouting that we looked over to the dock.'

'Was anyone else nearby?'

'A white man with a dog came up and ran away quick to find a telephone and call the police, and there were some children – colored children – playing a ways downstream with an old woman watching them while she cut river grass.'

'Were they closer than you to the dock?'

'No ma'am, they were downstream and we were upstream, and we were closer to the dock. But they could see better 'cause there wasn't no trees in the way. If they was to look, that is.'

'Did the police talk to them?'

He gave the question some consideration before answering. 'I think they were gone before the police got there.'

'What happened after the police came?'

'The older boy, he sobbed the story 'bout how his cousin fell in and he and us found him too late. The police took the boy's body away and the older boy with him. I don't know where. Some days later, the police gave our names to the boy's uncle, that judge, and he asked us to come to his house to give us fifty dollars. Each. You working for him now?'

'He died a few weeks ago. I've been working for his wife.'

Earl shook his head sadly. 'That too bad.'

The boss interrupted. 'Is that all you want to know?' he asked me.

'Yes. Thank you.'

'OK, hero, back to work.' He turned and stared at me like he could see all the way through me and out the other side. 'So what's all this to you?'

'I'm working for the Weidemanns.'

'I repeat, what's it to you?'

'I care about children.'

'Yeah? Well, in the future, care about your own and don't go snooping around with him. Someone might get hurt.'

Sticking the cigar back between his lips, he snapped his fingers and a wiry man with a dirt-streaked face scurried to his side. 'Paulo, take Mrs Pastore here to the nearest streetcar stop, and see that she gets on the next one.'

Before he could react, another man stepped forward. 'Tommy Pastore was a friend of mine,' he said. 'My truck's in the street up top. I'll drive her home. For Tommy.'

With a dismissive wave of his hand, the boss accepted the friend's offer and within moments, I was on my way up the alley toward the street, breathing normally again at last.

'You were Tommy's friend?' I asked. My escort was a sturdily built man of middle years with a confident attitude, curly dark hair, a two-day stubble on his chin, and, as I would soon learn, a ready smile.

'Yes, ma'am. Hank Russo's the name. Tommy and me go back to when he first got the job here. This your basket?'

'Yeah. Thanks.'

Well, that's that, I thought. I had considered asking Hank what he knew about Tommy's other wife, but it seemed like Hank and Tommy didn't go back but a couple of years. Most likely he wouldn't know anything about her, and I didn't want to risk giving out information he didn't already have. No sense in spreading the news around. It might put the idea into people's heads that Baby Tommy was illegitimate. Like Carlotta had said, if I didn't talk about it, no one would ever know. Still, I wished there was some way I could find out about that horrible woman who took everything we had. I knew Tommy didn't love her. He never loved her. But I needed to know for certain how awful she was and what had happened to make him marry her in the first place. Then I wised up to something, and I stood up straighter as the thought occurred to me: she may have gotten Tommy's house and Tommy's money, but I got what was important. I got Tommy's son. She'd never get one of those.

Hank was still talking. 'He was a good man, Tommy was.'

'I thought so too. Did he work here, at this warehouse?'

'Not here. Other places. Here, lemme carry the baby for you. Don't worry, my sister's got five kids, and I'm the favorite uncle.'

I smiled my thanks and handed him the baby. 'I named him Tommy, after his father.'

'It's a good, strong name.'

'And he looks like Tommy. At least, I think he does. He has Tommy's dark eyes and curly hair. Were you . . . were you there when he was shot?'

Even in the dark, I could see him give me a calculating look, trying to sum me up, before he answered with a vague, 'Mm-hm.' I figured I'd get further by not pushing, so I remained silent and so did he, until we reached his motorcar. It was a Ford, same make as Tommy's. It made me wonder if they'd bought them together, or talked about buying them. He opened the front door for me and handed in the baby, then climbed in the other side. For a moment, he just sat there, his arms folded over the steering wheel, staring straight ahead like he was in a trance, as if the seat beside him was empty. Baby Tommy whimpered and he came around.

'Yeah, I was there. Boss sent us to get back a stolen truck. The bastards were expecting us, pardon my mouth, ma'am. It was an ambush. They got Tommy before he could even get his gun out, but on my mother's grave, it happened so fast, he never knew he was hit. It was instant. No last words, no last thoughts, no suffering.'

'Thank you for telling me.'

'Where do you live?'

He cranked up the motorcar and drove me home.

EIGHTEEN

'How many old colored women do you suppose there are who cut river grass in the Forest Preserve?' I asked Freddy that same night as we were cleaning up after the séance. I'd just finished telling him about the Elgin Shoe incident, leaving out the factory's name in case he should accidentally repeat it. 'I'm counting on there being only one.'

'What are we gonna do? Go see her tomorrow?'

'First thing. Maybe she'll know something. And I really need her basket. The bottom gave out on my old one.'

'Yeah?'

'Tommy's just got too heavy for it. I hope this one is stronger. Anyway, soon he'll be too big for such a thing.'

'You need one of them baby buggy things to push him in.'

'I sure do.' We both knew I couldn't come close to buying one of those.

'You could look for an old one that wouldn't cost much. I'll keep an eye out.'

Freddy and I made a beeline the following morning to the Maxwell Street Market and the Basket Woman's stall where she sat among her wares, a woolen shawl wrapped tight around her head.

'There you are, sugar,' she greeted me. 'I have your basket ready to go. Lookahere, I made the bottom larger but not the sides, so it won't be too big for you to carry the little one.'

After admiring the workmanship, I paid her, then leaned against a nearby telephone pole and struck a casual note. 'Where did you say you got your grass?'

'Forest Preserve. I go there every week or two. A couple of my grandsons come along to help me carry home what I cut.'

'On the North Chicago River?'

'That's the one. There's good grass thereabouts if you know where to look.'

'I understand you were cutting grass last August near the dock where a boy drowned.'

She scowled. 'Never was! Who told you that?'

'One of the men who jumped into the river to help. He said you were cutting grass with some children and were closer to the accident than they were. He and his friend ran over when they heard cries for help. They tried to save him. They didn't actually see the boy fall in. I wonder, did you?'

'Did I what?'

'See the boy fall in. You were close to the dock, and there were no trees blocking your view.'

'That's what they tell you, is it?'

'That's what they say. I'm wondering if you saw the boy fall into the river. Is that what happened? Did a fish on the line pull him in? He lost his balance and fell, was that it?'

She ducked her head and resumed weaving in her lap. I waited patiently, rocking Tommy in my arms and humming a nursery tune, hoping she'd realize she wasn't going to drive me away with her silence. Freddy sat down at my feet and crossed his legs Indian style.

'What's it to you?' she demanded, echoing the words the Outfit boss had used last night.

'I have a boy. You have grandsons. This boy had an aunt and uncle who loved him, but the uncle is dead now and the aunt is ailing. There's no one to stick up for him. I will if I can, but I wasn't there to see what happened. Did you see? Was his death an accident? Or was he pushed?'

She raised the piece of basket she was working on and peered at it intently, stalling, I knew, while she considered my question. At last, she mumbled something under her breath.

'Pardon me?' I said.

'He might have been pushed.' I barely heard her that time, but it was enough.

'You saw the older boy push him?'

'I might of done.'

'You're not sure?'

'My eyes are old. I can't be sure of anything.'

'But you didn't mention this to the police?'

'What, me? You crazy? Like they'd listen to a poor old colored woman when the rich son of a big, important white family say the boy fell in? Who they gonna believe?'

'She's right,' mumbled Freddy. I gave him a gentle kick to keep quiet.

'Would you tell the police now?'

'I'm not telling *you* now, girl. You hear me say I can't be sure? That's the gospel truth. Maybe he push the boy, maybe he just pat him on the back and make him lose his balance. I mind my own business.'

I minded my own business by spending the next few hours in the public library tracking down newspaper obituaries about next week's clients. After digging up helpful information on Nicholas A. Draper, Mrs Severinus Rabincore, and Daniel Presley Poats, I was heading for the exit with my soon-to-be-hungry baby boy when I passed a library table that displayed a dozen books beside a sign that read 'New Acquisitions'. Not a place I regularly paused, but today, one word on one of those books caught my eye: Houdini.

The title? *A Magician Among the Spirits*. Its author? The Great Houdini himself. I was sure everyone in the world had heard of Harry Houdini, the master escape artist and magician who dazzled audiences with his miraculous, death-defying escapes and stunned them with his magic tricks. I knew how amazing he was. I saw him perform once, years ago. Equally well known was Sir Arthur Conan Doyle, the doctor who invented Sherlock Holmes and wrote down all his adventures. Oddly enough, Dr Conan Doyle, the darling of Spiritualists in both England and America, was fast friends with Houdini, the leading skeptic, in spite of their disagreement on this subject.

Intrigued, I paged through the table of contents – enough to realize what I was holding – until Tommy lost his patience and started howling. I couldn't stay in the library with a screaming baby, so, book in hand, I fled to the ladies room where I found a wicker chair in the antechamber outside the toilet. By holding Tommy to my breast with one arm and balancing the Houdini book on my knee with the other, I read the first chapter right there, growing more excited – and more anxious – by the minute. When Tommy had finished, I took the book to the checkout desk and handed the librarian my card.

'I found this on the New Acquisitions table,' I said to start the conversation.

'Yes, it's new.'

'How new? I mean, when did it arrive? Do you know?'

'Oh, several months ago. Earlier this year.'

'It sounds very interesting. Have you read it?'

'I hardly have time to read every book in the library,' she replied with a sniff.

'Of course not. I just wondered if you'd read this one. Have many people checked it out so far?'

She flipped to the back cover where they stamp the date due each time a book is checked out. 'Just look here and you can tell yourself. Two people have checked this out before you.'

Two people in several months didn't sound like a lot to me.

A short detour on the way home took me past one of Chicago's larger bookstores. I stepped inside and asked the sales clerk at the desk if they carried Houdini's new book, *A Magician Among the Spirits*.

'Why, yes,' said the hunched-shouldered man. 'Third aisle, on the right, under H.'

'Have you sold many copies?'

'Well now, let me see.' He turned to a bank of files behind the desk, pulled open one drawer, and walked his fingers through the index cards until he reached the one he was looking for. 'We bought three copies five months ago. Not sure how many are on the shelf.'

I checked. There were two. Breathing easier, I headed home.

'You won't believe it,' I told Freddy later that evening, waving the library book, 'but this is the story of Houdini's lifelong effort to prove that mediums and Spiritualists and telepathists are all fakes.'

'Uh-oh,' he said.

'At first I was worried too, but not many people seem interested in the subject. The bookstore had sold only one copy in five months and this library copy has been checked out just twice since they got it months ago.'

'Does that mean nobody cares?'

'Here's what I think: people choose to read what they already believe. Spiritualists like Sir Arthur Conan Doyle don't believe

Houdini, no matter what he says. Even when he proves they
are tricksters or when some medium confesses to fakery, the
Spiritualists say sure, there are some fakes but most are
genuine.'

'So you think people who come to mediums aren't going to
believe Houdini, no matter what he writes?'

I knew what he was thinking because I was thinking it too.
What would we do if Houdini's book put Carlotta out of
business? What would I do?

'That's what I'm hoping. Houdini's been using his magician's skills for years now to help him expose mediums for
the phonies they are – he's even offered ten thousand dollars
to any Spiritualist who can pass his honesty test. *Ten thousand
dollars!* None ever has. Yet there are still hundreds of mediums
in every city.'

'Gosh.'

'People who come to Madame Carlotta have made up their
minds to believe in spirits. They won't change because Houdini
can prove some are tricksters. They'll just say Madame Carlotta
is one of the genuine ones.'

'I hope you're right.' So did I.

'I saw Houdini perform on stage once, when Tommy and I
were courting. He was playing at a big theater downtown and
was he ever amazing! If he comes to Chicago again, we've got
to go see him, no matter what it costs for tickets.' I ruffled the
pages of the book. 'But here's what's really great about this
book. Houdini not only tells how Spiritualism started, he
explains some of the tricks mediums have used to dupe their
clients. We can learn some new enhancements, like this one
here: the slate writing trick.'

'But then everyone will know about it.'

'*Everyone* won't be reading this book. Houdini says right up
front that diehard believers make excuses for mediums, even
the proven tricksters, and they blame *him* for making the
mediums nervous! Let me feed Tommy first, and I'll start reading
you chapter one.'

NINETEEN

I t had been five months since my Tommy was killed, and there still wasn't a single hour that he didn't enter my thoughts. I dreamed of him often and the dream was usually the same: he came home. I was astonished. 'I thought you were dead!' I'd exclaim. How could I have misunderstood? How was it no one told me he was still alive? 'I got better,' he told me. 'I've been in the hospital.' My heart filled with joy. He had come home to our little house. Baby Tommy and I would be safe. We would all be fine. My body floated up like a bubble with laughter and delight in my discovery. As I began to wake up, I could feel the crisp bed linen on my bare skin, I could hear Tommy's breathing beside me. More important, I sensed his presence and felt the mattress give a little as he turned. I was not asleep. I was not dreaming. I was so happy.

Until I opened my eyes.

That was my psychic experience, and no one could tell me those visits weren't real. Tommy came back to me sometimes during the night. I could hear him in my head, I could smell his scent on his pillow, I could feel his warmth on the sheets. I didn't need Madame Carlotta, the Gypsy Queen medium, to summon his spirit. I did it myself.

So when Tommy came to me that night in a dream, I told him about the drowning that wasn't an accident. I told him how the Basket Woman had seen Noah Bristow push his cousin into the river, and how I thought he pretended to try to rescue him while really holding him underwater that wasn't deep enough to drown in. Then, once Dickie was gone and Bristow was set to inherit his cousin's portion of the judge's fortune as well as his own, he found he couldn't wait for his uncle to die a natural death. Explaining it all to Tommy made me see what I should have seen sooner: Noah Bristow had his back to the wall. He needed more money than stealing books from his uncle would bring, and he needed it fast. He'd been urging creditors to be patient, reassuring them that his uncle was sick and would die soon, leaving him a rich man with a trunk full of money, more than enough to repay everyone. But certain creditors had become impatient, and Judge Weidemann was a tough old bird who might hang on to life for months – even years. Bristow had to speed the inevitable.

I could almost feel Tommy asking me: But then how did he accomplish it? The newspapers reported only that the judge had succumbed to a sudden attack, which, for a man of his advanced years, probably meant a heart attack or a stroke. Whatever method Bristow had used, it had left no evidence, nothing to arouse the suspicions of the doctors who attended him. That eliminated things like strangulation or stabbing or a blow to the head. But a pillow over the face would leave no marks, and anyone strong enough to hold a thrashing boy underwater could certainly overcome the struggles of a frail old man. I didn't know exactly how Bristow had done it, but I was convinced he'd murdered two people, Dickie in August and the judge five weeks later. He'd planned the murders so cleverly that no one was suspicious at the timing. The boy's drowning was an accident. The judge's advanced age and poor health were common knowledge. It surprised no one that the loss of little Dickie would hasten the judge's decline. Bristow pocketed his double inheritance, paid off his debts, and from all accounts, had plunged into the creation of new ones.

Fully awake by now, I came to understand something else, something that made me gasp with horror. When inevitably the money ran low, Noah Bristow would see a new opportunity: his aunt. Her death would, presumably, release her half of the estate to him, assuming he was her only heir.

Mrs Weidemann was next in line. She had a life expectancy only as long as Bristow's money lasted. And she had lately been taken ill.

TWENTY

Rain showers had passed through hours ago, but they left Chicago's sidewalks and streets awash in puddles and the air smelling like musty wet wool. 'This isn't a good idea,' said Freddy for the third time as he trotted along beside me the next morning, heedless of the puddles I was trying to avoid.

'Then don't come with me,' I said, speeding up until I was passing others on the sidewalk.

'I don't think you should go to a police station alone.'

'They're the police, for pity's sake! They're supposed to help people.'

'That's not what they really do.'

I used the delay at the corner to give him a hard stare. 'Look, Freddy,' I said, lowering my voice, 'I know you had police troubles, living on the street like you did. I know you don't want to talk about it. That's fine. But I am convinced that Noah Bristow drowned his cousin so he could inherit his share of the judge's money. And I'm pretty sure he did in his uncle too, although I have no evidence, just logic. And what we need is the kind of rock-solid proof that puts murderers away forever. For that, I need the police. They aren't all bad,' I said, gesturing with my thumb toward the example of the cop in the middle of the intersection who blew his whistle and held back the stream of oncoming motorcars so we could cross. 'The cop who let us go last week might help us. I know his name: O'Rourke.'

The main hall in the precinct station was clogged with Chicagoans of all stripes, some weeping into handkerchiefs, others staring stoically into space, not many smiling. It wasn't the sort of place that encouraged smiles. I went to the public counter and waited in line behind three men for my turn.

'I'd like to speak with Officer O'Rourke, if he's on duty today.'

The man paged through a roster. 'He's on duty, but he's in the back. Who shall I say is asking for him?'

'Mrs Tommy Pastore.'

'And what is this about?'

'A serious crime that I believe has been committed.'

The officer pointed with his pencil to a bench against the counter, meaning I should wait there. I sat. Freddy twisted his fingers and paced.

Ten minutes by the clock on the wall and Officer O'Rourke came out from behind the barrier. The sour expression on his face suggested he wasn't pleased to have been interrupted. Freddy stiffened. I stood.

'Good day, Officer O'Rourke. I'm Mrs Pastore. This is my cousin, Freddy . . .' I realized with a start that I had never known Freddy's last name, if he even had one, so I left it at that. 'I wonder if we might have a moment of your time?'

'On what matter?'

'If we could talk somewhere more private . . .'

Without a word, he held open the swing gate that gave access into the front office and led the way to an empty desk in the far corner of the room. He was, as I remembered, a tall man, with the look of the Irish about him: a rosy complexion, blue eyes, and sandy hair dented where his cap had pressed. His accent showed no trace of the immigrant, so I concluded he had been born in Chicago's large Irish community. I set Tommy's basket on the desktop and glanced about, reassuring myself that the secretaries were wholly absorbed in their typing and the noise level from telephone conversations, typewriters, and switchboard operators would camouflage anything I was about to say.

'I want to report a murder. Two murders, actually.'

He didn't blink. This probably happened all the time for him; for me, it was momentous. I went on: 'You perhaps recall the death by drowning last August of a boy, Dickie Gettler, who was fishing on the North Chicago River?'

'Yes, ma'am.'

'It was considered an accidental drowning based on the word of his cousin, Noah Bristow, and the two colored men who tried to save him. But the two men didn't actually see Dickie fall into the river. An old woman did. She was gone by the time the police arrived so she never told them what she told me: that she saw Noah Bristow push his cousin into the water and then jump to the rescue. Instead of rescuing the boy, I'm sure what happened is that Bristow held him under until he drowned, all the while the other two men were searching underwater for him a bit south of the dock. One of those men told me the river wasn't that deep by the dock, meaning that the boy should have been able to touch the bottom after he tumbled in. Bristow did this because he knew his uncle's will left half the estate to the two of them, one quarter each, but if there was only one, that one would inherit the other's share.'

I paused for his reaction. There was none. Finally he said, 'That's it?'

'Not quite. Bristow needed the money badly. His gambling debts had grown so large that his creditors were threatening bodily harm. He stole valuable items from the Weidemann house and sold them, but his uncle, Judge Weidemann, forgave him every time. So it's even worse that he would kill his uncle, but to maximize his inheritance, he needed to kill his cousin first, last August. Then his uncle, in October, that's the second murder, so he could inherit the cousin's portion.'

'And what is your connection to all this?'

Why did everyone keep harping on that? Why couldn't I just be a concerned citizen who cared about children? I certainly couldn't tell him I had gathered this information in the course of my investigation of clients for a dodgy medium. 'I have been doing some work for the Weidemanns and have uncovered the truth about what's been going on. Two people were murdered. I'm certain of it. I would like to see justice served.' That came out a little more pompous than I intended, and I felt my cheeks grow warm.

He looked at me for a long moment and seemed to notice me for the first time. I may have imagined it, but I thought the muscles around his mouth relaxed a bit. 'Wait here,' he said, disappearing through a door with FILE ROOM etched on the glass. A few minutes later, he was back.

'What you've said matches up with the facts we have on file. You may be correct in your assumptions, however, there is one problem.'

'Proof?'

'Exactly. You have none, except for the old woman. What is her name?'

'I don't know. Everyone calls her the Basket Woman.'

'Was she certain she saw Bristow push Gettler?'

'Well . . . she said it might have been playfulness, but I'm certain.'

'Has she agreed to talk to the police and tell what she saw?'

'Not exactly.'

'What, exactly, did she agree to?'

I sighed. 'She said she wouldn't talk to the police, but I thought maybe if someone pressed her a little, she'd open up.'

'Open up and say the boy might have been pushed but they might have been playing?'

And that her eyesight was bad, but I figured there was no point in bringing up that discouraging morsel.

'You see, Mrs Pastore? You see what the problem is?' he said, gently this time. 'Your theory is all well and good, and it may be true, but without evidence, there isn't anything I or anyone else can do. The doctors who attended Judge Weidemann ruled that his death came from natural causes. Old age and a failing heart. They saw no evidence of foul play.'

'What kind of evidence would make the case?'

He gave me a speculative look. 'Eyewitnesses are always good. Willing eyewitnesses. A written confession. Physical evidence, like a murder weapon with blood on it or a gun that matches the bullet in the victim. Look, I'll make a note in the file that you came by and said that the basket seller was a potential witness, but I'm afraid that's all I can do. What is your address?'

I tamped down my frustration long enough to give him the boarding house address so as to keep Madame Carlotta out of the picture. Freddy and I took our leave.

'What now?' asked Freddy as soon as our feet hit the pavement.

I shook my head. 'I don't know, Freddy. I'm stumped. I just can't let this go. Noah Bristow is a double murderer who deserves to be brought to justice, and I am convinced that Mrs

Weidemann is in danger of becoming his third victim. We need proof. I'll keep my eyes and ears open for anything suspicious when I'm at the Weidemann house. Maybe the servants will know something or Bristow will say something incriminating.' The boy threw me a skeptical glance. 'I know, I know, that's pie-in-the-sky, but what else do we have?'

Outside the precinct station, we went our separate ways. Freddy had a séance to prepare; I had clients to investigate, and we were getting a late start on the day.

TWENTY-ONE

Armed with toothbrushes, a pile of rags, and a jar of silver polish, I stormed the mountain of hollowware that awaited me on the kitchen table, picking them off piece by piece, tray after tray, coffeepot after teapot after chocolate pot, sugar bowl after creamer, cake knife after pickle fork, as I chatted with Bessie, who seemed to enjoy the novelty of a new face in her kitchen. The Weidemann silver pattern was, sadly for their servants, a highly elaborate one with flowers and swirls creased with nooks and crannies where tarnish liked to hide, requiring arm-numbing hours of scrubbing with toothbrushes, followed by rubbing the smoother portions with a rag. Bessie had saved some of the breakfast bread and jam for me and the coffee was hot, so my stomach, at least, was content. I fed Tommy, then set him on his back on the floor with a soft towel folded under him, where he could kick his feet and amuse himself with a rattle of tin measuring spoons.

A couple of hours after I had commenced, Noah Bristow unexpectedly burst into the kitchen. According to Bessie, he preferred to breakfast in bed and never came into the kitchen. But today was different. I guessed he had stayed out most of the night and was only now rising. He seemed surprised to see me working at the table.

'Who's this?' he demanded. 'A new maid?'

'Mr Noah,' said Bessie, 'this is Maddie Duval, who your aunt hired to polish silver.'

He grunted. I said a cheery, 'Good morning, sir,' and kept my eyes glued on my work. There was not a chance in a million he would recognize me from that night at Ben's Confectionary, but why take avoidable risks?

Noah Bristow was dressed in casual daywear appropriate for a young man-about-town of his station – a single-breasted gray sack suit with liberally padded shoulders above full, pleated trousers. Clean-shaven except for a narrow, Douglas Fairbanks mustache, he wore his hair a bit longer than most men, parted it in the middle, and slicked it back with Vaseline. He had a long nose, wide, brown eyes, and pale skin marked by several red pimples so typical of his age. It was his mouth that gave him away: this was a young man whose fashionable dress and pleasant looks were ruined by the sneer on his lips.

'Where the hell are the coffee cups?' he snarled, looking around the kitchen helplessly, as if he expected them to leap out of the cupboard at his command. Wordlessly, Bessie got a cup and saucer and made to pour him some hot coffee, but he took them from her and helped himself.

Ellen bustled into the room. 'Good morning, Mr Noah,' she greeted him first, and then said to Bessie, 'Mrs Weidemann's awake and ready for her breakfast. Says she's feeling she could eat a bite of toast.'

Mrs Weidemann had spent most of the past week in bed. She had missed her séance appointment once again, sending an explanatory note saying she hoped to feel well enough to come the following week. Perhaps it was nothing more serious than a cold, and I was worrying about nothing. Nonetheless, I was worrying. She had seemed in good health, alert, and perky the night she had come to Carlotta's to observe the séance.

Taking one of the smaller silver trays I had just finished polishing, Bessie washed it in warm, sudsy water, dried it, and tricked it out with a lace doily, a bone china plate, and a monogrammed linen napkin. To that she added warm toast, a tiny pot of strawberry jam, a small silver coffeepot with matching sugar and creamer, the proper silver teaspoon, breakfast knife, and sugar tongs, and made room at the corner for a crystal vase holding a single delicate rose.

Ellen picked up the tray and headed toward the stairs. Noah intercepted her. Setting down his empty cup, he eased the tray from her hands. 'I'm going upstairs, Ellen. I'll take this to Auntie.'

'Are you having nothing to eat yourself, Mr Noah?' asked Bessie.

'Not feeling like food this morning, and I'll be lunching with friends at the club today. I want dinner at eight, and I'll be bringing three guests. I want to impress them, so make something good. For god's sake, none of that clear soup that tastes like water.'

'Yes, sir.'

When he had gone, I raised my head again. Bessie bustled around the kitchen, her lips shut tight against any retort, checking cupboards and icebox, compiling a list of what she would need for tonight's meal. I stayed quiet until she had sent Ellen off to the market, then offered my services.

'You're so busy, won't you let me fetch the empty tray from Mrs Weidemann's room? I need to stretch my legs, and maybe the lady would like to hear how the silver is coming along.'

Bessie nodded. 'She knows you're here today. Up the stairs, the first room on the right is Mr Noah's; the second room is hers. I'll keep an eye on little Tommy.'

It was my first, and perhaps only, chance to see what the house looked like beyond the kitchen, so I took my time passing through the dining room, with its matched pair of crystal chandeliers dangling above a gleaming mahogany table. In the entrance hall, a dark red Turkish rug lay on a mosaic tile floor and a huge portrait hung on the wall. I stopped briefly to examine the Judge and Mrs Weidemann, painted when they were in their forties, I guessed, and looking like they were off to a grand soirée, he a handsome man standing with one arm resting on the back of her chair, wearing a dark tailcoat with a shawl collar; she seated, dressed in a gold silk gown with puffy sleeves, holding a fan. The judge looked stern – having one's portrait painted was a serious affair. A Mona Lisa smile gave his wife a softer expression. She hadn't changed her hairstyle in all the years since; it was still arranged in two braids wrapped across the crown of her head. I wondered what she thought when she passed this portrait, as she must, every day. I know she grieved, but I wished I could tell her to be grateful for the many long years she had with her husband. I had had so few with Tommy. The floating staircase curved up to the second and third floors, seemingly without support, and as I climbed, I passed a dozen landscape paintings framed in heavy gold.

'Mrs Weidemann?' I called softly as I knocked on her door. I had to call three times before I heard her faint response. The elderly lady was propped up on a mountain of pillows in a large canopy bed surrounded with green velvet bed hangings that matched the draperies on the corner windows. The bedroom was quite dark inside, with no lights burning and the draperies shut. I had no fear she would recognize me from the séance weeks ago. Still I pitched my voice higher so it sounded more childlike.

'Good morning, Mrs Weidemann. I'm Maddie, the girl who's come to polish your silver. Bessie asked me to fetch your tray and see if there's anything else you'd like right now.'

'Hello, dear. How sweet you are. To help our Bessie!' she said, her voice weak and breathy – an entire sentence seemed too much for her at once. 'Have you finished? The silver?'

'No, ma'am, not yet. This is my second day. I think it will take another day after this. You have a lot of silver! And it's very beautiful.'

She gave a wan smile. 'Yes. Wedding presents. Many years ago. Happy years.'

'Yes, ma'am. Would you like more tea? Some water perhaps?'

'No.'

'Well, then, I'll just take this and leave you to rest.'

'Send Ellen. In an hour. To help. With my bath.'

'Yes, ma'am.'

I backed out of the room, balancing the tray as I closed her door behind me. A few steps down the hall, I set it on a table near the door to Noah's bedroom. I thought he'd left the house, but just to make certain, I knocked. When there was no response, I cracked the door, then pushed it open all the way.

The room was bright in contrast to Mrs Weidemann's, with its curtains tied back to let in the light, and it was similarly furnished with a canopied bed that Ellen had already made. A thick Persian carpet muffled my footsteps. Quick as I could, I went to the desk and opened each drawer, looking for something, anything suspicious that would suggest murder. Officer O'Rourke needed proof of murder? Well, I'd try to find some for him.

The desk drawers yielded nothing unexpected. I moved to the wardrobe and sorted through a dozen suits of clothes and shoes piled on the floor. Nothing strange or unusual. On each side of his bed sat a small cupboard with two narrow drawers. In the second drawer on the far side of the bed I found a yellow box, one that would be familiar to anyone who had ever lived in the city. Rat poison. Evidence!

But I knew what Officer O'Rourke would say: since nearly every house in every farm or city had trouble with rats and mice, rat poison could often be found in every room. What seemed out of place was its location. Why would a pampered young man like Noah Bristow concern himself with what was clearly the servants' problem? And why, if there were rats upstairs, was the poison in the drawer instead of in the corner on the floor? I was turning this over in my head when I heard footsteps on the staircase. For a second, I thought it was Ellen, but the cough I heard came from a man. It was Noah Bristow.

Panicked, I spun around. No time to leave the room before he reached the top of the staircase. I'd never reach the tray in the hall without him seeing me coming out. I needed an excuse to be in his room – and the coffee cup on the bedside table would have to do. I picked it up just as he reached the doorway.

'What the hell are you doing in my room?'

'Excuse me, sir,' I said, with a quick bob. 'I was told to fetch Mrs Weidemann's tray and see if there was any dirty dishes in your room.' I looked pointedly to the cup and saucer.

'Well, get it and get out,' he snapped. 'And if anything's missing, I'll be calling the police.'

Just like a thief to accuse others of stealing, like cheaters always assume everyone else is cheating too.

'I'm not a thief, sir.' Like you, I wanted to add. But Noah had nothing more to say to a lowly day maid, so I took the cup and slipped past him out of the room. My shaky knees rattled the tray things all the way down the stairs, but I had composed myself by the time I'd reached the kitchen. Without a word, I set the tray beside the sink. Bessie peered at it.

'Well, well, I see she ate some toast. Maybe this will be a good day. She seems to get better for a while and we get all hopeful, and then she takes a turn for the worse. Like Mr Weidemann did, bless his soul. Grief can do that to a person.' Grief didn't usually kill a person, though. 'What's this?' She pointed to the extra coffee cup on the tray.

'Oh, Mr Noah's door was open, and I happened to see the cup and saucer on the bedside table, so I picked that up too. Do you have a problem with rats here, Bessie?'

'What, here? Not lately. Why? You didn't see one up there, did you?'

'No, but I saw a box of Rough on Rats on the floor.'

'We get 'em sometimes, like everyone does. That's why I don't like food going up the stairs. But Mr Noah's got too big for his britches – he don't listen to me now that he's a man of means, and he's always leaving food around.' And she shooed me back to my polishing.

TWENTY-TWO

The rest of that week kept me in perpetual motion. Madame Carlotta handed me nine new client names to investigate, among them a banker seeking the spirit of his recently departed wife, a middle-aged woman looking to connect with her deceased parents, an engaged couple wishing to ask permission from her late father to marry, and a gambler wanting to see if his deceased companion could tell him which horses would win tomorrow at Washington Park. He would learn that Archangel Michael frowned on that sort of question.

Most of the time, we knew ahead of time which spirit the client wanted to contact because Carlotta would ask when the reservation was made. But sometimes it was tricky. Mrs Bentley Hamilton III wanted to speak to the spirit of her husband, whose name, obviously, was Bentley Hamilton III, and the rich were the easiest to research. But when Mrs Bentley Hamilton III wanted to reach her sister, whose name and address was unknown, we had a problem. For all we knew, the woman lived in Singapore. Sometimes, for one reason or another, Carlotta was unable to get the name of the deceased. Those cases took long hours of digging into newspapers and, when that failed, I would try to infiltrate the client's household and befriend a servant or pose as someone new to the area and talk with neighbors.

On my list that week were five names that came from a group of female friends who, I soon discovered, were all in their late teens and presumably out for a lark. Their age and sex made them nearly impossible to investigate, as they had experienced no recent deaths to research – or at least none I could discern through my usual methods – and young, unmarried women were not listed in any city directory. No doubt their flirtations with the Ouija board had paled, and they were seeking new thrills in Spiritualism. Freddy and I decided a standard perform-ance would be the safest course, with me providing the thrill through my now familiar, grieving-widow routine. Our only chance for any specific knowledge about the girls would come from clues found in their handbags immediately before the séance.

At the appointed hour, I met the gaggle of flappers in Carlotta's parlor where she introduced us as fellow spiritual travelers. They could not have been less interested in me, a mature woman whose old-fashioned hairstyle and mid-calf-length dress probably reminded them of their mothers, although they did coo briefly over Baby Tommy – something I was used to by now as he was an exceptionally beautiful baby, if I do say so myself. I listened carefully without appearing to, but since their talk was all giggles and gasps – 'You don't say!' and 'Copacetic!' and 'What Nora told me I wouldn't repeat for a thousand clams!' – I learned little of importance. As soon as Carlotta had herded them into the séance room, tottering on their high heels and giggling like children, I rummaged through their dainty beaded evening bags for clues.

I found cigarettes, handkerchiefs, lipsticks, powder, and some surprisingly large bills – someone had a rich daddy – but very little that was useful other than a bracelet bearing the charm depicting a high school where at least one of the girls had graduated in 1923 and a letter from someone named Minnie – an older sister, perhaps – who declared she was going to 'Keep Cool with Coolidge' when she cast her first vote. I reprised my routine on the stairs where I pretended to feel faint, and passed the meager results of my investigation to Carlotta. She wove those tidbits into her patter and thrilled the flappers.

My investigations could not distract my mind from what I had come to think of as the Weidemann murders. We had heard no more from Mrs Weidemann about her appointment, and I could only assume she was too ill to come. I suspected that Noah Bristow was the cause of her decline. On his aunt's death, he would inherit the remaining half of the Weidemann estate. I also suspected he was using rat poison or something that would undermine her health gradually so her decline could be attributed to her grief over the loss of her nephew and husband. It had worked before with the judge. But proof? I was haunted by the need for serious evidence that I could take to Officer O'Rourke, evidence that would send this killer to Carlotta's Far Beyond forever. A thousand times a voice inside my head called me to let go of this crusade, it didn't have anything to do with me, and I couldn't right all the world's wrongs, but it stuck in my craw that Noah Bristow was walking around free, living the high life on his uncle's money after having murdered a little boy and an old man. Every time I convinced myself to drop the issue, Tommy would steal into my dreams with new ideas on how to pursue it. That's how I thought of visiting the drug store. It was really Tommy's idea.

Chicago had exploded with drug stores in 1920 as soon as bootleggers caught on to the medicinal whiskey loophole in the Volstead Act. Doctors – and even dentists and veterinarians – could legally prescribe booze like any other medicine if they thought it would help their patient's ailments. It soon seemed like everyone had a backache or a female problem that would benefit from this tonic. It was a system that suited everyone: the docs got five bucks for prescribing a quart of the patient's favorite beverage; the drug stores and pharmacists where the prescriptions were filled thrived on selling the stuff at a healthy markup; and the patients got their booze. Every day at every drug store in the land, men lined up by the dozens to pick up their medicine. All completely legal. By now, Chicago boasted almost as many drug stores as speakeasies, and it could be hard to tell the difference.

I stopped by Walgreen's near Mrs Jones's boarding house as soon as I had a spare moment. I'd been there before to buy the basics: Bayer Aspirin, soap, bandages, talcum powder, and such, so the pharmacist, Mr Seibert, knew me well enough to greet me by name when I walked through the door.

'Good afternoon, Mrs Pastore. And how is young Master Tommy today?'

'Very well, thank you.' I picked up a box of Ivory soap flakes for laundry as I made my way to the counter. Mr Seibert rang up my purchase on the register.

'Mr Seibert, I wonder if you can tell me what the ingredients are in Rough on Rats?'

'Why, it's nothing much more than white arsenic. Why do

you ask, dear? Is Mrs Jones experiencing problems at the boarding house?'

I shook my head vigorously. It was not my intention to start a damaging rumor like that, even though I could hear the little creatures scurrying around inside the walls at night. 'It's pretty dangerous, then?'

'To people? Yes, very, and pets too. Depending on the concentration, of course.' He scratched his bald head and peered into the distance as he reflected. 'So happens I read in a pharmaceutical journal just the other day how arsenic is showing up in moonshine and bathtub spirits. I'm mighty afraid we're going to be seeing a lot more incidents of arsenic poisoning.'

'Is it fatal?'

'Can be. Again, it depends on the concentration. A little in some moonshine might just make a person sick, with stomach cramps, vomiting, diarrhea, and dehydration. More would lead to death. But even if there's nothing but a trace in some liquor and one drink of it wouldn't cause much harm, over time, you see, it would build up and kill you.'

'Gracious!' I pretended shock, but this only confirmed what I suspected.

Mr Seibert warmed to his audience. 'Some people say you can smell garlic on the breath of a person who's ingested arsenic. Folks are crazy to be drinking this bootleg stuff that's sold in gin joints these days. No one knows where it comes from. If you need reliable whiskey or other spirits, come to us with a doctor's prescription and you'll get the genuine article, made in government-bonded facilities.' He lowered his voice a little, although there was no one in the shop but me. 'If you need a prescription and don't know an obliging doc, I know one who will write one for a small fee, no questions asked.'

I thanked him, adding that I didn't need anything like that at present, and left the store.

Mrs Jones waylaid me as I came through the front door.

'Oh, there you are, Mrs Pastore. I'm glad I caught you. A man delivered a box this morning, for you. It's behind the staircase.'

A box? For me? Nothing like that had ever happened before. Intrigued, I located the cardboard box. It was large and too heavy for me to carry upstairs with Baby Tommy in my arms, so I carried him upstairs first and came back down to get the box. In my room, I cut the string and to my astonishment, found it full of baby things! Mostly clothing of various sizes, all clean and ironed, with hardly any stains or holes. A few soft blankets, four glass bottles with rubber nipples, a baby dish with ABCs around the edge, and two rattles. Not until I reached the bottom did I see the note, but I had already guessed as to the giver.

> Mrs Pastore, I hope you will accept these things for Tommy's son. My sister's youngest has outgrown them and she was happy to see them passed along to the baby of my good friend. Please let me know if there is anything I can do to help you in the future. It would be an honor.
>   Sincerely, Hank Russo

'Look, Tommy!' I cried. 'Look what Papa's friend sent you!' Tommy kicked his feet and waved his hands happily. I wiped the tears off my cheeks.

TWENTY-THREE

A large demonstration blocked my path as I made my way through Chicago's cold streets to the Weidemann house on Monday morning. I'd almost forgotten about tomorrow's election, although the campaign posters plastered on building exteriors and telephone poles that touted Davis or Coolidge – and even a few for La Follette – should have focused my attention. I'd cast my first vote ever for Harding during the last election – the first time women could vote for president – and I planned to vote again this time, probably for Coolidge. Most people I knew were leaning his way.

The crowd brought traffic at the intersection to a standstill. Horns honked, the streetcars backed up, and men shouted with impatience and pushed to get closer to the raised platform where a speaker was gesturing like a wild man. His voice didn't carry far over the din. It was obvious I wasn't going to penetrate that crush – especially not while carrying a baby – so I retraced my steps and took another, longer route to the Weidemanns. I arrived later than I'd intended.

'I'm sorry to be so late, Bessie, but the city is plugged up with campaigners. I had to go around some big crowds. They were all men, and I didn't care to try to push my way through.'

She clucked with concern. 'No indeed. The streets aren't safe anymore, even in broad daylight!'

'At least until the election is over. Will you vote tomorrow?'

'Wouldn't miss it. We worked too hard to get the vote for us not to take the time.'

I wasn't sure if 'we' meant women or colored, or maybe both, but I was curious, so I asked who she was voting for.

'Republican, the party of Mr Lincoln.'

'Me too. I don't pay much attention to the speeches, but since Coolidge is already president and hasn't done anything terrible that I know about, I figure he may as well keep the job. But I'm sorry to be late.'

'Never mind, I saved you a little something for breakfast. And the rest of this silver won't take you all day. Bet you finish before lunch. You're a good worker, Maddie. I'll call on you again when we need extra help.' She sighed. 'But that don't look likely any time soon.'

'I'm glad for work any time it comes,' I told her as I set Baby Tommy beside the warm stove, hung my coat and hat on a hook behind the door, and pulled off my gloves. 'How is Mrs Weidemann today?'

Bessie shook her head sadly. 'Doctor say she doing better, so she gets up, then she goes and has a bad spell and takes back to her bed; the stomach pains deviling her something fierce.'

Ellen came into the kitchen and gave me a cheery good morning before she scooped Tommy out of his basket, lifted him high above her head, and twirled around. 'Good day to you, Master Tommy! How are you this very cold morning? Very well, thank you, Miss Ellen, and you're looking pretty as any picture I've ever laid eyes on. Why Tommy, you handsome charmer, you! Next thing you know, you'll be asking for my hand in marriage. Yes, Miss Ellen, in twenty-five years, I'm going to do just that, so you be sure to wait for me, now.'

The levity broke as the door swung open and Noah Bristow came into the kitchen. I began gathering rags and toothbrushes, preparing the table where I would work. Ellen laid Tommy back in his basket, took a bucket and mop out of a closet, and slipped out of the room without a word.

'Would you like your usual breakfast this morning, Mr Noah?' asked Bessie.

'Yes. Bring it into the sunroom. My aunt is awake. I stopped in her room as I came downstairs, and she said she's feeling better this morning. She'd like toast and tea, as usual, also some scrambled eggs.'

'Right away, Mr Noah.' She took two trays from the pantry and began to dress them with lace doilies, napkins, and dishes, but no sooner had she set porcelain cups and saucers on each tray than Noah picked his cup up and went to the stove. He glanced about in a stealthy manner, which served to put me on my guard. Bessie had her back to him as she whisked eggs and milk, and I stared intently at the silver wine coaster I was polishing, so he would think no one was watching as he poured himself a cup of coffee. Why should anyone be secretive about that? And why should this spoilt young man be helping himself in the kitchen instead of being served in style in the dining room?

Reaching for the old toothbrush to get inside the flower nooks and crannies, I took the opportunity to steal another look in his direction. He stood by the stove, holding his coffee cup in his left hand and staring at the back door like he expected somebody to knock. I could see him from the other side of the table, out the corner of my eye, without seeming to watch him.

Suddenly, his right hand went into a trouser pocket and took out a bit of folded yellow paper. He looked around again at Bessie and me, but when he figured neither of us was paying him any mind, he reached toward the coffee pot with the hand that held the paper, fiddled with it a little – I couldn't see that part, his arm blocked my view – and put his hand with the paper back in his pocket. He stood there a while, leaning against the doorjamb, drinking his coffee like a man without a worry in the world. When he'd finished the cup, he set it on his tray and left the kitchen.

I waited for the sound of his footsteps to die away, then hissed, 'Bessie! Did you see that?'

'See what?'

'Mr Noah – he just put something in the coffeepot.'

'What!'

'Shhh. While he was drinking his coffee, he took a piece of yellow paper out of his trouser pocket and shook it into the coffeepot.'

Bessie was old, her hearing wasn't too good, and her bad knees made her lumber awkwardly, but there was nothing wrong with her brain. I followed her thoughts as she looked toward the coffee cup on Noah's tray.

'He drank that before he doctored the coffee,' I said. Then I took a deep breath and blurted out my fears. 'I think he's poisoning Mrs Weidemann.'

To my surprise, Bessie didn't bat an eyelid. She walked to the door that led into the rest of the house and peered into the adjacent dining room to make sure no one was behind it before she spoke in a hushed tone. 'I gotta say, I been thinking something like that for some time now, but I thought I was going crazy. I thought I was mean to think a young man would harm his own kin for money, especially since he was going to get the money soon enough anyway. And I couldn't see how he would do it. We all eat the same, drink the same.'

'Remember last week, when he took the tray up to Mrs Weidemann? Does he do that often? He could have added something to the coffee then.'

'He never took up his aunt's tray but twice. But what you say . . . it's possible. Then I'm remembering . . . one time, this was a couple of months ago, after Dickie drowned, the judge got real sick. So did I. He didn't get better. I did. At the time, I wondered . . . but I kept telling myself it couldn't be food or drink, since we all ate out of the same pot, as they say. That's what I told the doctor when he asked: I said, the judge drank coffee, I drank coffee, and Mr Noah drank coffee. Ellen, she's young and the Irish prefer tea, and Mrs Weidemann had tea that morning. That's what I told the doctor, so he said it couldn't be the coffee since Mr Noah drank that too. So he said it wasn't anything we ate or drank.'

'Did the judge die right after that?'

'Not right after. About a week after. I got a powerful bad stomach ache that day and was mighty sick. So was the judge. What was it you saw in Mr Noah's hand?'

'I don't know. It looked like yellow paper. He put it in his pocket.'

She considered that bit of information. 'When he gets home tonight, I'll get his trousers and say they need pressing. We'll see if there's any paper in the pocket. In the meanwhile . . . I have an idea.'

Without explanation, she reached for the coffee pot and, before I could stop her, poured the coffee down the drain.

'Wait!' I cried.

But it was too late. Any evidence was gone.

Bessie pursed her lips tight, realizing what she had done, but there was no retrieving the poisoned coffee – if it was, indeed, poisoned. She harumphed as she bustled about, grinding another batch of beans to make a fresh pot. Before she could wash the coffeepot, I snatched up a clean rag and wiped the inside, soaking up what little dampness remained at the bottom.

'This might be enough for someone to check for poison.'

I knew what Bessie was planning as clearly as if I had read her mind. We would have our suspicions confirmed in an hour or so, when the trays from Mrs Weidemann's room and the sunroom came back to the kitchen. While I waited, I picked up another rag and a piece of silver and continued polishing, but my thoughts were far from my work.

There were no surprises – Noah's tray came back with its coffee untouched. He didn't dare drink it, knowing what he'd put in it, but he'd made sure we'd seen him drinking the coffee that day, should the doctor or anyone else ask.

'That's it, then,' I said when I examined the tray with Bessie. 'There's no doubt about it. He spilled something – my guess is arsenic – into the coffee, which he was careful not to drink. That's how he's been poisoning his aunt. Gradually, every week or so, just as she felt better, he'd give her another dose, until she would soon be unable to rise from her bed. A few more doses and she'd die. Of melancholy, people would say. And that's what he did to his uncle.' I dipped the rag into Noah's cup to soak up more of the suspicious coffee.

The lines etched in Bessie's face deepened, and she shook her head in disbelief, muttering, 'Mm, mm, mm.'

I told her about my chat with the pharmacist. 'The symptoms he told me for arsenic poisoning are the same ones that the judge and Mrs Weidemann have experienced. I don't think there's any doubt.'

'I knew he was a bad boy when he stole the judge's books and the missus' jewelry to sell. But I thought, when he risked his own life to save little Dickie, I thought, well, he is a good boy at heart. I see now I was wrong.'

'I don't think he tried to save Dickie. I think he pushed him into the river, jumped in after him, and held him underwater.' Bessie looked at me like there were horns growing out of my head. 'But I don't have proof there either.'

'He's the devil himself! What'm I gonna do?'

I understood what lay behind her question. She could accuse

Noah Bristow, but his arrest was unlikely in view of the lack of evidence, and she'd be dismissed from her job at once.

'Will Mrs Weidemann believe you if you told her our suspicions?'

She gave this no consideration before replying. 'Never in a hundred years. She love that boy. She love both of those boys something fierce, like they was her own. When he stole those books, she made excuses. When her ruby ring went missing, she blame it on herself, saying she was careless and lost it and maybe it would turn up in the cleaning. She never can think bad of anybody, especially not him. No, if it was him or me, she'd believe him.'

'You need to be here,' I said. 'We can't say anything to Noah. If you accuse him, he'll go to his aunt and persuade her to dismiss you. Maybe he'll accuse you of poisoning the judge. You need to be here to protect Mrs Weidemann's food, at least until we can get more evidence that will persuade the police to arrest Noah. Maybe the coffee on this rag will do the trick.'

Ellen clattered into the kitchen, unaware of the drama that had just played out. 'Whew! I've finished scrubbing the hall floor and the porch both,' she said, dumping the dirty water down the sink. Behind her back, Bessie and I exchanged a look that agreed to spare her the details.

'Well now, girl, you get right to the marketing. Here's your list. And you get back to polishing, Maddie. There's work to be done, girls, no shilly-shally.'

TWENTY-FOUR

'I'd like to speak with Officer O'Rourke, please.' The cop behind the precinct counter ran his finger down a schedule on a clipboard and shook his head.

'Sorry, lady. He went off duty an hour ago. What's this about?'

'I have some information about a case he's working on.' Or, to be more accurate, a case I wanted him to work on.

'You can talk to Sergeant Baker,' he offered.

'No, thank you kindly. This is only for Officer O'Rourke.'

'You'll have to come back tomorrow morning then. He comes on duty at six. Or . . . you might find him down the block at Yancey's. He stops there sometimes after his shift.'

I thanked the man, got directions to Yancey's, and set out to walk the three blocks in the biting wind. As luck would have it, I saw O'Rourke the moment I stepped inside, sitting alone at a table, nursing a stein of beer and reading the newspaper. He looked up as I approached and frowned. Not a good sign.

I used my cheeriest voice. 'Good afternoon, Officer O'Rourke. Excuse me for interrupting you when you're off duty, but I have some information that just couldn't wait until tomorrow.' Taking his silence for encouragement, I set Tommy's basket on a chair.

Yancey's was a hole-in-the-wall gin joint with a corner bar, half a dozen tables, and a wall of crude wooden booths that looked like they'd been knocked together by a kid with a hammer. Two men sat in one of the booths, hunched over drinks and cigarettes, muttering in low tones and casting suspicious glances in my direction. O'Rourke was the only other customer. It was early hours yet.

'You wanted proof. I have some now.' I took the coffee-stained rag out of my pocketbook and handed it to him. 'This morning, Noah Bristow came into the kitchen, made a big deal about drinking a cup of coffee, then, while he thought no one was

looking, put something in the coffeepot. Arsenic, I'll wager. It
was something in a yellow paper, and Rough on Rats comes in
yellow paper. Also, I saw some in a drawer in his bedroom. I
soaked up some of the coffee with this rag. That's proof, isn't
it? If you find arsenic on it, I mean?'

My rag warranted a dubious glance, but he made no move
to take it. Nor did he invite me to take a seat.

'I think Bristow's been poisoning Mrs Weidemann just like he
did the judge, slowly, little by little, so it would look like they
died of something else like old age. I talked to a pharmacist
who told me the symptoms for arsenic poisoning included
stomach cramping, bowel troubles, and shortness of breath, and
the cook says that's what the judge suffered from. That's what
his wife is suffering from now. The doctor chalked up the judge's
death to a sudden attack of some sort, plus old age and grief.
They'll probably say something like that when his wife passes.'

'Mrs Pastore. How good to see you again,' he said, with
another look at the rag. A quick appraisal of the room's other
occupants seemed to make up his mind. 'Won't you have a
seat? Can I buy you a drink?'

If he saw any irony in a cop offering to buy a woman an
illegal drink in an illegal speakeasy, he didn't let it show by
any expression on his face. The bartender came over.

'Thank you,' I said. 'Some coffee, please? Or tea, if you have
it?' I looked O'Rourke straight in the eye. 'I wouldn't want to
get arrested.'

That brought a thin smile to his lips. 'No danger in that, Mrs
Pastore. I'm off duty. Now suppose you tell me what you expect
me to do with this evidence.'

'I should think that was obvious, sir. First, take it to a chemist
and see if it has arsenic on it. Then dig up the judge's body
and see if there's any arsenic in him. Then arrest Noah Bristow.
Fast, before he kills his aunt.'

He sighed. 'Here's the problem, Mrs Pastore. A murder charge
rests on three things: motive, means, and opportunity. And of
course, proof for all those. In this case, we have a young
gentleman from a prominent family who's never been in trouble
with the law—'

'He stole his uncle's law books and sold them. And Bessie

– she's the cook – says he stole some of his aunt's jewelry too.'

'So you say. But there were no charges filed.'

'The bookseller knows about this.'

'The bookseller knows the young man brought him his uncle's books. He could have done so with his uncle's approval. Ah, here's your tea. Thank you, Sam. So . . . where were we? We have a young man who was called a hero in the newspapers for trying to save his drowning cousin last August. He's the heir to his uncle's fortune. What is his motive?'

'He needed the inheritance quick so he could pay his gambling debts and avoid being murdered himself. He couldn't wait for his inheritance to come naturally.'

'People seldom kill debtors over debts; that would only make it certain the debt would go unpaid.'

'Well, they were threatening to break his legs or something like that.'

'Who was?'

'Ben, the owner of Ben's Confectionary.'

His startled expression told me he knew Ben. 'Bristow owes Ben money?'

'Used to. He paid the debt.'

'When?'

'Before the judge died. Bessie says the judge was kind enough to bail him out on more than one occasion.'

'So his debt was paid. Why would a young man poison the obliging uncle who paid off his debts?'

'There were other debts.'

'Where?'

'That, I don't know. I've heard there were others.'

'So Bristow's uncle paid his debts on at least one occasion and fails to press charges when the boy steals. The uncle sounds like a patsy, someone any sane person would want to keep alive forever.'

'Then there's the part about Bristow pushing his cousin into the river.'

'We've been over that. Possible, but no witness who will give evidence. Look, I'll grant you that this Bristow fella sounds like a rotter. And your theory is promising. But it lacks a credible motive and proof. He has no motive, and you have no proof.'

'The body will probably show signs of arsenic poisoning. I heard that arsenic can be detected for years after a person's death.'

'That's true. In a person's hair and fingernails, and in certain organs. Usually shows up in the liver and kidneys if it's a slow poisoning, and in the stomach if it's quick. But bodies aren't exhumed for the asking, especially when the doctor has no suspicion of poisoning.'

'But if the rag has arsenic and coffee on it, surely that's enough for suspicion!'

'A good defense lawyer – which young Bristow will certainly hire – will say many rags have arsenic on them. The rag could have been used to wipe up spilled coffee on the kitchen floor where arsenic was applied to kill rodents. Arsenic is available in every drug store. Why, I'll bet there isn't a house in this city that doesn't have a box of Rough on Rats in the basement or the shed or the kitchen. Look here, Mrs Pastore,' he said, probably noting my glum face, 'this isn't necessarily what I think. I'm just telling you what a lawyer will say. Everything can be explained away. And where does it leave you, if you make this accusation? You'll be dismissed from your job without a reference.'

O'Rourke paused to finish the last of his beer. 'But, to be honest, it sounds like you may be on to something. I'll take your rag. I'll give it to a chemist and get it checked it out. A rag with arsenic that two people can say came from doctored coffee might interest someone. I've got a friend at headquarters – a detective. I'll talk to him and see what he thinks about the odds here. Maybe some of the fellas at the station have heard something about Bristow and his gambling debts, if there are more. The details of that would be good to know. But I wouldn't get my hopes up if I were you. Bristow's got too many connections and too much money to be arrested without hard evidence. And I definitely wouldn't let this fella know you are meddling in his affairs, in case he is the murderer you suspect him to be.'

TWENTY-FIVE

The next day, Illinois went strong for Coolidge, and he won the election by a landslide. 'Silent Cal', as the newspapers called him – he didn't flap his lips as much as most politicians – would be staying in the White House for a full four-year term. He hadn't campaigned much or given a lot of speeches except over the radio, but no one I knew could afford a radio, so I didn't hear any of those. I wondered, as I walked through the city on my way to Hank's home, would the people who tacked up those campaign posters all over the city be as vigilant in taking them down now that the hoopla was past?

'Why are you going over there?' Freddy had asked. 'Wouldn't a letter be good enough?'

I had already sent Hank a letter thanking him and his sister for their generosity. 'I just want to pay a call on the family. Meet Hank's sister. See the kids.' His narrowed eyes told me he wasn't buying. And he was right.

I know what he was thinking. I had described Hank to him – a little older than me, good-looking, with black, wavy hair, dark eyes, a straight nose, and confident in the way Italian men are – and he figured I was looking ahead to another husband. I couldn't muster the words to tell him how wrong he was. There was never going to be anyone else for me, not after Tommy. But I did need Hank, and he'd offered to help me in any way he could.

The address led me to a brick row house on a Near South Side street not far from where Tommy and I used to live. In fact, I walked an extra few blocks out of my way just to avoid passing by our old house. I thought I'd die if I saw a stranger coming out of my front door. It wouldn't be *her*, of course. It would be someone she sold it to, but that didn't matter. It would hurt my heart all the same.

Darkness came early this time of year, so the streetlights had lit up even though it was only closing in on six o'clock. Tommy had usually come home by six, so I hoped Hank would too.

'Maddie! What a surprise!' Hank's face lit up when he saw me standing on their porch. 'Come in. Rita! Rita! Come down and meet Maddie Pastore! Come in and sit down. And you brought the baby!'

Rita came down the staircase from the kitchen, wiping her hands on her apron, beaming a greeting with her smile. Several children clambered after her. Introductions were performed and we made our way into a parlor that was shabby but clean. Tommy was wide-eyed at the sight of so many little faces, and I let the children prop him up on the rug to play.

'Look!' said a pert little girl of about six. 'He's wearing Julius's clothes!' The noise level rose as the other children chimed in.

'Yes, he is,' I said, 'and thank you, Julius, for letting Tommy have them.' I looked at Rita and said, 'I appreciate your gift more than you know.'

Embarrassed, she waved away my gratitude. 'It was nothing. I only hope those old things have some use left in them. Now, I have gravy on the stove and I must go back to the kitchen. You will stay and eat with us, of course, won't you, Maddie? We don't have many visitors and there is plenty of food.'

I protested firmly that I had come by only for a moment to speak to Hank. She was probably thinking the same thing Freddy was thinking, but I couldn't help that. 'Very well, then, but you are welcome to dinner if Hank can persuade you to change your mind. It would be a treat for us. Children, you be nice to the baby while Uncle Hank visits with his friend.'

Hank and I moved to a corner of the room while the children played with Tommy like he was a new toy.

'What is it, Maddie? Nothing wrong, I hope?'

I took a deep breath. 'At Tommy's funeral, Mr Torrio told me I could call on him if I needed to. Well, there is something I'd like to ask him, and I don't know how to reach him. I thought you might know where he works.'

Hank's eyebrows shot up. 'You what?'

'I want to speak to Mr Torrio.'

'Are you crazy?'

That was a distinct possibility. All last night, I'd fretted and tossed and turned, weighing the risks of getting involved with the Outfit against my strong hunch that Mrs Weidemann's life was in jeopardy. Was I firm enough in my belief that she was being poisoned that I would take the dangerous step of going to Johnny Torrio for help? It was a gamble. If he could supply the information necessary for the cops to arrest Bristow, well, surely her life was worth any unspecified risk to myself. After all, I wasn't asking for a favor for myself, so it shouldn't put me in debt to him.

'I don't think so.'

'You wanna get mixed up with them again? What for? You need money?'

'It's not about money.'

'What's it about?'

'I just want to ask him for some information.'

'Information about what?'

I squirmed. 'It's personal.'

Clearly frustrated, he ran his fingers through his wavy hair, making it stand up in front. 'Maddie, look here. People don't just drop in on Johnny Torrio. He's a busy man. And a powerful one.'

'But he liked Tommy, and he was kind to me. I think he'll not mind talking to me for five minutes.'

'If you could just tell me what it is you want to know, I could probably . . .'

I shook my head. 'I'm sorry. I can't. The less you know about it, the better. I won't let on I got the information from you.'

He paced the room for a minute before reaching a conclusion. Reluctance was written all over his face. 'All right, then, Mr Torrio spends most mornings at the Hotel Metropole. The feds raided his old headquarters not long before Tommy was killed – we figured O'Banion had a hand in that raid too. I'll take you there.'

I knew the Metropole. It was on the Near South Side, not far from where I was now. 'Thank you, but that isn't necessary. I can find it myself.'

'It isn't finding the hotel that matters; it's getting through the door.'

'I don't want you involved, Hank. If Mr Torrio gets mad, I'd rather it didn't fall on your head as well as mine. I'll go alone. I'll bring Little Tommy, to show Mr Torrio Tommy's son.'

He hadn't finished digesting that when I plucked Tommy from his circle of admirers and said my goodbyes.

Early the next morning we set out, Tommy and I, before I lost my nerve, for the Hotel Metropole on South Michigan Avenue. There was really nothing dangerous about my visit, I told myself firmly. Mr Torrio was a businessman; I was there on business. If he was in, I'd ask to speak to him briefly. If he wasn't, I'd ask when I might return. It was just business.

The elegant Hotel Metropole sat seven stories high on the corner of South Michigan and 23rd Avenue, taking up most of the block. An impressive redbrick building with bay windows jutting out of every floor, it set a high bar for style in this part of town. Men in black suits lounging around the main entrance off South Michigan gave me steely looks when I walked into the lobby, but no one approached me, so I went to the front desk like I was any normal customer wanting a room for the night. Surely there were some regular customers at the hotel, not just gangsters.

'Good morning,' I began, holding Tommy against my shoulder. 'My name is Mrs Tommaso Pastore, and I'm here to see Mr Torrio.'

The clerk, a thin man with his last few strands of hair plastered across his shiny scalp, gave me a slack-jawed stare. I tried again. 'I wonder if you could direct me to his office?'

This time, the clerk looked wildly about the lobby, as if he had lost someone. Then he dropped his head and began shuffling some papers. Suddenly, there was a man at my shoulder.

'You here to see somebody, lady?'

Startled, I spun around to face a burly man with a big red nose, a swollen cut lip, and a bruised eye. Another man stood behind him. I gave them my brightest smile. 'Yes, can you help me, please? I'd like to speak with Mr Torrio. I'm afraid I don't have an appointment, but he assured me at my husband's funeral that I could call on him whenever I needed anything. My name is Mrs Tommaso Pastore and this is my son Tommy.'

TWENTY-SIX

J ohnny Torrio leaned back in his chair, his narrowed eyes raking me from hat to shoes. He sat behind a great wooden desk piled high with papers and files in a paneled office on the top floor of the hotel. In one corner stood a stack of file cabinets, in another, a hat rack with a lone fedora perched on top and an expensive slate-gray overcoat hanging on a hook. The telephone on his desk rang its bell once, but he ignored it. Someone in a room nearby must have picked it up, because it didn't sound again. He said nothing to me, not even a token greeting, so I swallowed hard and started the conversation myself.

'Good morning, Mr Torrio. Thank you for seeing me without an appointment. I know you are busy, and I won't take much of your time.'

He examined me like someone would do if they were looking at a bug under a magnifying glass. 'How did you know where my offices are, Mrs Pastore?'

I was ready for him. I feigned surprise, like I hadn't given it any thought, and replied, 'Oh, gosh, I suppose Tommy must've mentioned it when you moved here from the old location. It isn't a secret, is it?'

'Let's just say I have several offices and would rather keep their locations out of the newspapers.'

'Well, I certainly won't mention this address to anyone, you can rely on me, Mr Torrio.' I cleared my throat. 'At Tommy's funeral, you may remember, you assured me I could call on you if I needed anything—'

'Sure. How much do you need, hon?' He opened a drawer on his right and pulled out a large envelope that bulged.

'Oh, no, sir. I didn't come for money. I have a job. We're doing fine, Tommy and me. This is Little Tommy. I named him for his father.'

This brought the shadow of a smile to his lips. 'He looks

like a good boy, Mrs Pastore. I like boys. Tommy would be proud. What job you got?'

'I work for a Spiritualist who connects the souls of the departed to their loved ones here on Earth.'

One bushy eyebrow shot up. 'A fortune teller?'

'A medium. Madame Carlotta doesn't tell fortunes. She doesn't look into the future. She connects the living with the dead. I help her with research, so she knows a little about her clients and can serve them better. And I help take care of her clients during the séances.'

He reached for a Lucky Strike and offered me one before he lit his own. I declined.

'She a fake?'

'To tell you the truth, Mr Torrio, I don't know. Much of what we do is bogus, but now and then, she seems to make a connection that I can't explain away. She has good instincts when it comes to people. Honestly, I just try to do my job and not think too much about it.'

'That's a good plan. More people should be like you.' He inhaled and looked at me with new approval. I'd stumbled on to saying the right thing. Now I needed to move on to the purpose of my visit.

'Mr Torrio, like I said, part of my job is investigating clients so Madame Carlotta knows a little about them, and while I was investigating this one client, I learned some things that make me certain that her husband was murdered by their nephew. The same young man almost certainly killed his cousin too and is trying to kill his aunt so he can inherit all the family money.'

He leaned forward in his chair. This was a topic he could relate to. 'Who is it?'

'The uncle was Judge Charles Weidemann who died last month. I think he was poisoned by his nephew, Noah Bristow.'

He blew a cloud of smoke. 'Hmmm. A judge. How was he poisoned?'

'With arsenic in his coffee. Slowly, so it would look like a natural death. He was old, so it didn't seem suspicious. I think he's doing that again with his aunt. He needs money because he's in deep.'

He grunted. 'They don't call it "inheritance powder" for nothing.'

'I went to the police, but they said I don't have enough evidence.'

'You want me to take care of it?'

'No! I mean, thank you, but I want to get more evidence for the police so *they* can take care of it. I wonder if you can help me with information about Noah Bristow's debts.'

'Information?'

'Like, does he owe money to anyone you know? Anyone in the Outfit? If I had evidence of big debts, that would show the police he had motive. It would be evidence they would pay attention to.'

At this moment, a door behind Torrio opened without a knock and his second-in-command, Alphonse Capone, stepped into the room. Capone seemed startled to see me standing there, a woman with a baby sleeping on her shoulder. I don't think he recognized me.

'Hey, Snorky,' said Torrio. 'You remember Mrs Pastore from Tommy's funeral, don't you?'

Mr Capone deserved his nickname that day – he cut a dapper figure in a snappy, loose, single-breasted sack suit of striped gray flannel, with padded shoulders, a matching vest, and wide trousers. He moved with the assurance of a man who knows he's dressed a cut above the rest. Tommy had told me a little about Capone: how Torrio brought him to Chicago from New York to help him run the Outfit, how his brother Frank got shot in April over an election the Outfit was fixing. Tommy said some of the guys called him Scarface behind his back, but Snorky was the moniker he preferred. Tommy had been smart enough to steer clear of him.

'Sure, boss. Pleasure seeing you again, Mrs Pastore. This Tommy's baby?'

'Yes. I named him after Tommy.'

Snorky came closer, supposedly to get a good look at Little Tommy, but I felt his eyes on me instead, like ants crawling over my skin. 'How old's the boy?' he asked.

'Four and a half months. He sits up now and has four teeth.'

As if that were a cue, Torrio stood. 'He was baptized, of course?'

'Um, baptized? I . . . uh . . . no.'

'Why not? You're a good Catholic, aren't you?'

'Um, yes. To be honest, Mr Torrio, I forgot. I've had a lot of things to think about lately, what with having to earn my way, and I just didn't think about baptizing him.'

'You know what? I like honesty. All too rare in a woman. You tell me the truth, and I appreciate that.' He took a wad of bills out of the cash envelope and handed it to me.

'Thank you, Mr Torrio, but I didn't come here for money. I came to find out if you knew of any debts—'

'I know what you came for, and those things aren't something I can discuss with a woman. You're a good woman, Mrs Pastore, a credit to your husband. And pretty too. Take this. Don't be proud. It's not for you; it's for the baby's baptism. You don't need it now, that's OK. Put it aside for later. And now Snorky and I have business to discuss, so we'll bid you good day.' And as he was talking, he took my elbow and walked me to the door where he handed me off to one of his bodyguards slumped in the outer office. 'Ron, escort Mrs Pastore out of the building and find someone with a motorcar to take her home.'

TWENTY-SEVEN

'So they hustled me out of the hotel and pedaled me home,' I finished. Freddy, hanging on every word, looked at me like I'd just slain a dragon. I downplayed the whole episode in order to spare him the worry.

'Geez Louise, Maddie, I can't believe you walked right into the gangster headquarters and out again and you're still breathing.'

'Come on now, Freddy. It wasn't that dangerous! Why would Mr Torrio want to harm me? He likes me! He likes my baby. He liked my husband.'

'Maybe so, but you don't want to go near that sort again, OK? They're not normal people. I've seen . . . never mind. What happens now?'

'Now? Nothing, I'm afraid. I've reached the end of my investigation. I've hit the stone wall you can't climb over, go around, or dig under. All I can do is hope Officer O'Rourke will get that rag tested for arsenic and his detective friend will be suspicious enough to request an autopsy on the judge . . .' Freddy made a face at the idea of digging up a decomposing body. 'I've done everything I can think of. I don't want Mrs Weidemann to die too, but if I told her that her nephew was feeding her arsenic, she wouldn't believe me, and it would only make things worse. I'm licked.'

'At least the cook believes you. And she's still there in the house to protect Mrs Weidemann.'

'She'll be doubly alert now. I don't believe Noah will be taking any more trays upstairs to his aunt.'

'Or helping make coffee in the kitchen.'

'That's for sure!'

Carlotta came noisily through the back door, calling out to us in a loud voice. 'Maddie! You have a visitor on the front steps. Freddy! Come help me get these parcels inside. My arms are full.'

I laid Tommy in the box I'd fitted out for his bed and scrambled down the stairs after Freddy. Who on earth would be calling on me?

'Oh, hello, Hank,' I said, opening the door. 'Won't you come in?'

Wearing a solemn expression, Hank Russo followed me into the parlor where he perched on the edge of a chair, his hat in his hands, and fixed his large dark eyes on my face. He cleared his throat before saying, 'I hope you don't think I'm poking my nose into your business, but I hardly slept a wink last night, so worried I was about you going to the Metropole. I never should've told you where Torrio was.'

'Don't worry, I told him I knew about the Metropole from Tommy.'

'I wasn't worried for myself,' he said indignantly.

'I'm sorry, Hank. Your worries were for nothing. Mr Torrio didn't seem angry at all. In fact, he was rather polite and insisted on giving me some money for Tommy's christening.'

'Well, that's good, but you never know about him. He's not predictable. I hope you won't be going there again.'

'No, I don't suppose I will. There's no need. He wouldn't help me.'

'Can't I help you?'

The less Hank knew, the safer it would be for him. 'Not unless you can tell me about who owes money to Outfit gamblers and how much.'

'Geez, no, I wouldn't know anything like that.'

I thought as much. Hank, like my Tommy, was a mere foot soldier for the Outfit with little knowledge of any significant business matters. 'Well, he brushed me off when I asked, so it was a wasted effort.'

'If you don't mind me asking, what are you involved in?'

'I was investigating a death that turned out to be a murder that turned out to be two murders, and I'm trying to prevent a third.' I sighed. I was painfully aware of my failure. And I had thought myself so capable! Upstairs, Tommy started to wail. I excused myself and went to change him and bring him downstairs.

When I returned, Hank was leaning back into the sofa, more

relaxed. I sat across from him, holding Tommy on my knees, rocking him back and forth.

'My sister was disappointed you couldn't stay for dinner last night,' Hank said. 'She told me to invite you to come tonight, or another night, if you're busy tonight.'

I sensed where this was headed. It was not Hank's sister who insisted on inviting me to dinner, although she would no doubt be pleased to have me. It was Hank. I know I should have been flattered by his interest, and at some level, I was, but the mere thought of another man paying court to me made me queasy. Hank was a decent man and Tommy's friend, though, and I didn't want to hurt his feelings. Not that I wasn't lonely. No sense in pretending otherwise. But I didn't want another man in my life, even one as kind as Hank. Tommy had his faults, sure, but he'd been more than my husband. He'd been everything to me: my best friend, my playmate, the only family I had. The friends I'd made at Marshall Field's over the years had drifted away after my marriage. Most were no longer working at the store, and we'd lost touch. I did want to make some new friends, though. Maybe Hank could be a friend.

'Does your sister's husband live there too?'

'Of course. You can meet Carlo when you come. Carlo Mancini.'

'And your parents?'

'They live a few streets over, with my two unmarried sisters. It's your typical big, Italian family,' he said with a smile. 'Lots of noise, lots of food, lots of babies, a little quarrelling.'

'I'm envious.'

'I know Tommy didn't have any family but some cousins in New Jersey. What about you?' I was right – Hank didn't know anything about Tommy's other wife.

'My family?' Baby Tommy felt my body grow tense and began whining. He needed to be fed. I looked out the side window where all I could see was the brick wall of the adjacent house.

'You don't have to tell me,' Hank said.

'It's all right. I can tell you. I couldn't have done so a few years ago, but I can now. My grandparents named Duval came to Chicago from Quebec when my father was a child. My grandfather repaired clocks. My grandmother came from Brittany in France where they make lace. She made the most beautiful lace you ever saw, mostly for priests' vestments for the church. They spoke French at home, and I learned a little French from them, but they died when I was young. Eleven or twelve, I think I was. My grandmother taught my mother to do some fancy needlework so she could earn some money at home, while my father worked for the newspaper in their print shop.'

'Are your parents still living?'

I nodded. 'But I don't see them anymore. There were nine of us: four girls and five boys. I'm the third. I don't think they cared a fig for any of us. I think about love and, well, I just don't believe they had any love in them to give. He – my father – was drunk most of the time he was home, and his hobby was throwing things and beating us. We all left home as soon as we were old enough to find work. I took a job at Marshall Field's when I was sixteen. As soon as I realized I could support myself, I left home too. I don't know where my brothers and sisters are. I could look the boys up in the *City Directory* – probably a few of them are still in Chicago – but we weren't close. I didn't know anything about love until I met Tommy. When I married him, my parents disowned me. Said I'd married beneath myself. They wouldn't meet Tommy. They didn't even want to see our baby.'

He reached across the space between us and laid a reassuring hand on my arm. 'Your father beat you?'

'At least one of us, almost every day. It was like we were taking turns. He drank before he came home, and he was always sorry the next morning, but . . .' I shrugged. What did it matter now? 'I used to go to a blind woman's house after school to read to her so I could stay away from home longer. He didn't lift a hand against my mother, but she never said a word on our behalf. Looking back on those years, I think there was an unspoken bargain there – he wouldn't beat her as long as she didn't take sides with us.' I met his eyes. 'My life began when I found a boarding house for girls who worked at Field's, and it became beautiful when I met Tommy at the store. Tommy was everything to me.' I looked Hank straight in the eye and said, very deliberately, 'No one will ever take his place.'

'I understand.' He gave a sigh, slapped his hands on his knees, and stood. 'Hey, so you didn't answer my question. Why not have dinner with my sister's family and see what a big Italian family is like? Rita would love to have a friend her own age, and she's a great cook – even better than our ma, although I'd get my knuckles rapped with a wooden spoon if I said so out loud. And the kids would love to play with Little Tommy again.'

'I'd like that.'

'Friday night?'

'Sure. Thank you.'

TWENTY-EIGHT

It was the very same young messenger boy from the Outfit who pounded on the front door of the boarding house on a cold, cloudy Thursday morning with a letter in his hand. Mrs Jones trudged up the staircase calling, 'Message for you, Mrs Pastore,' and before I could respond, she'd slipped it under my door. 'Boy says he'll wait for a response. Outside on the steps,' she muttered just loud enough that I could hear. 'Don't want nobody that grubby in my nice, clean parlor, thank you very much.'

'Thank you, Mrs Jones,' I called. 'I'll be right down.' Setting aside the cream of wheat I was spooning into the baby's mouth, I ripped open the envelope. Mr Capone would like to meet me for midday dinner at Zia Angela's, a restaurant on the Near South Side not far from the Metropole. If today was not convenient, I was to name a date that was.

I fooled myself for a few moments pretending I didn't know why he was inviting me to dine with him. I told myself I didn't know what he wanted. But it wasn't true. I did know. I'd sensed it when he eyeballed me that day in Johnny Torrio's office. Call it women's intuition, call it the sixth sense – the fact is, a woman can tell when a man is attracted to her, often before the man knows it himself.

I just didn't want to believe it. The very thought of Alphonse Capone, with his fat lips, little piggy eyes, and horrible scar, made my stomach heave. Trouble was, this wasn't Hank Russo or some decent fella who could be put off with a gentle hint. Capone wasn't a man you could turn down without serious repercussions. I took a deep breath. Stay calm and think of a way out.

First, I needed to send the boy back with the only response possible. I went downstairs. 'Please tell Mr Capone that I will meet him at Zia Angela's at one o'clock,' I told him. As I watched him run off through a flurry of tiny snowflakes that did not reach the pavement, I began to plan.

Never mind that I'd put away my black mourning dress weeks ago, I got it out and put it on for this occasion. Clothing sends a message. It had been a mistake not to have worn mourning when I visited Johnny Torrio at the Metropole. A widow in mourning commands a degree of respect that would have stood me in good stead. Mourning rules had become less rigid in recent years – many widows gave up black after a few weeks and some avoided it all together, and yet there was a woman at Jones's boarding house who had worn nothing but black since her husband died twenty-five years earlier.

I contemplated leaving Baby Tommy with Mrs Jones and Elsa, then decided his presence would be an asset, emphasizing motherhood rather than womanhood. 'You are coming with Mommy today,' I told him brightly as I dressed him in a sailor suit hand-me-down from Rita. He would be getting hungry again by the time I got to the restaurant, but I didn't intend to feed him before I left.

I had a plan. I could only hope it worked. If it didn't, I'd have to leave Chicago at once, something I didn't want to do. Chicago had been my home all my life. I'd never been anywhere else, even for a day. Regardless of its flaws, it was all I knew. I didn't want to start over in another city where I had no job and no friends.

A taxi happened around the corner just as I was leaving the boarding house. On an impulse, I hailed it. Tommy was getting heavy and I didn't want to arrive at the restaurant breathless and blushing, or to seem like I was so desperate for money that I couldn't afford a cab.

I spotted Zia Angela's as soon as the taxi reached the corner of 24th Street and Dearborn – the four dark-suited men loitering outside the restaurant gave it away before the sign was visible. Outfit bodyguards, well-armed against a possible ambush. One of them held the restaurant door for me. None of them spoke.

It was warm inside Zia Angela's. On an overcast day like this, the light coming in the windows wasn't strong enough to banish the gloom, but candles burning on each table gave the small dining room a welcoming atmosphere. With its paintings of the ruins of ancient Pompeii on the wall, it was the sort of place where you could be pretty sure Aunt Angela herself was standing over the stove in back, cooking the traditional family recipes that everyone would swear tasted just like Mama used to make back in the Old Country.

Mr Capone stood when I entered, but I set Tommy's basket down and quickly took off my own coat, hanging it on the rack by the door before he could help me. The message, if he could receive it, was that I didn't need any assistance from him.

'Mrs Pastore. How good to see you again.' Snorky Capone earned his nickname that day, dressed in a stylish striped, three-piece suit. Taking my hand as if to shake it, he held on longer than polite and looked deep into my eyes with what he no doubt thought was sincerity. I pulled away on the pretext of removing my gloves and hat.

'Thank you,' I said brusquely, setting the hat on the rack and patting the errant wisps of hair into place. 'I haven't been to a restaurant since Tommy was killed.'

He took in my clothes with a glance, and I believe I saw a flash of irritation when he realized I was wearing black. Or maybe it was because I'd brought the baby. Good. As he escorted me to our table, I noticed with dismay that we were the only customers in the place. No coincidence, I was sure.

The small table was set with gleaming white china and plain cutlery. Red-and-white checked napkins matched the tablecloth and an uncorked bottle of red wine wrapped in straw sat in the middle beside the candle. Faint strains of opera music – Caruso? – came from a record player in the corner. Taking a deep breath, I took my seat. Mr Capone sat across from me. He did not hold my chair, as Tommy always did. Reaching for the bottle, he asked, 'Want some wine?'

'No, thank you, Mr Capone. I'm a teetotaler.' And no fun at all, read the subtext.

I'm sure he winced. He paused for a moment, probably deciding whether he should indulge in a drink himself, then made up his mind and poured his glass full to the brim. He started to speak with a voice oozing with phony concern.

'Mrs Pastore – Maddie – I know it's been hard for you with Tommy gone. His loss hit us all hard. I know how it is to grieve – I lost my own brother Frank just days before your husband was shot. The O'Banion gang – they're nothing but a pack of rabid dogs. We'll be dealing with that scum pretty soon.' His gaze shifted to a spot over my shoulder. I turned to see a waiter hovering, unsure if he should approach. 'Yeah, you. Come here,' commanded Capone. 'Bring some menus, will ya?'

The waiter scurried to comply. I knew I'd throw up if I tried to swallow a bite of solid food but I had to order something. I motioned my menu away. 'No, thank you. I know what I'd like. Some hot soup, please. And a cup of tea with milk and sugar.'

'That's it? Christ, you're not much of an eater, are you? Well, I guess that's why you're not fat. I'll have the spaghetti carbonara and the steak and fried potatoes. And tell Angela to make sure it's rare this time.'

'Yes, sir.'

'Now, where were we? Yeah . . . I know how hard it's been for you, but I want you to know that we take our business responsibilities seriously. Tommy Pastore was a good man, part of the family, you might say, and we take care of our family.'

Baby Tommy's patience was wearing thin. His initial whimpering hadn't brought the desired result so he launched an angry protest that any mother would recognize as the empty-stomach cry. I brought him to my lap and bounced him gently on my knee, to no avail. Capone took the opportunity to drain and refill his glass of wine.

'Excuse Little Tommy, Mr Capone, his manners aren't developed yet. I know you understand. You have a wife and children too, don't you?'

'How did you know that?'

'Tommy told me. It must have been when he told me that Mr Torrio brought you to Chicago from New York to help him with the business. Do you have any boys?'

'Uh, yeah. One.'

'And what's his name?'

'Albert.' He shook his head. Clearly, this wasn't what he'd come to talk about. 'Now, that's what I'm thinking about. Your boy. That dump of a boarding house you live in is no place for you and the baby.' He raised his voice over the baby's cries. 'I've found a nice apartment for you with four rooms – a parlor, a kitchen, a dining room, and a bedroom. With windows in every room so the lake breeze can cool you off in the summer, not like the one-room-one-window place you're renting now. And it's not far from here, close to your old neighborhood.'

Was that a shot in the dark or did he really know what my boarding house room was like? Had he been spying on me? Or paying someone to spy? The errand boy, no doubt.

The waiter served my soup and Capone's first course. I set Tommy down – he was sucking hungrily on his fist – and took a tentative sip of the broth. Even if I couldn't eat it, it gave me something to look at and something to do with my hands. Capone plunged into his spaghetti. It wasn't pleasant to watch.

'And you don't have to worry your pretty head about rent. I'm taking care of that. All you have to do is move in and start living the good life again. Whattaya think of that?'

I was shocked that the offer was so blunt, but not surprised he made it.

I sipped my soup to give me a chance to compose my thoughts. 'That's very generous of you, Mr Capone—'

'I think we're on a first-name basis now, don't you, Maddie? You can call me Al.'

I gave him an insipid smile and avoided using his name at all. 'I'm really quite happy in the boarding house. It's small, as you say, but it's cheerful and I have friends there. And it's a short walk to work.'

'Work? Oh, that's right, your job with the medium . . . Johnny told me about that. But that's just it, Maddie girl. That's my point. You won't need to work a job anymore. Get it? I'll give you an allowance along with the apartment. You won't need to hand your baby over to strangers while you slave for pennies. You can stay home and give him the love and care he needs.'

'You know, that's the best thing about my job – I can bring Baby Tommy with me every day! And I enjoy the work and the independence it gives me.'

'Yeah? What exactly is it you do? Does the Church approve of this? Sounds like devil worship or something.'

'On the contrary, Madame Carlotta is a devout Catholic who opens every session with the Lord's Prayer. And her spiritual guide is the archangel Michael himself.'

'Who?'

'Book of Daniel. Revelation. Prince of the angels. So you see, I'm doing very well and, while I appreciate your concern, I'm pleased to say I don't need charity.'

'Jesus, Maddie, charity? Did I say the word charity? Did you hear charity come outa my mouth? No! Never! It's only what's owed you on account of Tommy's untimely death. It's like insurance. I'd count it an honor to look in on you when I could, when business was slow, to see if you needed anything now that Tommy's gone.'

Just what I was waiting for. Taking a deep breath, I gave him a big smile. 'Oh, Tommy's not gone. Not really. That's the real reason why I could never quit my job. You see, I help Madame Carlotta when she calls upon the Spirit World, and at nearly every séance, she brings Tommy's spirit into the room for me. I haven't lost him, not really. I talk with him almost every night.'

The waiter set Capone's steak in front of him. He was staring at me so hard, he didn't notice. 'You really talk to him?'

I pressed my advantage. 'Certainly I do. Oh, you and I both know that most so-called mediums are nothing but frauds. Fakes, charlatans, crooks who perform parlor tricks to swindle people out of their money. I thought as much too when I first met Madame Carlotta. But I can assure you – she is no phony. She's the real deal. She doesn't even charge her clients a fee! Through her archangel, I summon Tommy and tell him everything, and he advises me. It's comforting to know he's still there, watching over me and Little Tommy, taking care of us all the time, day and night.'

Capone gave a nervous glance around the empty room as if Tommy's ghost might materialize in the corner. I continued, 'He protects us from harm. I know he'll be grateful when he hears about your concern, Mr Capone, but he wants me to stay where I am. Oh, here's my tea.' I thanked the waiter then made myself meet Capone's eyes. 'My word, aren't you going to eat your steak while it's hot?'

Capone fumbled with his knife and fork and began sawing away at the rare hunk of beef on his plate. He ate fast, shoveling bites into his mouth before he'd swallowed the last one, and pausing only to lubricate the process with a swig of wine. The minutes passed in silence as he wolfed down the meat. I picked up Baby Tommy and fished limp bits of pasta out of my soup for him.

Suddenly Capone snapped his fingers. The waiter appeared.

'Was everything to your liking, Mr Capone?'

'Yeah. Tell Angela she did good.' He stood. So did I. Evidently there would be no check. 'Listen, Mad— uh, Mrs Pastore. You gonna talk to my friend Tommy tonight?'

'Yes, as a matter of fact, Madame Carlotta has a séance scheduled at eight. I'll tell Tommy all about seeing you. But he probably already knows. I have the feeling he's with me almost all the time.'

'Yeah?' He directed another furtive glance around the empty room. 'Well, be sure to tell him how his pals avenged his death. And tell him from me . . . tell him his brothers in the Outfit are looking after his wife and son. Tell him that, OK? I don't want any misunderstanding.'

'I'll be sure to tell him.'

The next day, the grubby young man delivered a message to Madame Carlotta from Mr Capone, asking to attend one of her séances at her earliest convenience. He wanted to contact his deceased brother. I nearly lost my lunch.

TWENTY-NINE

The morning mail brought a letter from Officer O'Rourke, typed on crisp white stationery with the official City of Chicago seal at the top. He wrote that he had some information for me, if I would be so kind as to stop at the precinct station between noon and three o'clock today or tomorrow. What on earth was so secret that he couldn't just type me the information? I lost no time in dashing over to Carlotta's house to tell Freddy.

'I don't want to wait 'til tomorrow,' I said. 'Curiosity is killing me. They must have found arsenic on the rag, don't you think? Why else would O'Rourke ask to see me?'

'To lock you up for good?' he teased. 'Or maybe he likes you. Seriously, though, you want me to come too?'

'I was hoping you would. I hate to ask, knowing how you feel about the cops, but I'd appreciate it. And we can stop by the courthouse to look up some wills while we're out. Wear your suit.'

At the Cook County Courthouse, Freddy requested the wills of the three people whose relatives were scheduled for séances next week: two who had died earlier this year and one who had passed on thirty years ago. He bounced Tommy on his knee while I read the contents and jotted down details I knew would help Madame Carlotta, and we were out of there in just under two hours. 'It's only eleven o'clock,' I said. 'Too early to get to the police station. I know a lunch counter on the way – shall we stop for a sandwich first, or is it too early for you to eat?'

It was never too early for Freddy when it came to food. How he remained stick thin with the quantity he packed away, I'll never know. When I once mentioned his bottomless stomach to Carlotta, she said he was making up for his years on the street when he was always hungry.

We reached O'Rourke's precinct station shortly before noon. I gave my name to the duty officer, and we were promptly

ushered into a dingy office at the back of the building. O'Rourke
joined us after a few minutes. After exchanging minimal pleas-
antries with my 'cousin' and me, he got down to business.

'The chemist who tested the rag you gave me discovered
traces of arsenic.' I couldn't help it – I clapped my hands with
glee. Vindicated! Now they would act! O'Rourke continued,
'I took the results to Detective Benderski, who agreed to ask
the court for permission to exhume Judge Weidemann's body.
We'll see what that tells us.'

At long last we were getting somewhere! 'And then what?'

'Depending on the results, we bring Noah Bristow in for
questioning. I wanted to warn you – you'll be questioned too.
And the cook at the Weidemann's house.'

'And the Basket Woman?'

'If she'll talk to us. There will be a number of people to
question, some who've already given statements.'

I gave a deep sigh of satisfaction. Surely this would all happen
soon, in time to prevent Bristow from killing his aunt. 'When
do you think the autopsy will take place?'

'No telling. Getting permission to exhume the body comes
first.'

I nodded. I understood, but my patience had its limits. 'Does
that take long? Remember, Mrs Weidemann is in danger, so
please tell people they need to get this done fast.'

I knew Bessie would be taking great care with the food Mrs
Weidemann ate, but I didn't dare let that blind me to other
ways a frail, older woman could be harmed. A pillow over the
face would leave no marks. A fall down the staircase would
be chalked up to an unfortunate accident. I let Officer O'Rourke
know my concerns but there was little he could do to speed
the process.

I couldn't wait to get to the Weidemann house to tell Bessie
the news. We'd been right! Perhaps I could stop by tomorrow.

O'Rourke wasn't finished. 'I also wanted you to know that
you'll probably be called in to testify in court if the matter goes
to trial. And I wanted to tell you that . . . well . . . I should
have taken you more seriously sooner. It looks like your suspicions were correct.'

After that almost-apology, I fairly floated out of the police station. The burden of providing proof, catching the murderer, preventing another death – everything I'd been carrying around for weeks – now left my shoulders and soared into the sky. The cold, wet wind on my face felt like a fresh spring breeze as Freddy and I walked home.

'I've made a meatloaf tonight, Maddie,' said Carlotta, 'if you want to join Freddy and me for dinner. We can call it a celebration.'

'Gosh, two dinner invitations for the same night!' I said. 'But I'm going to Hank Russo's sister's house for dinner tonight.' Carlotta arched her eyebrows and cocked her head to one side. 'No, no,' I hastened to add, 'it's not like that. Rita has invited me. It's the whole family.'

'I haven't said a word,' said Carlotta, sending a broad wink to Freddy. 'Not a word. I'm just glad to see you going out a bit, that's all.'

As Hank had said, Rita Russo Mancini was a superb cook. We were four adults and six children at the table, counting Little Tommy – it was a meal of happy chaos. Rita's muscle-bound husband, Carlo Mancini, a switchman in the railroad yard, sat at the head of the table, with Hank at the other end. After the meal, I tried to help Rita clean up the dishes, but she wouldn't hear of it. 'Carlo and I can work faster by ourselves, thank you for offering, Maddie.' Hank steered me into the parlor where the Mancini girls were busy propping Tommy up with pillows to play house.

Banishment to the parlor suited my ulterior motive, so I didn't protest.

'Did you vote Tuesday?' I began, steering the topic of conversation to the elections.

Hank shook his head. 'I thought about it. I didn't have any real feeling for any of the candidates except La Follette, and he didn't have an ice cube's chance in summer, so I didn't bother.'

'What was it you liked about him?'

'Fighting Bob's a union supporter. A socialist. I like that. You vote for Coolidge?'

'Yeah. No real reason, but I wanted to vote.'

'Well, you picked the winner.'

'It wasn't hard. All the newspapers said he was going to win big, and he did. I guess you didn't vote in the earlier election either, the Democratic primary last spring?'

'No, ma'am, I voted in that election. Had to. Bosses ordered us to vote for Klenha, the Outfit man.'

'That was the day Frank Capone was killed, wasn't it? April first? Were you caught up in the shootings?'

He shook his head. 'Frank's death happened at the polling station at Cicero and Twenty-second. I was nowhere near there that day. Lucky for me or I mighta been pushing up daisies by now.'

'Did you know Frank?'

He shrugged. 'A little.'

'He was older than Al, right?'

'Yeah. So's Ralph. That's the other Capone. Mr Torrio brought the brothers here from New York.'

'So Al's the youngest? He was born in America, wasn't he? At least, he doesn't have an accent, like Mr Torrio. I wonder . . . was Frank born in New York?'

'Gee, I dunno. Asking too many questions around work don't look good.'

'If he spoke with an accent, that would probably mean he was born in Italy, wouldn't it?'

'I guess. And now that I think about it, Frank did have a little accent. But that don't necessarily mean he was born over there. I know people born right here in Chicago who grew up speaking Lithuanian or Polish or something at home and talk with an accent.'

'I suppose you're right. A shame about him being shot during the election.'

'Yeah, well, Frank was no Boy Scout.'

'Did he have any nicknames, like his brother? I know they call Al Snorky or Scarface.'

'I heard Al and Ralph call him Salvatore sometimes. That wasn't a nickname though. It was his real name. He probably changed it to Frank to sound tougher, more American.'

'Was he married?'

'Dunno. Never heard of any wife or kids.'

'What happened that day, when Frank was shot?'

'Like I said, I wasn't there. Me and Tommy were making deliveries like usual. I only heard about what happened from Charlie Fischetti who was there. Frank Capone had put sluggers at all the Cicero polling booths to . . . you know . . . make sure the voting went the way Torrio wanted. All armed to the teeth. Then some men in suits showed up. Our boys thought they were O'Banion's boys and someone started shooting. Turns out they were cops, although Fischetti swears he saw some of O'Banion's boys with them. Anyway, the official report said it was justifiable shooting 'cause Frank was resisting arrest.'

I knew most of this from the newspapers, but Hank was adding a few things to my meager stash of personal information. Like my Tommy, Frank Capone had written no will, so I was on my own when it came to digging up details for Carlotta.

Hank went on. 'That was a bad day for the Outfit. Those Capone brothers are tight. Why the interest in Frank?'

'Oh, I don't know . . . morbid curiosity, I suppose.'

'You aren't thinking about getting mixed up with that family, are you?'

'Heavens, no.'

'Those Capone boys, they'd just as soon shoot you as look at you. No regrets.'

'I understand. I was just asking.'

Hank turned to face the children playing on the floor. 'Hey, kids, listen up! Do I hear the Good Humor man? I got too many pennies in my pocket, and I'm wondering if anyone wants to help me spend 'em?'

THIRTY

The first chance I had, I bundled Tommy up in a warm blanket and set out through the city to the Weidemann home. Gray skies threatened rain and a gust of wind blew the hat right off my head. Luckily, the man behind me caught it before it hit the gutter and returned it with a flourish. I hadn't seen Bessie or Ellen since I'd finished the silver polishing, and I was bursting to give Bessie the news about the police investigation. I knocked at the rear door. Ellen opened it. Shooting me a cold stare and no greeting, she stood aside. 'I suppose you're here to see Bessie. I'll just leave you two alone.'

Right away, I knew what had happened. Bessie had told her about our investigation, and Ellen was hurt that we'd kept it from her.

'No, Ellen. Stay. Please. I have news you'll want to hear.' I sat at the large kitchen table with Tommy's basket at my feet. 'I want you both to know the good news. The police are investigating Judge Weidemann's death! You told Ellen about our suspicions, didn't you, Bessie?'

'I had to, Maddie. I needed her to help me watch Mr Noah.'

'I'm glad you did. Listen, Ellen, we weren't trying to keep secrets, honest. We were trying to protect you. If word gets out that Bessie and I suspect Mr Noah of poisoning his uncle, he could harm us – and you, if you're in with us. At the very least, he would dismiss Bessie and you. And that may still happen. It's very, very important to act as if nothing has changed.'

Bessie put the kettle on to boil. 'I think we all need a cup of tea, fixed like you like it, Ellen. And there are some biscuits left from breakfast – not warm but still fresh.'

'Thank you, Bessie. Well, here's my good news: I talked with a policeman on Friday. I gave him the rag that we used to wipe the coffee pot. You know about the rag, don't you, Ellen?' She sniffed and looked away. I read that as a 'yes' and went on. 'It was just as we suspected. The chemist who tested it found arsenic and coffee on it. The cop took that information to a detective who agreed to request an autopsy on the judge's body to check for arsenic poisoning. I'm sure that's what they'll find, but it may take a little while. They have to go to court and get permission.'

'I hope Mr Noah doesn't get wind of this,' Bessie said with a frown.

'It's unlikely . . . unless he has friends inside the police department.'

'Do they need to ask Mrs Weidemann for permission?' asked Ellen, drawn into the conversation in spite of her resentment. She leaned forward on her elbows with a worried frown. 'If they do that, she might refuse. She won't believe her darling Noah could do anything so despicable. She didn't believe the judge when he told her about Noah stealing his books and things.'

'She sure believed him when he said Ursula had run off with the silver,' Bessie pointed out.

'The police never found Ursula or the silver, did they?' I asked.

'No,' said Bessie, 'but they didn't expect to. Stolen silver gets melted down quick so it can't be traced to anyone, and as for Ursula, she probably used the money to get far away. Mr Noah had been bothering her something fierce. But what about the permission?'

I shook my head. 'Luckily, they don't need the next-of-kin's permission to dig up a body when they've got suspicions of foul play. And I hope they're smart enough not to bring it to Mrs Weidemann's attention, in case she tells Noah Bristow. The cop told me it's something a judge has to order, assuming he agrees with the coroner and the state's lawyer that there's a good reason to do it.'

'What if the judge doesn't agree?' Bessie asked.

I held my palms up in a helpless gesture. That was my last real worry, that something would go wrong in the process and the judge would not see what seemed so obvious to me. I had to trust that Officer O'Rourke and the detective could make the case.

'When does all this happen?' asked Ellen.

'No telling. Could be days. Weeks, even. So it's real important that you both keep a sharp eye on Mr Noah when he's
home. Watch every bite of food and drink Mrs Weidemann
puts in her mouth. Don't let him be alone with her.' I relayed
my fears about smothering or a fall down the stairs. Both
women shuddered. They were too decent to harbor such
thoughts. I was not.

Bessie straightened up in her chair. 'I have an idea! I'll try
to persuade Mrs Weidemann to invite her nieces for a visit. The
more people around, the harder it will be for Mr Noah to try
anything.'

'Nieces?' I vaguely remembered that the judge's will
mentioned some other bequests, but I couldn't scrape the
details out of the corner of my brain.

'Rosalee and Fannie Abbott. They've not been to Chicago in
years. I don't think the oldest is twenty yet, but they're getting
close to marrying age.'

'I've never even heard of them,' said Ellen, 'and I've been
here two years.' Tommy started fussing and, before I could
reach for him, Ellen plucked him from his basket and bounced
him on her knees – a clear signal that I'd been forgiven.

'The judge wasn't fond of them,' explained Bessie. 'Not on
their own account, mind you; it was their father who married
Mrs Weidemann's other sister that he didn't like. The Abbotts
live in Milwaukee. I bet I can get Mrs Weidemann to send the
girls an invitation, maybe to come this week and stay for
Thanksgiving. 'Course, she couldn't entertain, what with her
in mourning, but she could ask some of her friends to include
the Abbott girls in their parties and theatrical evenings.'

'What an excellent idea! You think you could persuade her?'

Bessie pursed her lips and nodded solemnly. 'She's doing
better now – now that she's not eating arsenic with her meals!
She's up out of bed every day. I think a nice visit from the
nieces would perk up her spirits. She never shared the judge's
opinion of the Abbotts, but of course, she couldn't gainsay her
husband.'

'One thing I don't understand,' said Ellen, looking at me. I
braced myself. There was a large hole in my participation in

this affair that I was hoping no one would notice. No such luck. 'How did you come to suspect Mr Noah in the first place? That is, before you saw him fiddle with the coffee?'

Out of the corner of my eye, I saw Bessie give me a speculative look. She hadn't thought of that before now. I had to tread lightly.

'Good question. I suppose the things I read about in the newspapers made me suspicious and then, when I was working here with the silver, I heard more . . . things that didn't add up neatly. Two deaths so close together, with money benefitting the same person. A person who had stolen before to cover his debts. And I saw that rat poison in his room the day I went to fetch the tray. That looked odd, since Bessie said the house didn't have a rat problem. Put it all together, and you have motive and opportunity. But until I saw him stand right by that stove and fiddle with the coffee, I had nothing to back up my hunch.'

A faint bell chime that floated into the kitchen like a message from heaven saved me from further questions. Ellen handed Tommy to me and made for the door. 'She'll be wanting help with dressing,' she explained for my benefit. 'Mrs Parsifal is coming to call this morning, now that she's feeling herself again. Good day, Maddie. Don't be a stranger.'

THIRTY-ONE

The sun had chased away most of the clouds by the time I emerged from the Weidemann house. I made my way south in a leisurely fashion. My investigative work for Carlotta was current – she had good information about her upcoming clients – so I decided to take my time and enjoy a walk down State Street, Chicago's busiest shopping district. Hoisting Tommy on my shoulder, I ambled along the sidewalk, navigating through the waves of pedestrians, all of whom seemed to be surging upstream while I was going down. Pausing frequently, I showed Tommy the pretty merchandise in the windows and let him absorb the noise of the motorcar engines, the squeals from the streetcar brakes, and the babble of foreign languages that characterized this city of immigrants. Tommy would be a child of the city, like me, born and raised in Chicago, but it would be a different Chicago than I had known as a girl.

Back when I was little, I remember seeing parts of the Chicago elevated train – the famous L – being built above the streets. I remember those same streets paved with wood, cedar wood blocks soaked in creosote set in a checkerboard pattern in tar and gravel. Now most of those had been paved over with macadam. When I was a girl, old people in our neighborhood were still talking about the Great Fire of 1871 that destroyed the town and brought on a building spree during the next couple of years that beat the band. Little Tommy would never see the streets full of horse-drawn wagons and carriages like I recall. He'd think nothing of buildings that stretched more than ten stories high on every street. When he was old enough, I'd show him some culture at the art museum and the theater and the Field Museum that Mr Marshall Field paid for. Chicago was my city. I knew nothing else. I'd never traveled outside it in my life and didn't need to. We'd be fine in Chicago, Tommy and me. I was beginning to believe it.

Something unusual was going on along State Street. Men were unloading sawhorses from the back of trucks and piling them at the corners. A woman in a smart blue suit must have noticed my puzzled frown, because she paused to answer the question that was on my mind.

'They're settin' up for the parade tomorrow, dearie.'

I gave a rueful smile. 'Of course! I wasn't thinking.'

Tomorrow was Armistice Day. How could I have forgotten? Just six years ago, at the eleventh hour of the eleventh day of the eleventh month of 1918, the guns of war went silent. The Great War ended. No one knew how many millions of men had died in battle – I knew two of them myself, men who had once worked at Marshall Field's, had gone to fight in France and never come home – and that number didn't count the uncountable civilians who died of starvation, injuries, and disease. But everyone knew that this war was so costly and so horrific that humanity would give up war for good. I'd watched the carnage for years from the comfort of a theater seat courtesy of Pathé newsreels, far away from danger in the trenches. The images of death and devastation brought Europe's misery across the world to our own theaters, dispelling forever the lie that war was a noble adventure.

Last year, Tommy and I had gone to the parade together. We'd cheered the marching soldiers, applauded the bands, waved our small flags, and talked solemnly about the boys who didn't come home. Tommy had been a soldier, and he could have marched in the parade, but he refused to take part. 'It's for heroes,' he told me. 'I don't deserve to share the honor.' He'd been drafted into the Army in 1918, trained for sixteen weeks as an artillery gunner, and shipped to France in October. His unit arrived the first of November, ten days before the war ended. They saw no action. They did see the front with its rat-infested trenches and hospitals crammed with wounded and shell-shocked boys, for their unit was assigned to help with demobilization. He was there for nearly a year after the fighting had ended. When he told me about it, he seemed embarrassed. I hadn't known what to say at the time, so I said nothing.

If he were with me today, though, I'd say, combat or no, you served your country to the best of your ability, and I decided

right then and there that I would take Little Tommy to the
parade tomorrow. Afterward, we would go to the cemetery
where they handed out American flags to put on the graves of
veterans, and I'd give Tommy a flag. At that moment, right
across the street, I saw the striped awning of Schofield's florist
shop.

'Come on, Tommy, let's buy some flowers for Papa's grave.'

I had to stand at the corner for several minutes before the
traffic cop signaled to our group to scurry across the street.
The sidewalks were jammed on account of the sawhorses, and
some people spilled into the streets, which wasn't any better
since they were full of motorcars and trucks jostling for position. Clutching Tommy against my chest, I ducked and threaded
my way through the confusion to the other side.

I entered Schofield's on the heels of three men who looked
like they were together. The same colored assistant was there;
he looked up and greeted us with a smile that suggested he
remembered me from last time when I'd come in with Ellen.
One of the men said they'd come for the Merlo funeral flowers.
The assistant told them Mr O'Banion was finishing up those
arrangements in the back room. As they filed behind the counter
and out of sight, he turned to me.

'And what can I help you with today, miss?'

'I was thinking of taking something to a grave tomorrow.'

'For a soldier?' I nodded. 'You might consider poppies, miss.
People are buying them for Armistice Day, for the veterans,
remembering the poppies of Flanders fields like in that poem
that's so—' We were interrupted by a man barging through the
shop door.

It was Hank Russo. Of all people!

'Why, Hank! What—'

'Quick! Come—'

Two very loud shots rang out from the back room. There
was a shout and two or three more shots followed, then, after
the space of one breath, a final bang by itself. I had never heard
genuine gunfire up close before, but I knew instantly what it
was.

I froze on the spot. Hank did not. He grabbed me around the
waist, put a hand on my head, and pushed me to the floor

against the counter, shielding me and Tommy, squashed against my neck, from easy view. The assistant dropped to the floor at the same moment.

My heart pounded like a big bass drum. Tommy began to squeal. I heard the scramble of feet as the three men rushed out of the back room to make their escape through the front door. I prayed they wouldn't stop to shoot us on the way out.

They stopped.

Hank stood. 'Go! Go!' he yelled at them.

A raspy voice said, 'What about—?'

'She's one of us. Go! Quick!'

I kept my head down against Little Tommy, whose screams told me he sensed his mother's terror. I tried to cover him with my own body so if they shot me, the bullet wouldn't hit my precious boy.

Scuffling footsteps told me the men were fleeing. Afraid to move, I cocked my head just enough to see through the open door into the street where the four men walked purposefully to a black motorcar idling at the curb, trying to strike a nonchalant air even as their heads were bobbing in every direction. Hank looked up and down the street as if to judge whether they'd aroused any suspicion, then slid into the driver's seat as the others piled into the back. He sped off before they had time to slam the doors.

Not until we were certain they'd gone did the assistant and I straighten up off the floor. Trembling like a man with palsy, he scrambled into the back room where he began to moan, 'Oh, lordy mercy! Oh, lordy mercy, Jesus.'

Seconds after the gangsters' motorcar pulled away, several pedestrians stepped cautiously into the shop. 'Lady, what the hell?' said one man, looking around the shop and seeing nothing disturbed. 'We heard . . . well, is everything all right?'

Words failed me. I could only point a shaky finger toward the back room.

Before five seconds had passed, the front room was jam-packed with curious people pushing to see the dead body. Men shouted, 'Get back!' and 'Call a cop!' and 'Get a doctor!' but I knew without seeing the corpse that six bullets going into a man at point-blank range were not going to leave him merely

wounded. One man came out retching, his hand over his mouth.
A woman outside the door fainted.

My own limbs had turned to mush, so I leaned against the
counter and took deep breaths of fetid air. I couldn't have pushed
my way out of the shop anyway – a crowd was blocking the
door. I held Tommy tight against my chest, unable to hear
through the din whether he was crying or not. Seconds, maybe
minutes passed, and two policemen pushed their way inside.

'All right, folks, get outa here,' one shouted, grabbing people
by their shoulders and shoving them out the door. 'This ain't
no theater play.'

'Move along or you'll get arrested for obstructing justice,'
said the other, who reached the back room before his partner.
'Jesus H. Christ, it's O'Banion!'

Word spread like a prairie fire. 'They got O'Banion!' everyone
was saying, thrilled, excited, and horrified at the same time.

'Serves him right.'

'He had it coming to him.'

'I wanna see!'

'Move out the way!'

I wanted to explain that it was the wrong O'Banion, not the
gangster, just an ordinary man, a simple florist, who happened
to have the same last name. I wanted to tell the police that the
gangsters had killed him by mistake, but they were busy herding
people outside, out of the suffocating shop, out of the way.
Including me and Tommy. I tried to catch the attention of one
of them to make them understand their mistake, but he just
grabbed my arm and shoved me along with the others. I waited
on the sidewalk in the midst of a growing crowd as strangers
exchanged information with strangers.

'They got O'Banion this time,' said a man behind me.

'Christ, this'll set off a battle to rival Verdun,' said another.

'What happened?' asked a woman to my left.

'Someone shot the North Side Gang boss,' answered another.
'Probably Torrio's boys or the Gennas.'

'Good riddance to him.'

'You don't think this is the end, do you? Hell, no, things are
just heating up.'

As soon as I'd caught my breath, I took my bearings and

struck out toward the nearest streetcar stop. I'd come to my senses. It wasn't my job to set people straight. The last thing I needed was for anyone to know I'd been a witness to the poor florist's murder. I didn't want the police or anyone else to find out I'd seen the faces of the three gangsters and Hank Russo, or in no time, I'd be as dead as the harmless flower arranger who liked to flirt with Ellen.

THIRTY-TWO

Next day's headlines set me straight. Every newspaper in the country ran the story. In Chicago, big black capital letters shouted from the top of all the local dailies: **Arch Criminal of Chicago Slain in his Flower Shop**. **O'Banion Is Murdered in his Florist Shop by Three Gunmen who Escape**. **O'Banion is Slain in his Shop**. Turns out the murdered man at Schofield's *was* Dion O'Banion, the North Side mob boss himself. I was stunned. Nice looking, friendly, not much older than I was, with a gentle voice and a flair for flower arranging . . . how did a man like that become the boss of a murderous organization that made millions in crime? One paper quoted a police chief crediting O'Banion with at least twenty-five killings. Was Tommy counted as one of those? And Frank Capone? And the others in Johnny Torrio's gang?

My heart skipped a beat when I saw another headline: **Girl an O'Banion Death Clue**, but I breathed easier when I read the girl they sought was blond and had something to do with a feud. Not me, thank heavens. The police had mounted a citywide search for the three assassins and the fourth man who drove the getaway car. No names were mentioned, but surely, in those crowded streets, someone had seen enough to identify the men. Poor Hank, his liquor delivery job had turned into driving a getaway car for murderers. If Tommy had been alive, would he have been roped into this?

Reports described O'Banion's bloody corpse lying crumpled on the floor amid a profusion of chrysanthemum blooms that he had been arranging for Armistice Day, his dead right hand still clutching his shears. The colored porter, identified as William Critchfield, was being questioned by the police. If he knew what was good for him, he'd say he didn't recognize the men who shot his boss. I could only hope he'd forgotten about the woman and baby who had wanted to buy flowers for a soldier's grave.

I was poring over the newspapers at Carlotta's house with Freddy. She'd bought every daily she could find, and she and Freddy were talking about the crime and its probable consequences. I said little. The less they knew, the safer they would be.

'When is Al Capone's appointment?' asked Freddy. 'Tonight?'

'He wanted tonight,' replied Carlotta, 'but I told him the eleventh was reserved for families of our boys lost in the Great War. He'll be here tomorrow night.'

'Who with?'

'Alone. He requested a private séance.'

'Aren't you afraid?'

'Afraid of what? He's like any other client, just wants to contact his brother's spirit. 'Course I'm not afraid.'

Maybe not, but she didn't know Al Capone. I did, and I was afraid. The man was unpredictable and violent. No telling what he would do if he heard something from Carlotta he didn't like or didn't hear something he expected to hear.

A few years back, when Tommy had started working for the Outfit, I hadn't thought much about it. The money was real good, and all he was doing was delivering liquor, for pity's sake, something that had been perfectly legal until a stroke of the pen made it a crime. Most people didn't think drinking was a crime. Catholics certainly didn't. How could drinking an alcoholic beverage be a crime when wine was a critical part of Holy Communion? But I knew now that Tommy and I had been naïve. Getting involved with these gangsters – even with something as harmless as deliveries – pulled you into their sticky web little by little, until you were part of the whole and guilty of helping with white slavery, brutal beatings, robberies, extortion, and grisly murders. Even with Tommy gone, I was still tangled up in their rat's nest. I wondered if I would ever be free.

My best efforts had turned up precious little information about Frank Capone for Carlotta to use at Al's séance. Frank had lived in Chicago only a few years. He'd come from New York with some of his brothers. No one seemed to know how many Capone brothers there were, and asking questions like that wasn't prudent. He left no will that I could find. His obituary had been short on personal details – evidently the family wasn't forthcoming. Freddy and I had worked up some enhancements, but for the moment, we were focused on tonight's séance.

It would be a full table with seven clients eager to communicate with their slain soldiers: two widows, one sister, a brother, two mothers, and a son. Carlotta had been preparing herself for the ordeal all day, resting in her room with shades pulled and reviewing the information I'd compiled on each man. One had died only last year from injuries sustained during a German gas attack years earlier; the others were killed seven or eight years ago during the war and were buried in France or Belgium, or at sea. Two had been officers: a captain who had received the Croix de Guerre for an assault on a German machine gun nest and a major in the artillery who was killed at Chateau Thierry. One had flown a spotter airplane; another was a medic who died when artillery fire hit his field hospital. Two of the men were privates killed at the battles of Belleau Wood and Cantigny. The lone navy man had been a gunner's mate on a destroyer escorting eastbound convoys.

We never knew what Carlotta would do during these sessions or how she would approach each spirit. She always insisted she was merely the vessel for Archangel Michael and that he would determine the success or failure of any séance. I'd coached Freddy with a couple of sentences for each man, things he could rasp out in his low voice if Carlotta's patter faltered. We would perform the usual tricks with the candle and bells to get started, and at the end, Freddy would let fall a handful of fresh poppy petals I'd plucked from their stems. They would flutter silently down to the table in the dark, becoming visible only when the séance had ended and the lights came up. A fitting final touch.

Not much Latin was required that night as Carlotta implored Archangel Michael to find the spirits of the brave men who had died for their country. '*Dulce et decorum est pro patri mori*,' she chanted. Michael arrived promptly and, as the one who carried souls to heaven, he gathered the spirits we wished to contact and let them speak through Carlotta. Sometimes she used information I'd provided; other times she found words of her own to impart. In each case, she seemed to sense the right thing to say, optimistic words that would bring the most comfort to the bereaved family members. Even if she wasn't truly clairvoyant, she did have a gift in that way.

The clients left, grateful and satisfied. Carlotta's donation basket held over a hundred dollars.

Now it was time to start preparing for Al Capone's séance. Now it was time to be afraid.

THIRTY-THREE

As Freddy and I watched from the second-story window, a black motorcar pulled up in front of Madame Carlotta's house. Before it came to a stop, a second motorcar eased along the curb behind it. Two men in suits, their hands buried in coat pockets, stepped out of each vehicle. They scanned the dark, quiet neighborhood, finding nothing more menacing than a man walking his dog past a dim gaslight, a couple crossing the street, and a trio of flappers giggling down the sidewalk on their way to a smoky speakeasy. When they had verified the all clear, another man – stocky, with a face obscured by a hat pulled low over his brow – exited the second motorcar and hurried up the front steps. The door opened before he reached the top, and Madame Carlotta ushered Al Capone into her home.

Two bodyguards accompanied him inside. Two remained on Carlotta's front steps, back-to-back, as they kept watch down opposite ends of the street. Two others, the drivers, remained inside the motorcars, ready to peel away in case of an ambush. Night had fallen hours ago. Even a cat couldn't have seen very far. Freddy and I could hear voices from downstairs, but no distinct words. We knew the two bodyguards would be left to cool their heels in the parlor, while Mr Capone was shown into Carlotta's séance room for his private session. We heard the door between the rooms close. That was our cue to move into position.

I gave Freddy a silent thumbs up sign and crept downstairs on stocking feet into the kitchen where I opened a cupboard mounted on the wall dividing the kitchen and the séance room. Inside the cupboard, a secret door opened to the other side, where the wallpaper pattern concealed its existence. I didn't rush to open it. First I leaned into the cupboard and peered through a peephole to see whether Carlotta had cut the lights. She had not. She was speaking to Capone. I could hear her clearly. That meant they could hear me, I reminded myself. Scarcely daring to breathe, I waited.

'. . . and I can make no guarantees, Mr Capone. The archangel Michael does not serve me; I serve him. Some of my clients find it helpful to return a time or two if the preliminary visitation disappoints.'

He grunted.

'Now, if you'd care to remove your coat to be more comfortable . . . no? As you like . . . then, would you kindly take a seat – this one – while I extinguish the light.'

Only the candle that Carlotta placed in the center of the table relieved the darkness. We had switched out the large, round table for the smaller one we used for private séances, one that allowed Carlotta to reach across to hold her client's hands, with the candle between them.

'Now, you and I will join hands in our endeavor to reach the Spirit World, and so you will rest assured that I have no tricks to play.'

Freddy, I knew, was watching through a similar peephole from his position above the chandelier and would be opening his secret door now, as I opened mine.

Carlotta began her routine as she always did, with several deep breaths and eyes closed. She would not be rushed. She hummed a little, like a cat purring. No recognizable tune, just two or three notes repeated over and over. I grew nervous. Al Capone was not known for his patience. Finally, after what seemed like longer than her usual introduction, she began to speak. 'Our Father, who art in heaven . . .' Capone joined in the prayer. Like all the Outfit boys, he was a good Catholic.

'Michael . . . dearest archangel . . . spirit guide of the heavens . . . favor us tonight with your presence . . . *Magnificat anima mea Dominum . . . et exsultavit spiritus meus* . . . prince of the angels, guide us into the Spirit World . . . bring us the soul we seek tonight . . . *in Deo salvatore meo . . .*'

Freddy chose that moment to lower his speaking tube. From my position in the kitchen, I could hear the faint swoosh of the bellows that mimicked the rush of the wind, and I knew Carlotta and Capone could feel the breeze as Freddy aimed it toward them and then toward the candle. The flame flickered and went out.

'Come to us tonight, dear Michael . . . *gloria Patri, et Filio, et Spiritui Sancto* . . . lead those in your realm of glory to us tonight . . . bring the comfort of a visit to the bereaved soul here tonight . . . *sicut erat in principio* . . . we are all believers here . . . seek your assistance in connecting to the brother of one here tonight . . . *saecula saeculorum* . . .'

I couldn't see it or feel it, but I knew from past séances what that sudden break in her patter signified. So did Freddy. The muffled tones of a distant bell sounded. Archangel Michael had arrived.

'Dearest Michael . . . thank you for bestowing your presence on us unworthy mortals . . . there is among us a man who seeks his beloved brother, Frank Capone, who departed the world of the living seven months ago . . . deign to assist us tonight, dear Michael, bring the soul we seek to us tonight. Reassure his loving brother that he is content in the afterlife.'

There was a long pause as Carlotta waited for inspiration. Nothing happened. I wasn't concerned – yet. I knew Freddy would wait a bit longer before stepping in with two or three sentences he could deliver in a low, gruff voice with a slight accent we trusted would sound enough like Frank to convince Al Capone he had contacted his brother.

Capone whispered, 'He was baptized Salvatore, not Frank.'

'Archangel Michael knows this. It is he who carries the precious souls up to heaven. He knows every one of them.' Nonetheless, she used the given name in her next appeal. 'Salvatore Capone . . . is he willing to communicate from the Spirit World with his brother, Alphonse?'

I readied my enhancement. The voice of Frank Capone – from Carlotta or Freddy – would come soon.

It had been simple to create the glowing head prop. We searched magazines until we found a full-page image of a man's face. I cut it out and painted over the facial features with Undark, an almost magical luminous radium paint that glowed in the dark. Next, we mounted the paper face on cardboard and fastened that to a stiff, black wire that I could stick through the opening into the séance room. Moving it slowly up, down, and around created an eerie effect that we'd used to great advantage in past séances. Al Capone had been positioned in the chair directly across from me, so he could not miss seeing his brother's disembodied face glowing in the dark. Holding tight to the end of the wire, I waited for my cue: the vocal introduction of Frank Capone.

A long silence. More silence. Then from Carlotta, another plea. 'Please, Michael, we entreat you . . . find Salvatore Frank Capone . . . bring him to his brother who mourns his absence.'

Carlotta stopped talking and I thought I heard a soft snore. Ordinarily I would have squeezed her hand to jostle her awake, but I wasn't acting as a shill now, I was in another room for this séance. I held my breath, hoping she'd wake up, when at last I heard Archangel Michael's unidentifiable, gravelly accent coming from her throat. 'Heeee issss not here.' There was a long delay, then she repeated, 'Heeee issss not here.'

A minute, perhaps two, ticked by. Impatient and probably confused, Capone whispered, hesitantly at first, 'Whattsamatta? Can't Frank talk?'

'Heeee issss not here.'

'What's that supposed to mean? Are we supposed to come back another night or something?'

'Heeee issss not here.'

'Whaddaya mean, not there?' Capone's voice grew sharper with every exchange. 'You saying he's not dead? Jesus, I buried him myself!'

'Heeee issss not here.'

All of a sudden, it struck me. Carlotta couldn't have understood what she was saying. Or how it could be interpreted. Or how unspeakably dangerous it was that she was saying it. Raw terror surged through my body like electric current. Mentally, I urged Freddy to chime in with his prepared sentences, but I knew he never interrupted if Carlotta was holding forth as Michael.

'Where the hell is he, then?' demanded Capone in a louder voice that cracked with horror as he realized he'd supplied his own answer.

I stopped breathing. A lethal silence lasted for the space of four or five heartbeats, then there was a crash as someone – it had to be Capone, but I could not see – overthrew the whole table and a chair.

At the noise, the two thugs in the parlor burst through the

door, flooding the séance room with light, pointing their guns into the room as they looked every which way for someone to shoot. In the split second before I slid the panel closed, I saw Carlotta in her chair, looking rather dazed, and a seething Al Capone standing beside the overturned table, his fists clenched, his thick lips snarling foul curses. Praying Freddy would have the presence of mind *not* to pull up the speaking tube at that moment – movement of any sort would draw the eye whereas a fixed object would receive less notice – I set the unused glowing face on the kitchen floor and flew on stocking feet out of the kitchen toward the séance room, thinking to protect Carlotta from Capone's violence. But when I wrenched open the hall door that led into the séance room, I saw only the backs of the bodyguards as they hustled their boss through the parlor and out the front door. My presence went unnoticed.

Freddy came thundering down the stairs, nearly colliding with me as he burst into the séance room.

'Are you all right?' he gasped.

Carlotta had that glazed look about her that told me she'd been jerked out of her trance too quickly and wasn't fully conscious of what had just occurred. I knelt down beside her and took her hand. 'Oh, Carlotta! Why did you do that?'

'Do what?'

'Make him mad. Why did you make Al Capone mad? He stormed out. He didn't like the message.'

'Wh-what was the message?' she asked. She didn't remember what she'd said. That was the first time she'd been in such a deep trance that she wasn't aware of her own words.

'You – I mean, Archangel Michael kept saying, "He is not here". He wouldn't say anything else. It sounded like . . . I think Capone understood it to mean that his brother was not there, not in heaven, but in hell.'

Carlotta watched Freddy, who had begun righting the table and chair, as she nodded slowly, considering my words. 'Sometimes messages get confused.'

'Was this one confused?'

'I don't think so . . . I can't always tell.'

Trying to smooth over the calamity, I reassured her. 'It might turn out to be a good thing. It might mean he doesn't come back again. Or better yet, maybe the message will frighten him into mending his ways.' More likely it would prove a very bad thing, if he decided to murder Carlotta, burn down her house, or take revenge in some other vicious manner. Or . . . would he be too afraid of angering the Spirit World to harm one of its mediums? I left those fears unspoken.

THIRTY-FOUR

The minute I heard Mrs Weidemann had asked for a séance on Friday night, I pinned a clean diaper on Tommy, dressed him in a thick flannel suit, and set out for the Weidemann house to learn what was what. Bessie gave me a warm greeting at the back door.

'Why, if it isn't Miss Maddie and her gentleman friend, Master Thomas, in the flesh! Come in, come in.'

'Where is everyone?' I asked.

'Ellen will be back from the market in a spell. Mrs Weidemann is getting dressed for a women's club meeting at the church.' She lowered her voice slightly. 'And Mr Noah hasn't come out of his room yet.' The roll of her eyes gave me to understand that he was sleeping off a late night.

'Mrs Weidemann must be feeling better, then?'

'Praise the Lord. Each day finds her stronger. She got out of bed a few days ago. Yesterday she sat in the conservatory for the first time in weeks and then went to a lady friend's house for tea.' And in a whisper she added, 'Ellen and me, we watching her like hawks. I still worry about her come night-time, though, up there alone on the second floor with just *him*, but we've outfoxed him, we have. I go to bed right after supper and Ellen stays up until he gets home – that's usually about two or three in the morning. She wakes me up and goes to bed herself, and I go sit in the front hall where I can hear any footsteps in case he travels during the night. I stay there until she's awake in the morning.'

'I'm glad to hear she's well enough to get out now and then,' I said, hoping to prompt Bessie to tell me about tomorrow's séance. It worked.

'Remember that time I told you about, when she wanted to go see a mystic person? And she couldn't go because she was feeling so poorly?' I nodded. 'Well, she's going tomorrow night. She thinks she's gonna see the judge's ghost. She told Mr Noah at supper last night.'

'What did he think of that?'

'He made fun of her. Said there was no such thing as talking to the dead. Said hold on to your wallet, Auntie, 'cause those people are out to rob you blind, telling you the ghost said give all your money to them.'

'I suppose that does happen with some mediums.'

'If it does, it happens to foolish folk who got no more sense than a baby, and no offense intended, Master Tommy.'

'I hope the séance helps her find some peace.'

'That poor lady . . . bless her heart. But Mr Noah, he wants to protect her money, all right. He wants to make sure no one steals it before he can get his hands on it!'

Ellen bounded through the door, a bundle of warm energy on a cold Chicago morning. Expressing her delight at seeing me and Baby Tommy, she insisted we stay long enough to share some coffee and a slice of Bessie's pound cake. After I'd fed Tommy, he and I set out for Carlotta's house so I could fill her in on what I'd learned.

By the time I arrived, it was nearly noon. She and Freddy were in the kitchen preparing a simple meal of vegetable soup with bread and butter. The mood was unusually jolly.

'Join us, Maddie, won't you? I have something for Tommy too, some of these peas – would he eat 'em if you mashed 'em up good?'

'I can try, thank you very much. He's a good eater – he takes most food as long as it's mushy. And I have some news about Mrs Weidemann.'

'That can wait,' said Carlotta. 'I have some news too.' She batted her eyes and gave a superior smile. 'Mr Pearson has given notice.'

I think I'd seen Mr Pearson, the traveling salesman who rented Carlotta's front bedroom, three times in as many months. A genial, middle-aged bachelor who sold plumbing fixtures wholesale, he had a territory that brought him to Chicago about two days a week. Traveling as much as he did, he found the comfort of a homey bedroom and a home-cooked meal preferable to a cheap hotel.

'What happened? Did his sales route change?'

'Exactly. He'll take over all of Chicago, not just the South Side, so he plans to settle down in a place of his own.'

'How very nice for him,' I said, not overly interested in a description of Mr Pearson's sales territory.

'And nice for us,' Carlotta said triumphantly, 'because now we have an empty bedroom to offer you and Tommy. If you care to move out of your boarding house, that is.'

Carlotta laughed at my startled expression. I had often envied Freddy his simple pallet in the enhancement room, but I'd never considered that I might join the family, so to speak. Carlotta and Freddy had become almost like family, and for someone like me who had none, it meant the world to be invited to move in. But I knew in an instant that it would not be possible.

'I don't know what to say, Carlotta . . .'

'Say yes,' said Freddy.

'Of course, I'd love to move here. But . . . I'm afraid I can't afford it. I pay Mrs Jones only ten dollars a week and that includes dinner. I really can't afford more than that, and I'm sure Mr Pearson paid you considerably more in rent.'

'Rent? Who said anything about rent? Business has been good, thanks to you and Freddy. So good I was planning to give you a raise in pay. But if you like, instead I can give you the room rent free. You'd have to pay only for your share of the food.'

Such a stroke of good fortune hadn't come my way since my world fell apart with Tommy's death. I could finally leave the grubby world of Mrs Jones's boarding house! It was almost too much to swallow at once. My eyes stung with hot tears. 'Are you sure? The baby won't be a bother? He doesn't cry much but sometimes at night, he might keep you awake.'

'Lordy mercy, Little Tommy is such a placid child, he couldn't bother anyone if he tried. This'll feel like a real home with a baby in it. Mr Pearson will be gone in two weeks, so you have time to think it over—'

'I don't need time. I'd love to move into Mr Pearson's room!' The front bedroom was half again as large as the one I had at Mrs Jones's, and I'd have the run of a parlor, a kitchen, and a small back yard as well. Farewell stinking toilet room, flying roaches, and contagious diseases! Heaven couldn't have sounded any better. 'Thank you . . .' My voice broke. All I could think of was how much I wanted to tell Tommy that his son and I were going to be all right now, just like he kept promising me in my dreams. Maybe . . . just maybe he had something to do with my change of fortune.

'Well, good, then,' said Carlotta gruffly. She pulled a handkerchief out of her sleeve and mopped her eyes. 'I'm glad that's settled. Now, we need to get back to work. Here are some more names for you to check for next week's séances: Dr Phineas Jones, Donald A. Mickel, Mrs Roland T. Blake, and Master Samuel Cruickshanks – I always hate to see the names of children. What could be worse than losing a child, I ask you? Now, what was it you wanted to tell us about poor Mrs Weidemann?'

Everything.

Freddy and I had kept from Carlotta our discoveries and concerns about the judge's homicidal nephew so as not to burden her with unnecessary information, but now that Mrs Weidemann was on the schedule for tomorrow night, we would have to come clean. We needed her help, or at least her acquiescence, if we were to carry out our plan.

I took a deep breath. 'Carlotta,' I said, feeling like a child caught snitching cookies, 'there's something I need to explain about the Weidemann case. I probably should have told you sooner, but I didn't want to worry you needlessly when I wasn't sure if she'd ever really come back. When I started investigating her husband a few weeks ago, I learned about another death in the family, one that took place shortly before his own. Mrs Weidemann's nephew, a boy of twelve who was like a son to her, drowned in August.'

'Yes, I know,' sighed Carlotta. 'That poor woman has had a heavy load to bear.'

'The circumstances were very suspicious,' I said, wishing I could let that subject slide. Hearing about the death of a child disturbed Carlotta so much that Freddy and I avoided the topic whenever possible. I told her about Dickie's drowning and my belief that Noah Bristow had done the deed. 'You see, he would inherit Dickie's portion if he was the only nephew alive at the time of the judge's death.'

Next, I painted her a picture of the judge's death, telling her about Noah's debts, how his uncle's symptoms matched those of arsenic poisoning, and how the court was getting ready to decide whether or not to exhume his body.

'That's not the end of the story either,' I continued. 'I am sure Noah Bristow is trying to kill his aunt now. She inherited half the estate, and I think it all comes to him at her death. That could be years away, and he doesn't want to wait for it to occur naturally.' I told her about the coffee rag that had traces of arsenic on it. 'Arsenic in food or coffee was his weapon of choice, but now that the cook and the maid are watching him closely, it has become more difficult for him. I fear he'll try some other method.'

'Like smothering her with a pillow,' Freddy added. 'Or pushing her down the stairs. Ways that will look like an old lady's accident.'

A dazed Carlotta sat motionless for a few moments after we had finished, her tender heart unable to cope with such wickedness. Finally, she said in a timid voice, 'My word, and her coming tomorrow. Whatever shall we do?'

It was precisely the opening I had hoped for.

'I've given that a good deal of thought, Carlotta, and I have an idea. Mrs Weidemann is so taken with her nephew, she won't hear a bad word against him from anyone, but I'll wager she'll listen to a warning from her husband from the Far Beyond.'

'Yes, of course. I'll try my very best to contact Judge Weidemann's spirit tomorrow. Surely he'll warn her about this evil nephew.'

'Exactly my thought. And if your powers are not as strong as they could be, Freddy can enhance the visit with his own voice – he does such a convincing imitation of an old man. We can work up Freddy's message. Something that tells her she's in danger and pushes her to throw the bum out before he can kill her too.'

'I know!' said Freddy eagerly. 'How's this?' The boy cleared his throat and lowered his normal, high-pitched voice to a gravelly rasp. 'Beware . . . beware the danger living in our house. Beware the greedy nephew who hastened my death with poisoned drink. Send the evil lad away at once! He plots your own death as he plotted mine.' Reverting to his normal voice, he said, 'How's that? It'll sound better coming through the speaking tube.'

'That's good, Freddy. And afterward, we can have a visit

from the drowned boy. He can warn his aunt too. I'll be seated at the table next to you so I can handle that water trick we do for people lost at sea. Freddy will do a good voice there too.'

Carlotta was frowning so I hastened to add, 'Of course, this is only if the real spirits fail to show.'

'Of course,' she replied uneasily. 'Of course . . .'

THIRTY-FIVE

When I arrived at the séance shortly before eight o'clock, one client was already in the parlor talking with Carlotta. It was Anthony Wood, a carpenter (yes, that was his real name!) seeking to contact the spirit of his brother. I'd investigated the brother, Howard Wood, last week. Anthony Wood would be an easy client.

I had dressed carefully for tonight's part, putting on one of my best dresses, an emerald wool with a drop waist and eyelet cuffs and collar that I'd bought at Marshall Field's the year before I got pregnant. A light brown wig with a bun disguised my black hair and made me look older. Mrs Weidemann had seen me only twice, once here at Carlotta's when she had come to observe and again in her darkened bedroom when she was ill. I had little fear that she would recognize me, but there was no point in taking risks. I made myself look as different as possible from the drab young mother who had spent three days polishing her silver.

Those two were the only clients scheduled for this Friday. Mrs Weidemann had not requested a private séance this time, perhaps embarrassed about her previous cancellations. As the minute hand ticked past eight, I started to think she would fail to appear once again, but finally, just as Madame Carlotta was about to begin without her, a motorcar pulled up to the curb. I heard the engine die and a door slam.

Decked in her gay gypsy finery, Carlotta met her client with a flourish. 'Good evening, Mrs Weidemann, and welcome to my humble home. I am so glad to serve as your guide to the Spirit World tonight. And so gratified about your return to good health.'

Mrs Weidemann offered a limp hand. 'Thank you, Mrs Romany, I'm pleased to see you again. And so pleased, at long last, to be able to attend one of your séances. My health of late has prevented me from leaving my home, but I am quite well now. May I introduce my dear nephew, Mr Noah Bristow? I trust it is not a problem to include him tonight?'

Noah Bristow stepped out of the shadows and strutted into the parlor like a cock sure of his hen. I stifled a horrified gasp. Panicked, I turned my face away from the newcomers and clutched my shawl tight around me. My heart raced. Thinking fast, I analyzed my predicament: unlike Mrs Weidemann who had seen me only in low light, Bristow had met me and spoken to me several times in the Weidemann's well-lit kitchen. However, I had a baby with me then and did not now, and I was dressed very differently tonight in much nicer clothes. I was wearing a wig. It would have been beneath this self-absorbed young man to have paid close attention to a lowly serving girl. I took several calming breaths and told myself I was safe. Still . . . it is often a person's eyes or voice that triggers a memory, so I made sure that shy Mrs Duval didn't meet Noah's gaze when Carlotta made introductions around the room. When my turn came, I murmured, 'Good evening, sir,' and promptly moved into the corner away from the lamplight. In a moment, we would be in total darkness in the séance room. Once the séance had started, I would speak very little and lower my voice when I did.

Only then did I grasp what his presence would do to our plan. Was there some way I could get to Freddy before the séance began?

I dragged my attention back to Carlotta in time to hear her say, 'Naturally, Mr Bristow is most welcome.' With all she knew about him, I was amazed she could behave as if he was one of her regular clients, but she knew the stakes. 'We'll pull an extra chair to the table. Come this way, please, and we'll begin.'

Bristow didn't budge. He was dressed casually in a padded-shoulder, double-breasted sack suit with the widest Oxford bags I'd ever seen. His hair, combed back in a pompadour, was kept in place with liberal amounts of hair oil. 'I feel obliged to warn you, madam, that Mr Bristow is a skeptic,' he said, pompously referring to himself in the third person. He rocked unsteadily from side to side, and I wondered if I was the only one in the room who could smell the liquor on his breath. That should work in our favor.

'We welcome skeptics and believers alike, Mr Bristow,'

replied Carlotta, unruffled as always. 'I predict you will be a believer before the night is over. You will find nothing amiss in our practice.'

'*Our?*' he said, raising one eyebrow.

'The archangel Michael and I will be your spiritual guides tonight.'

'Who's that? Some ghost?'

'The archangel Michael is not a ghost. Look in the Book of Daniel. Also Revelation. Now, before we have a seat, would everyone please examine the spirit cabinet so you can reassure yourself that it is empty.'

'What's a spirit cabinet?' asked Anthony Wood.

'Sometimes . . . I never know when . . . but sometimes a spirit will leave something in the cabinet, a memento or a sign that carries special meaning for someone in the room. We'll see if anything comes to us tonight. You'll want to reassure yourself that it is empty at the moment.'

The small wooden cabinet sat on a table beside us. It was a pretty box, quite old, decorated with mother-of-pearl inlay and accessed through a door with ornamental brass hinges and latch. One by one, we approached the cabinet, opened the door, and satisfied ourselves that the cupboard was indeed bare. Anthony Wood, the carpenter, gave it a professional inspection. 'Quite nice workmanship,' he commented to Carlotta. 'A skilled craftsman made that, madam, perhaps a hundred years ago.' Noah Bristow didn't stop there – he picked up the cabinet – which was quite heavy – shook it, then knocked on all sides as if searching for hidden compartments.

'It's been serving my family for generations,' Carlotta replied, paying the young man no mind.

I was last to examine the cabinet, as always. Using my body to shield my hand, I laid a copper penny dated 1873 on the floor of the box.

'Looks empty to me,' I said softly as I latched the door.

Seating was never left to chance. 'We'll take our places at the spirit table now,' said Carlotta. 'Mr Bristow, bring that chair for yourself. You'll want to sit there, beside your aunt. Mr Wood, you may sit here and Mrs Duval, take the chair on my left and we'll exchange electricity for flame.'

'Wait a minute,' said Bristow. 'I want to look around first.'

'Be my guest, sir.' Carlotta's gentle voice amazed me. She had more patience than anyone I'd ever known. 'You are welcome to search and satisfy yourself that everything is as it should be. We have all the time in the universe.'

Someone calm and deliberate with knowledge of the typical Spiritualist's hocus-pocus methods – someone like Harry Houdini – would have made short shrift of Freddy's efforts to disguise his enhancements. Fortunately, Noah Bristow had none of those qualities, and he was drunk besides. He ducked under the table, knocking his forehead in the process, and rapped on all the surfaces. He examined the chairs for hollow seats or secret compartments, something I hadn't thought of but would consider in the future. Carlotta had not turned off the electric light above us, but a thick curtain shrouded the window and the bulb was dim, which goes a long way toward explaining how he missed the trapdoor under the table. Freddy had cut it along the lines of the floorboards, not as a regular square or rectangle, so it blended in convincingly. Bristow neglected to look up, but even had he done so, the tiny door cut into the ceiling beside the chandelier chain would not have been visible, so cleverly had Freddy worked it into the design on the decorative ceiling medallion.

Bristow pulled back the heavy curtain to assure himself that no one was lurking behind it, tripping over his own feet in the process and clutching the curtain to save himself from a fall to the floor. He raised the two large pictures on the wall to see if they hid anything – they did not, but his hand came very near the panel door that led to the kitchen. I held my breath, but the floral wallpaper pattern had effectively concealed the seams. He missed the two pinhole openings in the wall between the parlor and the séance room, which were also camouflaged by the wallpaper pattern. Houdini would not have been fooled, but Bristow was. It's funny how suspicious people will always look for secret hiding places and hidden doors but never suspect that a shill might be sitting beside them.

Freddy, who was surely watching through a pinhole in the ceiling medallion, would be puffed up with pride.

'So far, so good,' said Bristow as he swaggered to his chair.

When everyone was seated, Carlotta lit the candle in the center of the table and pulled the chain to switch off the chandelier lights.

'Now, we will all join hands to link us together and we will begin our journey.' I took Carlotta's hand in my right and Mrs Weidemann's in my left, as she continued her patter. 'Breaking this bond will damage our ability to communicate with the spirits. Our energy is greater together than alone, so please don't break the spiritual chain. Now, we begin. Clear your minds of mundane aspects of everyday life and concentrate on the loved one you wish to contact. Hold their image in your head. Remember the sound of their voice, their mannerisms, the way their eyes sparkled when they laughed.'

Several minutes of silence followed. I spent the time thinking hard about how Noah Bristow's unexpected arrival was going to affect our plan. Having the judge's spirit warn his wife about their nephew would not be calmly received by the nephew sitting beside her. How would he react? With rage? Would he upset the table and chairs as Al Capone had done? Would he storm out? Or would he deny the allegation or laugh it off? Should we postpone the visitation until we could get Mrs Weidemann here by herself? Was that even remotely realistic? I thought it unlikely that Bristow would permit his aunt to return alone. He would insist on accompanying her, 'for her own protection'. I decided we had no better option than to go through with our plan, regardless of his reaction. Mrs Weidemann needed to hear about the danger now, from someone she trusted. And she trusted her husband. After all was said and done, there was no way to help the judge or the boy, but we could still save Mrs Weidemann if she would only believe us.

I was pretty sure Freddy would have reached an identical conclusion. He would bide his time, see how the séance progressed, and make up his mind whether or not to speak in the judge's voice at the moment when Carlotta faltered.

Carlotta was whispering something. I focused my attention on the fragile words that floated through the darkness like soap bubbles. She began quietly as she always did with the Lord's Prayer and some Latin folderol, then started imploring the archangel Michael to draw near. I sensed more than heard

Freddy's speaking tube being lowered from the ceiling. I squeezed Carlotta's hand in encouragement. My other hand held Mrs Weidemann's.

'Dear Michael, bestow your presence on us mortals tonight, we beseech you. We are five tonight who wish to contact loved ones in the Spirit World. We are all believers.' Well, that clearly wasn't true, but Noah Bristow did not contradict her.

Small gusts of wind came out of nowhere as Freddy sent air through the tube, turning it in a circle so we all felt the breeze come and go, and then directed it at the flame, which flickered wildly and went out. No one made a sound. We were enveloped by total darkness now.

'*Esto nobis pregustatum in mortis examine*,' chanted Carlotta. 'Come, dear Michael, archangel over all angels . . . *cujus latus perforatum* . . . visit us this night. Lead to us the spirits we seek. Bring them to their loved ones so they can be reassured and informed.'

She continued in this vein for several minutes longer than usual. I waited to learn which spirit would appear first or, as had happened on rare occasions, find that Archangel Michael would not appear at all. Carlotta usually preferred to begin with me because I could set the stage for a successful séance as I asked my late husband whether or not I should move in with relatives.

Tonight, Archangel Michael had other ideas.

'I am here.' Carlotta's growly foreign accent signaled that Michael had arrived. I tensed. My part on the séance stage was fast approaching. 'There is an unbeliever among you. He will believe before the night is over.' Nice touch, Carlotta, I sent her mental encouragement through my thoughts. Then her voice changed to its normal tone. 'I sense a spirit. I sense a spirit in the room with us now. A man. A kind man. A man who had troubles in his life. He is close. He is among us. He wants to speak but cannot. Can you speak, sir? Can you speak? No, he cannot. I sense peace and contentment. He wants to tell someone he is content. He wants to tell his brother.'

'That's Howard!' said Anthony Wood. 'My brother! Howard, are you there?'

There was no response.

This was my cue. I let go Carlotta's hand, raised my right arm as high as I could, and opened my hand so the palm faced out.

'He is here,' said Carlotta. 'He does not speak. He wishes—'

'Look!' said Mrs Weidemann. There was a gasp. 'What is it?'

According to his obituary, Howard Wood had been a Mason, and it was my assumption that his brother was a member too. At the library I learned that one of the Masonic symbols was the eye of God, so Freddy drew an eye on the palm of my hand with our radium paint. When I waved my arm gently above my head, the glowing eye seemed to float in the distance. A splendid enhancement, if I do say so myself.

'I sense incompleteness. Unfinished business. A road untraveled,' said Carlotta.

'His friend,' said Anthony Wood in a hesitant manner. 'He had a friend. Do you mean Ralph, Howard? Is it Ralph? It must be Ralph, his friend. Howard was a bachelor, but he had a good friend, a very close friend, another bachelor, who was away when he passed. It's Ralph, isn't it, Howard? What shall I do?'

'I sense grief,' said Carlotta. 'Confusion. Loneliness.'

'It's about Ralph, I'm sure. I'll go see Ralph and explain about . . . about . . . the confusion. It was accidental, wasn't it, Howard? You didn't mean to take all those pills, did you? Is that what I should tell Ralph? Is that what you want, Howard? They were very close,' he said to no one in particular. 'I should have thought of that myself. Is that it, Howard?'

'I sense confusion. A misunderstanding. An accident.'

'I knew it was an accident,' said Anthony Wood. 'His illness confused him and he took too many pills. He didn't mean to do it.'

I put my hand down as Carlotta said, 'I am sensing nothing more. Your brother has moved on.'

THIRTY-SIX

A period of silence punctuated by Latin mumbling followed as Carlotta sank deeper into her trance until nothing but a one-note hum came from her throat – a nice touch of suspense I hadn't heard before. Several impatient sighs and throat-clearings came from the direction of Noah Bristow. I found I was holding my breath. No telling what this young thug would do when Freddy began his accusations.

Suddenly Carlotta straightened up with a jerk. 'Someone has arrived,' she whispered, sounding surprised. 'Someone is with us. Michael, who has come down to communicate with us mortals tonight? A man . . . I sense a man whose love for his wife is stronger than death . . .' Was she signaling me to speak to my late husband, or was this a cue for the judge? My heart pounding, I dared not say a word for fear of making a mistake. I held off for a few seconds, hoping for further instruction. Freddy did not wait. In his shaky, old-man voice, he began what we had rehearsed.

'Light of my life . . . dearest one . . . I come to you with fear in my heart . . . danger stalks . . . beware the menace lurking in our own home . . . I am murdered, poisoned by the one we took to our bosom and nourished . . . our nephew . . . the love of money is the root of all evil.'

The moment I knew the spirit had come to speak to Mrs Weidemann, I let go of Carlotta's hand and dug into my pocket where I had secreted a few dozen rose petals – the widow's favorite flower in her favorite color – and sprinkled them on the table in front of her where she would see them when the room became light again. At that same moment, a fist smashed the table, nearly cracking it in two and making me jump almost out of my seat.

'What's that you say? Filthy lies!' cried Noah Bristow. Freddy did not let this outburst interrupt his spiel. Mrs Weidemann gave a sharp cry of alarm.

'He seeks to poison you too, my dear wife,' continued Freddy, heedless of the interruption. 'Cast him from our house! He is a murderer . . . wicked . . . poisoner!'

Now Freddy pitched his voice higher, like a boy's. That was my signal to squeeze the rubber bladder under my arm and let the water dribble through the tube in my sleeve, on to the table.

Mrs Weidemann gasped. Noah Bristow made some strangled noises. Freddy's voice shifted higher, like a little boy's. 'Auntie? Auntie? Help me . . . he'd holding me underwater until I drown. I am drowning. All for money . . . my inheritance . . . he is wicked . . . evil . . . murderer. Help me, Auntie.'

'What . . .?'said Mr Wood, startled. 'What's this? Water? What's happening?'

'Liar!' screamed Bristow. In the pitch dark room, I could not see his movements, but I could hear enough to know he had lurched to his feet, knocking his rickety chair to the floor, and stumbled backwards against the spirit box, which also crashed to the floor. He must have had more to drink than I'd thought. 'Fakes!' he shouted over Freddy's continued patter. 'Tricksters! Frauds! Nothing's true. I'll prove it!' He lurched against the walls, searching, I presumed, for the door to the parlor so he could get some light into the room.

Next to me, Carlotta took a long, rattling breath and her hand clenched mine as if she had just felt a stab of pain. She said, 'Another . . . wait . . . another comes . . .'

What did she mean? There was no other. Freddy's monologue did not let up. 'Murderer,' he rasped, 'evil doer . . . poisoner . . . for money.' Then I heard a second voice over his, a woman's voice, coming from Carlotta. This was unexpected. This was Carlotta on her own, trying to help us in some manner. We hadn't asked her to help – in fact, we didn't want her involved in case she unintentionally botched our plan, but there was no controlling Carlotta in the middle of a séance. I squeezed her hand, hoping she'd interpret it as a signal to stop talking. No dice. Noah Bristow continued ranting and sweeping the walls with his arms, searching for the doorknob.

Carlotta's voice quivered. It was unlike Archangel Michael's, one I hadn't heard her use before. I squeezed her hand again and implored softly, urgently, 'Madame Carlotta,' but either she didn't understand the message or she was too deep in the trance to draw out of it. She sounded confused.

'I am the messenger for one who wishes to speak,' Carlotta said. 'I sense her presence . . . a young woman, a laborer perhaps, in a gray dress . . . scuffed shoes . . . a violent death . . . I see silver . . . many pieces . . . valuable . . . I see a man is stealing the silver . . . heavy candlesticks, heavy, heavy . . . Stop, thief! Blood on my head . . . falling, falling . . . blood on the floor . . . a demon from hell . . .'

Could it be the maid who had stolen the silver candlesticks months earlier and disappeared? What was her name . . . Ursula? She had run off, or so everyone said. Was she dead? This was all impossible – Freddy and Carlotta didn't know about her. Only I knew the story of the maid who had absconded with the candlesticks. I'd not told them about that. I'd not seen any connection to the judge's death.

There was no time to ponder this new development, for at the same moment, Bristow found the doorknob and wrenched it open with a scream of frustration. Enough light came into the séance room from the parlor to give everyone a dim view of the surroundings. Carlotta was still seated, her eyes shut, paralyzed by the unfolding drama. Mrs Weidemann had gone rigid with shock and confusion. Freddy had pulled up the speaking tube, so there was nothing to see there. But Bristow was casting about for the pendant chain that would turn on the overhead light. At last he spied it and gave it a yank. 'Foul lies!' he shouted, wobbling from side to side and spewing flecks of foam from his mouth like a man possessed. 'Fakes! Charlatans! Trying to ruin me!'

The sudden glare had us all squinting and blinking in pain. Within seconds, Mrs Weidemann's eyes focused on the rose petals in front of her. Hesitantly, she reached out with a finger to touch one, as if she could not believe they were real. 'Pink . . .' she said softly. 'My favorite. He always brought me pink roses . . .' Her brow creased with uncertainty as she pondered the messages and the rose petals and then searched her nephew's face for some explanation. 'All this time, I've been ill . . . can that have been your doing, Noah?'

'All these mediums are fakes!' he cried, appealing to his aunt. 'You can't believe a word they say. They don't know anything about what really happened. They can't know. I'll prove it. Just watch me.' Thrusting me roughly aside, he stumbled to his knees in his haste to turn over the table. I held my breath. Would he find the trap door?

Because there was nothing tricky on the underside of the table, Bristow found nothing. He rocked back and forth on his knees, his rage dissolving into sobs of frustration. 'It wasn't my fault! I had to protect myself. They were going to kill me if I didn't pay up. That horrid slut of a girl, she threatened to tell . . . she taunted me . . . what else could I do? I didn't hit her very hard, I promise . . . I had no choice, don't you see? It was her or me.'

'Here, here, young man,' said the mild-mannered Anthony Wood, who seemed to have just woken up to the very real danger simmering inside this violent creature. To no avail. No one even glanced in Wood's direction.

After looking wildly about for a few moments, Noah focused his rheumy eyes on Carlotta who by now had shaken off her trance and was on her feet, holding on to her chair for support. Leaping up, he seized her shoulders and began shaking her until her head wobbled, crying, 'Liar! You've made this up. Who told you? I did nothing wrong!' until Mr Wood and I managed to pull him off her. With one fist clutching the back of Bristow's collar, Mr Wood half-carried, half-pushed the young man out of the séance room and into the parlor.

'He was old anyway!' screamed Noah, his arms flailing ineffectually against the older man's grip. 'Old and sick and dying anyway! He wouldn't do anything for me!'

'That's quite enough, you miserable ruffian! You'll sit here until the police arrive, or I'll sit on you myself! Ladies, quickly, the telephone!'

There was only one of us alert enough to move toward the telephone. As I did, Bristow tore free of Mr Wood's grasp and threw a wild punch in his direction, hitting him in the shoulder and knocking him to the floor. Snatching an umbrella from the stand by the door, he swung a blow at my head that I managed to duck before he escaped through the front door, leaving the rest of us in shocked silence. Mr Wood recovered first. 'There,' he said, rubbing his shoulder. 'I think we're all right now. What an evening!'

I reached for the telephone and called the precinct. 'They said an officer would be by momentarily,' I said as I replaced the receiver.

'Madam,' Mr Wood addressed Mrs Weidemann, 'my sincere condolences on the deaths of your husband and your nephew at the hand of that despicable young man. Who could believe such perfidy was possible? Why, only the spirits themselves could have known. You are fortunate your husband warned you in time to save yourself.' Looking about for something to do while we waited for the police, he righted the little table and picked up the pieces of the spirit cabinet. 'A pity about your spirit cabinet, Madame Carlotta,' he said gently. 'It's a shame to lose such a pretty thing. I think it can be repaired, however, with the right— here, now, what's this?' Underneath one of the pieces lay a coin. 'Why, it's a penny. It was in the spirit cabinet, I believe.' He examined it more closely, then gasped. 'It's dated 1873. Upon my word, that's the very year my brother was born! This must be from Howard. It's from Howard!' He looked at each of us in wonder. 'It's a message, isn't it? Of course it is. What does it mean, madam?'

Carlotta blinked hard, as if trying to remember what she was supposed to say. 'I've seen such coin messages before,' she replied – correctly, since I had made that a specialty of the house. 'I believe it conveys his love and his wish that you know he is happy in the Great Beyond.'

Mr Wood clutched the penny in his fist like he would never let it go. 'Upon my word, I'll be showing this to Howard's friend, Ralph. He'll be so relieved. Thank you, Madame Carlotta. Thank you from the bottom of my heart.'

'Pink,' murmured a dazed Mrs Weidemann as she stooped to gather up the petals that had fallen to the floor and press them, one by one, to her lips. 'Pink. I'm so sorry, Charles, I didn't know . . .'

'And I'm sorry, too, Mrs Weidemann,' Carlotta said as she stooped to help with the petals. 'I know this must be a shock to you, hearing such dreadful news from your husband like that. His love for you transcends time and space. Nothing could hold him back from his warning.'

'Yes . . . his warning,' she said absently. 'It's so hard to believe . . . three deaths . . . all of them murders? What am I to do? I'm quite alone in the world.'

'Believe your husband,' I urged. 'Would he say such things about your nephew if they weren't true?' Poor lady, she could only shake her head, too distraught to reply.

By now Carlotta had regained enough composure to make her way into the kitchen for a glass of water for Mrs Weidemann. Suitably fortified, the widow dithered – how could her nephew, a boy with all the advantages they could give him, be guilty of such heinous crimes?

'And the female spirit. Do you know who that was, Mrs Weidemann?' I asked.

'It can be none other than Ursula, our maid who ran away with our silver candlesticks earlier this year. It never occurred to me that she might have been a victim of violence. We all blamed her for the theft when in fact, it was Noah who . . .' She looked at me with shocked eyes and I knew what she wanted to say. It was Noah who had put the idea in their heads that the maid had stolen the silver to throw suspicion away from himself. 'But what happened that night? How could it be that she was murdered, when she took her clothing with her? I myself saw her empty room.'

I thought I knew. 'Perhaps Ursula caught Noah in the act of stealing the candlesticks and threatened to expose him. He struck her on the head with one of the candlesticks and killed her, maybe unintentionally. Then, to make it appear as if she was the thief, he removed the clothes from her room and told everyone she'd run away with the silver. He probably left her body in some remote place and sold the silver later on. I expect the police will make him tell where.' And getting away with Ursula's death, accidental or not, gave him the courage to plan little Dickie's 'accidental' drowning and his uncle's slow poisoning, all accomplished in a sequence that left him with half of the judge's estate. His aunt's death would have given him the other half.

Mrs Weidemann wrung her hands. 'I shouldn't have believed him. Why, oh why, did I believe him? I knew he had taken my jewelry, but I thought . . . I said to myself that he was a good boy underneath. And I thought . . . I believed he tried to save his cousin in the river. Oh, why didn't any of us see him for the killer he was?'

Love is why. We see what we want to see, especially in those we love. We make excuses or look past what doesn't conform to the image fixed in our heads. Like Freddy rationalizing Carlotta's fakery because he loved her like the mother he never knew. Like me blinded to Tommy's flaws, making excuses for his bigamy, putting the blame on his first wife, pretending his work for the Outfit was an ordinary delivery job. Like the Spiritualists clinging to their fake mediums and Ouija boards, ignoring Houdini when he exposed their methods.

The policeman arrived. It wasn't O'Rourke. We gave him an account of what had happened and what we believed Noah Bristow to have done. He said little but took careful notes.

It was Anthony Wood who first noticed that Bristow had escaped in the Weidemann motorcar. Realizing that Mrs Weidemann would have no way to get home, he offered to drive her back in his own motorcar and to make sure she was safe. 'I'll speak to the servants,' he told Carlotta quietly. 'We'll make sure all the doors are locked, in case he should try to come back. Which I doubt, but you never know what a deranged man will do. I spoke to the policeman and he has agreed to set a guard on the house tonight. Upon my word, it's been quite a night, hasn't it?'

Yes, it had.

As soon as the house had cleared, Freddy padded down the stairs in his socks.

'I was so worried,' he said, 'I nearly . . . never mind. But you're safe.' He hugged Carlotta. 'And she listened, didn't she? I mean, she believed what we said about that bum?'

I nodded. 'You were great, Freddy. Your Judge Weidemann was so old and believable, it would have persuaded anyone. And your Dickie voice was perfect. But' – I turned to Carlotta – 'how did you know about Ursula and the silver theft? Who told you about that?'

She frowned. 'No one. That is, I don't know. I don't remember saying anything about silver.'

'You don't remember? You spoke of seeing a young woman. You spoke of candlesticks and murder.'

She shook her head. 'No, I heard Freddy do the two warning voices. I . . . I don't know anything about candlesticks.'

'You don't remember because you were so deep into your journey.'

Carlotta nodded absently. 'The dead woman's spirit must have spoken through me. Like Archangel Michael does.' Freddy and I stood there, sharing the same thought as a slow smile lit up Carlotta's face. 'I did it, didn't I?' The wonder in her voice was genuine. 'I broke through to the Far Beyond and reached someone. I knew I had the power!'

THIRTY-SEVEN

The following day, a fisherman found Noah Bristow's body floating in the Chicago River, not far from the place where Dickie had drowned. The newspapers said he got drunk and fell in. The police said it was suicide, a desperate action taken by a young man wracked by guilt. I wondered if Johnny Torrio's men hadn't done it as a favor to me. Carlotta claimed there was only one explanation that fit the facts: she had for the first time actually succeeded in summoning a spirit to her séance, and that spirit had lured Bristow to the edge of the river and frightened him so badly, he fell in. Or was pushed. Freddy believed her implicitly.

I was torn apart by doubts. Since that first night when I sat in Carlotta's séance room and heard her confuse my brother's wedding with mine, I had known she was a fraud. A genial fraud, a caring fraud, but a fraud who deluded herself as much as she fooled her clients. She had no special power to contact the spirits of the dead.

But when I'd returned to my boarding house and put Baby Tommy to bed, I lay beside him for hours as I examined everything I'd learned about Spiritualism in recent months. Harry Houdini had proved that every Spiritualist he'd tested over thirty years was a fake. He'd offered huge rewards to any medium who could make genuine contact with the dead, and no one had ever claimed the money. He'd tried himself, many times, to reach the Spirit World, without success. But he never claimed it was impossible, just that he had never found anyone who could do it.

In the opposite corner was his friend Sir Arthur Conan Doyle, who maintained that he had contacted the dead on many occasions through authentic mediums. Both men were honest, educated, and intelligent – could both be correct? Was it possible that some mediums were genuine? Could Madame Carlotta – née Myrtle Burkholtzer – be one of the few who really could contact the souls of the departed? How else had she known about Ursula, when I myself did not suspect the maid's disappearance was connected to Noah's other two murders? I could no longer dismiss the possibility that Carlotta was a genuine mystic. Had it been a one-time event? Or would she be able to summon an actual spirit again?

Two weeks later, the results of Judge Weidemann's autopsy came in. The condition of the corpse – specifically the lack of deterioration – shouted the presence of arsenic even before the doctor had begun his examination. The judge's lungs, kidneys, and liver showed visual signs of arsenic poisoning, and chemical tests turned up significant arsenic in those organs. The official ruling was arsenic poisoning. Too late, of course, since the murderer had already met his final reward, but it was enough to convince anyone who still harbored doubts that Noah Bristow was a remorseless killer. Ursula's remains were never found.

Mrs Weidemann did not return to Madame Carlotta for further reunions with her husband or her nephew. I heard later from Ellen that she did invite her nieces to come with their parents to Chicago from Milwaukee for the Thanksgiving holiday, and that the visit was such a success, the family stayed on through Christmas and later moved in with her.

Baby Tommy and I moved too – into the front bedroom of Carlotta's house. Later that day I resumed my investigations with two new client names.

FACT OR FICTION?

When I started reading historical novels as a child, the blend of history and fiction fascinated me. But what part of the story was true and what part was the author's imagination? Usually curiosity took me to the encyclopedia where I would look up Napoleon or Genghis Khan or Sitting Bull to learn the answer – and also find out whether the author had played fast and loose with the facts, something that offended my sense of fair play. If you share my curiosity, here are some of the basics about this story to get you started.

Maddie Duval Pastore, Carlotta Romany, Freddy, Noah Bristow, Officer O'Rourke, and the Weidemann family are products of my imagination. Most readers will recognize Al Capone as a real historical figure. Although he was only twenty-five when he took over the Chicago Outfit from Johnny Torrio – also a historical figure – and was in prison by the age of thirty-one, Capone is probably the most famous of all American gangsters. Why is that? Because he wanted to be. He loved giving interviews to the press and seeing his picture in the newspaper, and he pursued publicity every chance he got. The scene with him and Maddie in the restaurant is, of course, fiction, but it's plausible – Capone was a noted womanizer and consorted with prostitutes. He went to prison for tax evasion – they couldn't get him for the many murders he committed – and was released eleven years later. Almost at once he was hospitalized with advanced syphilis, then an incurable disease that resulted in a gruesome death he richly deserved.

The other gangsters were a bit more circumspect: Johnny Torrio actually 'retired' from the mob when he turned it over to Capone. He died of natural causes at the age of seventy-five. Most gangsters died young and violently. The Outfit gang's main rival was the North Side Gang led by Dion (or Dean) O'Banion who was murdered just as I have described it, in his flower shop as he was finishing an arrangement, although no one except his African-American assistant was there to witness the act. The headlines in chapter thirty-two are the actual ones from that day's newspapers. Al Capone's brothers are real, although far less is known about them than Al. The Hotel Metropole was the headquarters of the Outfit during those years.

Jane Addams was a Nobel Prize-winning philanthropist who pioneered the idea of settlement houses, a place where immigrants and the poor could find help and a better life. Hull House is a museum today. A picture of it – and pictures of Capone, O'Banion, and others relevant to the story – is available on my Pinterest page. Just search for *The Mystic's Accomplice*.

Harry Houdini, probably the greatest magician of all time, was passionate about debunking scam artists and fraudulent Spiritualists who preyed on gullible people. Just as passionate was his friend, Sir Arthur Conan Doyle, the creator of Sherlock Holmes, who believed wholeheartedly in fairies and in communicating with spirits. Houdini's book, *A Magician Among Spirits*, published in 1924, was carried in many libraries and bookstores. It's still available, if you'd like to read it. In it, Houdini describes many ways fake mediums used to trick clients. I borrowed some of them for my story. Thank you, Houdini!